TRUST IN LOVE

Aleesa was aware of the concern in Miles's eyes, but she knew she couldn't tell him the truth about herself. Maybe tomorrow, after he met her parents. So she spoke as firmly as she could, hoping he would accept her answer.

"There's no one else, Miles. If you sense there's a chasm between us, I don't know what to tell you. I will always be honest with you, as I hope you'll be with me. Can't we let our relationship grow, like I said before?" she pleaded.

He couldn't stop himself. He kissed her then, gently at first. As his lips touched hers, he sensed a palpable hunger from her as if she wanted, needed more. He held her head with both hands. She fused her mouth to his. What was going on? Was Aleesa denying her reluctance to commit to him, yet still showing that she really cared? What was it? Impatient, needing to know, to love her more, he thrust his tongue forward to taste the inner sweetness of her mouth. She sighed and sought to caress his lips with her own tongue. He welcomed the gesture.

"No matter what it is, love, you are the only one for me and always will be," Miles whispered in her ear.

TRUST IN LOVE

Mildred Riley

ARABESQUE

BET BOOKS

BET Publications, LLC
www.msbet.com
www.arabesquebooks.com

This is a work of fiction. All characters, places, and incidents are products of the author's imagination. Any similarities that may occur are purely coincidental.

ARABESQUE BOOKS are published by

BET Publications, LLC
c/o BET BOOKS
One BET Plaza
1900 W Place NE
Washington, D.C. 20018-1211

Copyright © 2000 by Mildred E. Riley

BET Books is a trademark of Black Entertainment Television, Inc. ARABESQUE, the ARABESQUE logo and the BET BOOKS logo are trademarks and registered trademarks.

First Printing: May, 2000

10 9 8 7 6 5 4 3 2 1
Printed in the United States of America

Prologue

1935.

"Sorry son, cain't use ya. School board sez to on'y hire teachers wi' 'sperience. Boy, yew jes' a new grajiate!"

"But, sir," Ambrose Miller protested, "I did practice teaching as part of my college curriculum." The white man's eyebrows arched at the word he had never heard before. Undaunted, the applicant pressed on. "If you'll look at my grades," he pointed to his transcript record on the desk, "I have all honor grades. I was the top graduate in my class."

The heavy-set man, perspiring profusely, swept the papers up and handed them to Ambrose.

"Don' make no neva min'—the board of this here county sez 'sperienced teachers gotta be hired. Kno' we want our Negro students to hev' same as the rest." His voice trailed off with a sly grin.

Ambrose was seething inside. He wanted to reach across the desk that separated them and pummel the man's beefy, florid face into bloody bits of bone and tissue. But he knew he faced a lost cause. It did not matter that he had a degree in agricultural science from Macota Agricultural College, that his transcript showed the honor grades he'd received—his four years of higher learning meant nothing to the man who knew with arrogant certainty that he controlled the young black man's future.

"Here's yo' resume." He mispronounced it *resoom*. "Cum back, hear, when ya gits *work* 'sperience."

Ambrose had hoped for a different outcome when he'd applied for a teaching position in the town's segregated high school. He knew he'd better leave the office quickly. He took the papers, tipped his hat, and left. As he walked outside to his father's old Ford, he felt prickly perspiration trickle down from his armpits. His blood boiled furiously as he tried taking deep breaths to calm himself. Because an uneducated backwoods farmer was white, owned a piece of land, could vote, and was a member of the county Board of Education, he could control Ambrose Miller's life and future. Bitter rancor rose within his body, but if he allowed his actions to reveal how he really felt, he might be killed.

When he heard the knock on the door of his laboratory where he was working, Dr. Felix Holmes, agricultural department head at Macota College, removed his head from the hooded microscope he was working with. "Come in," he said. "Please come in."

He stood, watching as the door opened and his visitor approached. He had been told to expect a Russian dignitary.

The man did not look Russian at all. He looked British or American. He wore his hair in the slicked-back style of Rudolph Valentino. Dr. Holmes did not know that the Russian wanted to appear as Western as possible. His suit was well tailored, his shoes had been polished to an exquisite shine. His elegant grooming was enhanced even more by a gleaming white shirt, blue and white striped silk tie, and gold cuff links.

By contrast, Felix Holmes's frumpy lab coat and down-at-the-heels comfortable old shoes embarrassed him a bit. But he quickly dismissed the feeling. After all, this was *his* office, *his* department, and it appeared, from what he had been told, that his visitor wanted something from him.

The man bowed slightly and accepted Dr. Holmes's handshake with a firm grasp. His nationality was revealed when he spoke with a thick accent.

"Dr. Holmes, it is a pleasure to meet you! Piotr Petrovsky is my name and I am pleased that you would permit me to call on you. I am deputy director of the Agricultural Collective Union in Ukraine. We have been informed that you have developed a specific type of cotton plant that can mature in a short growing period."

"Yes, that is so. Please have a seat."

He gestured to a chair beside his desk. He sat down, placed his hands tent-like before his mouth, and listened closely to what the Russian had to say.

"Since the revolution, we have been seeking help with our farming, cotton growing, poultry farming, and other endeavors. We wish our country to grow and develop. We are willing to pay for such help in our development. I have been authorized to offer you a salary of five hundred dollars—U.S. dollars—a month, a full professorship at the university, a paid round-trip to Russia and back, and a month's paid vacation if you would be willing to come and teach us. We need help from experts like you."

"Mr. Petrovsky, sir, that is a very generous, very tempting offer, especially for someone like me, who has spent a lifetime teaching and developing new plant strains. However, I must tell you that I am not a young man and I plan to retire within the next year."

"Ah, so perhaps when you retire. The offer would be the same."

"No, I think not, tempting though the offer you propose is."

"Of course, Dr. Holmes, I am deeply disappointed. It would have been a significant honor for me to have recruited someone of your stature to help in our developing agricultural program."

"Regretfully, I must decline."

Both men stood, realizing that the meeting had ended. Dr. Holmes escorted the Russian to the door. He shook hands with the departing Russian official.

"It just occurred to me, sir, that perhaps some of our young graduates might be interested in the opportunity you speak of. Some of them have worked with me, and are knowledgeable in the growth and development of a smooth, long-staple cotton that is adaptable to a short growing season. Some of them have studied poultry farming as well. Would you be interested in interviewing some of them for your program?"

The Russian answered quickly, realizing young college graduates would be cheaper to hire, and his personal star would thus rise higher in the collective. He pumped Dr. Holmes's hand vigorously.

"But of course, Dr. Holmes. I would be interested in your graduates!"

"So, you didn't get the teaching job at the high school."

Felix Holmes saw the look of despair, of hopelessness, on his former student's face.

"No, sir, I didn't. Was all I could do to keep from killing that damn redneck. Here's a dude that can barely read, yet *he* has the power to keep me *down*— from even earning a living! What can I do? There're no jobs, thanks to this depression we're in, and I tell you, sir, I'll starve before I go to work in the cotton fields! What good is my college education, picking cotton?"

His disappointment at the injustice he had experienced hung in the room. Dr. Holmes understood. He spoke gently to his young friend.

"You really want to teach, don't you?" He placed his hand on the shoulder Ambrose, who looked up at his mentor expectantly, hopefully.

"You know I do, sir. I want to share what you've taught me with others."

"Well, I think I can find you such a job . . . if you're willing to take it."

"Take it!" Ambrose's eyes widened at the possibility. "I'd jump at the chance. Where is this job?"

"In Russia, son. The Ukraine, to be exact."

A month later a contingent of thirty Negro college graduates who could not find suitable employment in the United States sailed into the city of Odessa on the Black Sea. So began an unheard of, most unusual adventure of young black Americans living and working in Red Russia.

One

His beady black eyes bore into hers like steel bits. He glared at her from his high perch on the judge's bench, his hawklike nostrils flaring menacingly.

"You *do* understand, counselor, that *this* court expects the highest quality of defense preparation."

"Yes, your honor. I try to come to court prepared, your honor."

"See that you do!" He slammed the gavel down. "Court adjourned until Tuesday morning, nine A.M., being Monday is a holiday."

Living up to his reputation as a tough chauvinist, Aleesa sighed to herself as she shuffled her papers into her briefcase. Where on earth could she find a physician to concur with her theory? She *had* to win this case.

Balancing unwieldy bags of groceries in each arm, Aleesa kicked the door shut. The light on her answering machine was blinking with the persistence of a strobe light. She slipped out of her shoes and dropped the bags on the sofa, happy that she hadn't purchased anything fragile. She punched the Play button.

Miles's deep, rich baritone voice comforted her like a soft warm blanket.

"I'll be at your place 'round seven-thirty, okay? Love ya, babe."

Aleesa rested her head on the back of the sofa. She thought how lucky she was to be in love with such a wonderful man. Since he'd come into her life, everything seemed more wonderful—her life had more meaning, more purpose. She admired his self-confidence—positive without being ego-driven. As an airline pilot, she supposed he *had* to be courageous and self-confident.

Tonight was going to be a special night for Miles, and she was happy to be sharing it with him. The national chapter of the Tuskegee Airmen was having a black-tie dinner party and dance to honor Miles, as well as several other black pilots. Miles was a senior pilot for WIN, World International Network, a well-known cargo distribution company.

She checked her watch. It had been an unusually harrowing day at court, and she was weary. Sighing, she pushed to her feet and wrestled with the heavy bags to the kitchen of her one-bedroom apartment.

She had just placed the last item in the kitchen cabinet when the phone rang again. She let the answering machine pick up. It was her mother.

"Leese, think you and Miles can get here early on Saturday? Dad's got tickets for Tanglewood—Wynton Marsalis and his young people's jazz group. Don't want to miss that. See you, and drive carefully."

Her mother was always planning something, but Aleesa decided to respond to her mother's invitation only after she checked with Miles. He was usually agreeable, but he ought to have a chance to agree or disagree when plans were being made for him.

Aleesa's face flushed as she recalled their first meeting. It had not begun well at all.

It was at a junior high school. A classroom had been reserved for the school's Career Day. People were milling around a long table set with coffee urns, cups, pastries, and glasses for fruit juice. At a nearby smaller table each of the volunteer speakers were being given name badges and assignment schedules.

Aleesa was just pinning her badge to her jacket lapel when she heard a deep masculine voice. "So nice to meet you, Aleesa Haskins."

Startled, she looked up into the face of a very handsome man. He had soft, melting-like brown skin with dark, piercing eyes shadowed by ink-black eyebrows. As he looked down at her, his mouth twitched at the corners, revealing an infectious grin.

"I'm sorry." He extended his hand. Reluctantly, she accepted it. It was warm and smooth.

"I'm Miles Lewis Kittridge, Jr." He continued, "You may call me M.L., or Miles, but I'm hoping that you will call me."

Taken aback by his bold approach, Aleesa dropped his hand.

"I'm Aleesa Haskins, but, of course"—defiance registered in her voice—*"you've* already *read* my name tag. And I must say, so far, I see no need to call you anything."

Miles stepped back, raising both hands as if to ward off a blow. "Whoa, whoa, time out!" He made a T-sign with his hand and forefinger. "I didn't mean to insult you." He bowed slightly. "Let's start over." He flashed his disarming grin again.

"Miles Lewis Kittridge, Jr."

This time she extended her hand and he shook it. "Aleesa Haskins," she said.

They went to dinner that evening. She wasn't sure

what made her accept his invitation. She surprised herself when she agreed to have dinner with a man she'd met only that day. It had been months since she had dated anyone. Not since her years-long affair with Arthur Bradley had soured. They had started dating in high school, continued into college, and been considered "a pair." Since Arthur and she had parted, there had been no significant man in her life. Perhaps, she thought, her reason for accepting Miles's invitation was that she needed a change. Things were not going well at court. Something new was needed.

"I can't believe I let you talk me into this," she said when Miles held the car door open for her.

Miles felt his heart take a sudden jump as the soft fragrance she wore enveloped him. It increased his anticipation of an exciting evening ahead.

He hurried to the driver's side of the car, slid in and fastened his seat belt.

"So you can't believe you let me talk you into having dinner with me tonight?"

"Right. I'm not usually so . . . so impulsive."

"Well"—he turned his head sideways and grinned at her—"we'll just have to say it was my persuasive charm that impressed you, eh?"

He noticed her hesitation before she answered him. She stared out the car window as they drove out of the city. He wanted to reassure her, touch her soft auburn hair that curled gently around her face. The black silk pants suit that she wore with a white silk blouse set off her lithe, trim figure. Her aura of winsome delicacy intrigued him, but from what little he'd seen, he suspected that there was an innate strength behind that gentle facade. He was dying to get to know her.

"You're very sure of yourself, and I find that interesting, but no . . . I think I decided I needed something . . . someone interesting in my life . . . right now."

"So . . ." Miles prompted.

"I think it's because I'm knee-deep in this court case—need to come up for air—get a fresh perspective. I'm not sure just why I thought you'd fit the bill."

"Glad to help anytime. You'll find I can be a very helpful fellow."

"You certainly aren't short on ego," she said. She looked out the car window. "I see we're headed for the south shore. Where are we going?"

"A really nice seafood restaurant. The Whale's Tale. T-a-l-e, not t-a-i-l," he spelled it out. "It's one of my favorites, down on Bankshead Harbor. Ever been there?"

She shook her head. "No, I haven't, but I'm glad it's a seafood place. I love fish."

"Good. What's your favorite?" he asked.

"Everything . . . lobster, shrimp, scallops, clams. You name it. Flounder, haddock, scrod. I'm a maniac, you know."

"Maniac?" he frowned, thought for a moment, then threw his head back with a laugh.

"I get it! You're from Maine!"

She nodded. "My folks raised me in Portland."

"Did a good job, too."

"Well, I guess . . ."

"What do you mean, *guess*? Here I've only just met you, but I'm impressed."

Aleesa's heart pounded in her chest. She didn't want to talk about her parents just yet. She also thought it was arrogant for Miles to make such a judgment. He didn't know her, not really, or her parents. She changed the subject.

"What about you? Where are you from?"

"Me? Right here . . . good old Boston. Raised up

on 'Sugar Hill,' we called it then. Humboldt Avenue, Harrishof Street, Townsend Street, Monroe Park . . . those streets were home to me and my friends."

"How did you become an airline pilot?" she asked. "Were you in the service?"

"No, I just always wanted to fly. I grew up on Superman, couldn't get enough of him. We lived on the third floor. Mother said she was always checking to see that the windows were locked." He chuckled. "Afraid I'd tie a sheet around my shoulders and try to fly out."

Aleesa could visualize a small boy running around, trying to fly like Superman. She smiled at the thought.

"You must have worried her a lot."

"Hmmm, maybe. Anyway, I took flying lessons as soon as they would let me. Got my pilot's license before I got my driver's license, went to MIT, got a degree in aeronautical engineering, and applied for a job with a commercial airline."

"They turned you down," Aleesa said quietly.

"Damn straight they did. Looked at me like I was crazy—had come from another planet. Said they didn't know how their passengers would react if there was a black pilot at the controls."

"So you don't mind flying cargo?"

He shook his head as he checked his rearview mirror and flicked on his signal to make a right turn.

"It's flying I want, Aleesa. Makes no difference, passengers or packages, as long as I'm well paid, that is." He smiled at her. "The career coordinator at the school today told me that you're a defense lawyer."

"That's right."

"Isn't that some kind of stretch for a woman, defending criminals?"

Miles knew that he'd said the wrong thing when he saw Aleesa stiffen in her seat. He offered an apology. "As usual, I've put my big foot in my mouth."

"Don't apologize. I don't take exception to what you said. You're not the first male to say that—probably won't be the last."

He could see that she was upset by his comment.

"Gosh, what I really meant was it's rare to find a woman defense lawyer . . . isn't it?"

"Not really."

"I shouldn't have made a dumb remark like that. You've every right to choose any career you want," he apologized. "But can I ask why?"

She remembered her father's reaction when she'd told him of her intention to be a defense lawyer. The answer she gave Miles was the same one she had offered her father.

"Someone's got to help the brothers. They're being sent off to jails and prisons like it's a rite of passage, like it's expected. I want to change that if I can by defending them."

Miles took note. There was strong determination in her voice.

"Have to admire your courage. You're a brave young woman to try," he admitted as he negotiated his way past a lumbering eighteen-wheeler on Route 3.

"If we don't help our own, who will?" Aleesa said thoughtfully. "Did you know that our children, especially physically active boys, are tracked into the 'special needs' category?"

"Don't believe I did know that."

"Well, it's true. No wonder so many of them do poorly in school—end up in juvenile detention centers."

"It's not fair, is it?" Miles said as he drove into the restaurant's parking lot.

"I never thought so," Aleesa agreed. "And maybe I can't do very much, but I can try."

They passed beneath a brightly lit canopy and Miles

surrendered the car keys to the parking valet, who had already opened the door to allow Aleesa to get out.

Miles took her elbow, inwardly delighted to be escorting such a beautiful young woman. He hoped he hadn't alienated her with his chauvinistic remarks. He was certainly attracted to her. Highlights of burnished gold spun through her soft auburn hair. It seemed to shimmer around her face like a delicate veil when she turned her face to stare at him. His next words jolted her, almost into speechlessness.

"Aleesa, you are lovely, brave, and very, very intelligent, and you may as well know from the start, I intend to marry you."

Her eyes widened and she stopped dead in her tracks.

"That has to be the dumbest line I've heard in a long time! I don't even *know* you! You must be crazy!"

"Not really. And I do plan on giving you time to get to know me—get used to the idea." He smiled as he led her into the dining area.

"Thanks a bunch, buster, but no thanks! This is just a friendly get-acquainted date, that's all. I have no interest in marrying *anybody.*"

"We'll see," Miles said, "we'll see." He told the waiter, "A table by the window, sir, if that's available."

"Indeed, right this way, sir."

"Aleesa," Miles whispered, "you're going to love this place."

"Maybe, as long as you don't think having a meal with you means I have to marry you. Because if that's the case, you'd better take me home right now."

"Not a chance, little lady. I promised you a seafood dinner and that's what you're going to have."

The waiter led them to a table in front of a large floor-to-ceiling window overlooking Bankshead Harbor. The setting sun, a gold-flamed orb, hung low on the western horizon. The orange-red glow reflected on the placid water, on the sailboats and cabin cruisers that swayed gently at their moorings. Early shore lights glowed softly in the waning daylight and added to the peaceful atmosphere.

The tables were set with sea-green tablecloths and mauve napkins. Crystal goblets, elegant silverware, and low votive candles flickered in the center of delicate flower arrangements.

The waiter seated Aleesa and handed her a thick velour-covered menu. She opened it to an attractively designed list of entrees. She smiled her thanks at him. Soft music murmured in the background and added to her comfort. She looked out the window and felt herself relax.

She remembered that first date so well. She remembered too, feeling overly burdened with the law cases assigned to her. There was the one of a teen-aged boy accused of arson at his high school. His frantic parents had retained her to defend him and were deeply concerned about the future of their only child. And there were the pressing problems she had with the client she was currently defending. As she reflected back on that first evening with Miles, she recalled how comforted, how 'cared for,' he had made her feel. Did that mean he was going to be in her future?

Two

Aleesa rushed down the stone stairs of the law library in downtown Boston. *Thank God,* she thought, *it maintains some weekend hours of admission.* Thank God, too, that she'd been able to find a parking space on a nearby side street. Just like every other city, Boston had its parking problems. But, after all, this historic city had been laid out on cow paths.

She located her car, tossed her hair away from her sweaty face, threw her briefcase onto the front seat, slid in behind the steering wheel, fastened her seat belt, blew out her cheeks in a puff of breath, and switched on the ignition.

Good old Bess, she thought as she pulled away from the parking space. As long as she took the eight-year-old Volvo to the mechanic for regular maintenance, the car gave her good service.

She was relieved that her research had given her some answers. Now she was ready to proceed with her client's case, and just maybe had a good chance of winning. And, yes, indeed, for a one-hundred-fifty-dollar stipend for his time, Dr. Bissell would testify as an expert witness.

Her thoughts turned to Miles. For the first time since their meeting six months ago, he was coming to her place for dinner. His busy flight schedule and her varied court activities made time together hard to come by. But whenever he was out of the country, he sent small gifts.

"It's just so you won't forget me," he told her with the impish grin which was beginning to have an effect on her. It might be a Japanese print, a beautiful jade pin from Bangkok, a silk scarf from the Hermès shop in Paris, or perhaps a fragile cup and saucer carefully wrapped from one of London's most famous stores, Harrods. Always the message with the gifts was, FROM THE MAN IN YOUR LIFE, EVER AND ALWAYS, LOVE, MILES.

The gifts were very nice, but accepting them had bothered her. She planned to tell him so tonight.

Miles's eyes widened when he saw her kitchen. "Wow! This is some kind of kitchen! Sure you're not a professional chef?"

Her answer was quick. "You'd be happy if I happened to be some kind of domestic, I take it, not a lawyer, if I hear you right."

"No, no, not at all," he protested.

She waved her hand. "Anyway, Miles, welcome to my sanctuary." In a more somber tone, she explained, "This is where I work off *all* my frustrations, hostilities, calm my fears and work through my disappointments. When I can beat up a mean chocolate cake, fuss over a beef stew, or fry up a pan of fried chicken, I always feel a whole lot better."

"You certainly don't eat all that food from the look of that beautiful figure of yours," he complimented.

"No, I don't, but I do have friends who seem to enjoy my cooking, and I share with them."

"I've never seen such a well-equipped kitchen in an apartment. You've enough pots and pans to cook for an army." He tossed an appreciative nod toward the gleaming pots and pans that hung from a rack over the butcher block island.

Aleesa looked up and nodded. She was putting the finishing touches on a casserole.

"I never like doing things halfway," she admitted. "And whenever I get the chance to cook, I want to have everything I need and not have to make do or settle for substitutes."

"An artist is only as good as his . . . um . . . her tools, eh? Tell you what, next time I'm in Paris, I'll pick up a few gourmet utensils, now that I know you like to cook."

Aleesa turned to face him after placing the casserole in the oven. "No, Miles, really, I don't need any more utensils, and besides, I wish you'd stop sending me gifts."

He stared at her. "Stop sending . . . ?"

"Right, stop sending. The gifts are exquisite and it's thoughtful of you, but . . ."

"But what? What you talkin' 'bout, girl?" Miles challenged. His eyebrows rose with questions. He continued angrily, "You mean I can't give presents, tokens of my affection, to the woman I love? You mean you're goin' to deny me *that* pleasure? Nonsense!"

Aleesa sighed, leaning back against the sink. She breathed deeply before she answered. "I know I seem ungrateful, Miles, and I'm sorry if I've offended you, but I can't help it. I like taking care of myself, being independent, not . . . you know what I mean, like . . . being bought or something," her voice trailed off. She turned back to the sink.

"Bought or something!" Miles thundered at her.

He strode over, took both her hands in his, and held them gently. He shook his head.

"You're so wrong," he said quietly. "I'm not trying to 'buy' you, Aleesa, I'm trying to show how much I care, that even though I'm many miles away, I think of you. Don't you know how much pleasure that gives me?"

She didn't trust herself to answer. She knew he was sincere, and *her* feelings bothered her. She had never felt that she had what people call 'gracious skills,' or even the ability to share her deepest feelings with anyone else.

She freed her hands from his grasp and returned to washing the lettuce. "Well, please stop sending me things. Like I said, it makes me feel . . . well, anyway, I don't like the feeling. It . . . it overwhelms me, somehow."

Standing beside her at the sink, watching her, Miles noticed the disturbed look on her face. He saw even more. Concern, fear—what *was* she afraid of? Commitment? Certainly not of him. Instinctively, he reached for her. He wanted to reassure her, comfort her, but she moved quickly to get something from the refrigerator.

Aleesa was disturbed because she knew she was becoming attracted to Miles. She knew, too, that she wasn't ready for a real, steady relationship. She had her own priorities—her present court case, for one, and the other unresolved, overwhelming burden that she had to reconcile before she could make any commitment. She wondered, could she maintain a simple, friendly, platonic relationship with this man? Maybe that was why she wanted to reject his gifts. Perhaps she shouldn't have invited him to dinner, she thought. But he'd been away so often, and she really did want—no, *needed*—a friend.

She took a cheese tray and a small platter of shrimp with cocktail sauce from the refrigerator. She led Miles into her small but inviting living room. A white leather love seat had been placed in front of a large window.

On a glass-topped coffee table were a decanter of wine and an ice bucket. Wrought-iron torchieres flooded the room with soft light that reflected off the high ceiling. An elegant tapestried wing chair in the opposite corner had a small table beside it. Miles noticed a pile of what appeared to be law books on the table and scattered on the floor.

"Been studying?" he asked.

"Yes, I have," she said, relieved that they had left their disagreement back in the kitchen. At least Miles was considerate of her feelings. That made her a bit more comfortable. And God knew, he *was* handsome. She watched as he sat down on the love seat. His movements were smooth and easy. His body had no muscular bulges, only a firm, subtle, invigorating energy. He was built like a track star. He told her once, she remembered, that he had run the four-forty hurdles at the Penn State Relay Races while in college. Track was also her favorite sport, and she could envision Miles's long legs flashing over the wooden hurdles.

She had also noted his calm, patient attitude. He always seemed to know what he wanted. For example, whenever they went out to dinner, he would be pleasant and firm with the waiters, but he would make it very clear what it was that he wanted and how he wanted it served. He was never intolerant or overbearing, and she was always comfortable with him. Would dinner tonight change that comfort level? Despite her rejection of his gift-giving, would she be able to keep the evening's activities on a "friend-to-friend" level?

She responded to his question. "I'm working on a pro bono case. My firm, Carter, Evans and Goode, frequently assigns cases, free cases, to newcomers to the firm, like me.' "

"And you're defending?"

"A poor soul."

"Tell me about him." Miles poured wine into the glasses, handed one to Aleesa, and moved so she could join him on the love seat. She did, then took a sip of wine and offered crackers and shrimp to him. He shook his head. She was hungry, so she ate a shrimp and sipped more wine before she turned to face him. "You'd better help yourself to shrimp and crackers." She glanced at her watch. "Be a few minutes before the casserole will be ready."

"That's fine. I'll pick at something in a bit, but I'm interested in your case."

"Well, Miles, you know, of course, I can't reveal the client's name." He nodded in agreement. "But I can give you the gist of the case. M. T. has been accused of robbery."

"Robbery?"

"Robbery. He was arrested for robbing an ATM machine. He was identified by a photograph . . . the ATM camera. But I can prove that this is a case of mistaken identification. You know *they* say we all look alike."

"I know," Miles conceded. This time he helped himself to some shrimp. "These are excellent shrimp," he said, and took a few more.

"Glad you like them. Miles, the reason I know it's a case of false identity is because I can prove my client was in another place at the date and time the ATM photo was taken."

"Where was your client?"

"In the hospital."

"Hospital?"

"Right. He was a patient at a psychiatric facility in downtown Boston on the same day and at the same time the picture was taken. He couldn't be in two places at one time. I plan to subpoena his hospital records, as well as have testimony from the staff physician that treated him while he was hospitalized."

"And you can get him off even with the picture?"

"I'm betting on it," she assured him.

The timer went off in the kitchen.

Aleesa jumped up. "That bell means the casserole is ready. Sit, Miles, sit," she told him. "I'll have the food on the table in a jiffy. Relax, finish your wine. I do want you to enjoy yourself tonight."

Miles could hear her working about in the kitchen, placing dishes on the table, removing items from the refrigerator. He speared another shrimp, dipped it into the cocktail sauce, and popped it into his mouth.

An enjoyable evening, eh? he wondered. What was all that "not accepting gifts" about? How else could he show her how much she meant to him if he couldn't ever give her things? He'd have to find a way to let her know how much she meant to him and . . . he would not give up, not until she accepted him and his love. Somehow. He had figured their relationship was moving forward when she'd invited him for dinner tonight. Could he be wrong? He'd never had problems before getting women to understand him. But, he realized, Aleesa Haskins was different from most of the women he had known. He knew the attraction was real—for him.

He picked up the tray of shrimp and crackers to take into the kitchen. Placing the hot casserole on a trivet, Aleesa looked up as he came in. Her face was flushed from the oven's heat, her hair curled in tendrils around her face. Miles was stunned, almost speechless. God, she was so beautiful! He let out a soft breath, placing the tray on the kitchen counter. It was sheer willpower that kept him from grabbing her, holding her close, kissing her. He felt himself harden. *God knows how much I want to make love to her, how much I need her,* he thought.

He forced himself to calm down. Aleesa was not the

naïve girl-next-door type, that he knew. He observed
her precise movements as she placed the food on the
table, lit the candles, turned out the overhead light,
and beckoned him to the table. He smelled the pro-
vocative cologne she wore, a sophisticated floral es-
sence, and he visualized her lovely naked body close
to his in candlelight. *Go slow,* he warned himself. *Man,
go slow.*

Three

Aleesa hurried into the courthouse. Alan Bissell, the psychiatrist who had treated her client, promised to meet her a half hour before court so she could review his deposition. She expected it to be straightforward and very convincing. And it was.

"Dr. Bissell," she questioned her expert witness, "will you please give the court your full name, and please spell your last name?"

"Certainly, ma'am," he answered in a firm tone. "My name is Dr. Alan J. Bissell. That is B-i-s-s-e-l-l," he spelled.

"And your education?"

"Undergraduate degree from Harvard University. My medical degree was from Harvard Medical School."

"Are you Board Certified?"

"Yes. My Board Certification is in Psychiatry. I specialize in obsessive-compulsive disorders."

Aleesa had chosen to wear a black tailored suit with a simple white silk blouse. A large bow tied at the neck framed her face. She wanted to look professional, so she wore small pearl earrings—her makeup was soft and subtle. Her nails had been manicured with only clear nail polish. She had known firsthand that the judge in this case was a well-known misogynist. Whether she liked it or not, he was the judge she had drawn on the case. He believed women should be kept at home, certainly not in his court. For the sake of her client, Aleesa did not wish to jeopardize the case by upsetting him. She had to be careful.

"Dr. Bissell, would you describe in layman's terms the psychiatric condition of my client?"

"Yes. Your client has been diagnosed with a rather unusual obsessive-compulsive disorder known as Self-Induced Water Intoxication Syndrome. Called SIWIS, for short."

"And can the patient become quite ill from this disease?"

"If not treated, yes."

"How can drinking excessive amounts of water make a person so sick, Dr. Bissell?"

"Because although water is an extremely vital part of good health, extreme amounts of water upset the proper balance of electrolytes, normal blood levels, and other parameters of good health."

"Your treatment for such cases, Doctor?"

Aleesa noted that the judge was paying rapt attention to her witness and his answers.

"To be successful in treatment, the patient should be hospitalized and his intake and output of fluids carefully monitored and measured twenty-four hours a day."

She handed the witness a picture. "Dr. Bissell, was my client a patient at your hospital the day this photograph was taken at the ATM machine?"

Dr. Bissell checked the date on the picture, then handed it back to Aleesa. "My hospital records document that your client was at the hospital being treated the day this picture was taken."

"Thank you, Dr. Bissell."

* * *

Later, she told her father that there was no way the prosecutor could discount the medical records the doctor had presented. Subsequently, the judge dismissed the case and her client was returned to the hospital to complete his treatment.

Her father was jubilant.

"I had every confidence in you, my dear. I knew you would win your case!" Her father's voice boomed congratulations over the telephone. "Too bad you can't get up here and go sailing. The weather is beautiful, and I can think of no better way to celebrate your success."

"Dad, I wish I could. It's getting real hot here in Boston, but my supervisor insists that I file a lawsuit against the city . . ."

"For false arrest of your client?"

"Right."

"Well, get up as soon as you can. Bring that young man with you . . . that pilot fellow."

"Maybe, Dad, if he's free. Say hi to Mom."

"Will do. Bye, honey. Proud of you."

Aleesa replaced the receiver. She sat still for a moment. Her father was proud of her and she believed that Miles would be, too, but what about *them*? Would *they* have been proud of her?

With her hand still resting on the phone, suddenly it became clear to her that she wanted to share this triumph with Miles. How come? Where had that feeling come from?

She went into her kitchen, cleared a space on her work counter, and gathered papers and reference materials she would need for her brief.

Harrison Butterworth, a senior partner in the firm,

had insisted that she start preparation for a suit on her client's behalf against the city.

"Your client's rights were violated . . . false arrest, and he should be compensated for that loss. Just because he has a severe illness makes no difference. Get right on it, this weekend, and we'll see what we can do to retrieve some money for the poor man. You don't mind a little weekend work, do you? You can report your billable hours."

"No, Mr. Butterworth. I'm free this weekend and I'll get started."

"You're sure? I know the weather indicates it's going to be a good weekend for sailing." He knew about her hobby.

"There'll be other weekends, I'm sure, sir."

Tall, red-haired, with the impeccable grooming and manners of a successful attorney, he gave her a brief smile.

"You do good work, Ms. Haskins. Action against the city will not only teach the police to do better work, but it will make our firm look more humane to the average Joe. *Look at Carter, Evans and Goode . . . how wonderful for a big firm like that to look out for the little guy.* I'm certain the news media will pick up on that fact."

And the publicity will not hurt the firm, Aleesa thought.

So she worked from eight Saturday morning until she took a lunch break: a peanut butter sandwich and a glass of skim milk. She spied a container of strawberry-flavored yogurt, but decided that would do for a snack later.

Weariness overcame her late that afternoon. All at once she'd had enough of M. T. and his problems. She stood and stretched slowly, as if trying to put some vigor back into her body. She felt as creaky as an old woman. *My God, I'm only thirty-two, I shouldn't be this stiff.*

She decided to check her E-mail before she called it a night. There was a message from the college alumni chairperson reminding her to please forward a financial contribution ASAP so they could meet their goal. A message was there from her cousin, Judd, about the upcoming celebration for his parents' fortieth wedding anniversary. And . . . there was a note from Miles.

In LA. Will arrive Sunday. I will call you when I get in town. All my love, Miles.

It would be good to see him, to see his reaction when she announced she'd won her case. She imagined his eyes would widen, not in surprise, but in his delight in sharing her happiness. And his all-encompassing smile would make her know how much he cared.

After her shower and shampoo, Aleesa sat facing her mirror and took inventory. Attending law school at night had taken four years while working days waitressing. Even now, a few years later, she maintained her figure. One hundred-twenty-five pounds on a five-foot frame was not bad at all. Her skin, a rosy honey tone, glowed from her steamy shower, and her reddish-brown hair tumbled to her shoulders. But it was her gray-green eyes that puzzled her. Who had given her those eyes? Well, she reflected, creaming her face, when you were adopted there were some things you never knew. What had Miles *seen* when he looked at her? Whatever prompted him to tell her on their first date that he was going to marry her? *What* had he seen in her? After all his travels, the many women in all the cities that he visited, what

made him think that *she* was the one? Wasn't she
like all the rest, except "adopted" and unsure of who
she was. Growing up, her folks said she was theirs,
their "chosen" one, but wasn't that like shopping for
a car or furniture? "We choose *this* one. Always
wanted a green car. Like, always wanted a *girl.*"

And what about her birth parents? Were they alive
or . . . dead? Ghost-like angels hovering somewhere
around her shoulders, invisible but guarding her nev-
ertheless. Or were they? She wondered.

She went around the apartment, checking the door
locks, and the stove to make certain no burners had
been left on and all lights were turned off. *For a person
who is so practical, a lawyer who deals with facts and reality,
I ought to push aside the distraction of my birth and get on
with my life,* she thought to herself.

She couldn't see the man's face, but there was no
mistaking the angry gestures he was making at the
woman whose long auburn hair fluttered as her shoulders shook. The woman was sobbing, "Please, please,
no, don't, don't say any more! Please!"

Aleesa sat bolt upright in bed. Her hair was wet, her
nightgown clung with dampness to her skin. The nightmare again. She hadn't had one since she was a teenager. Why now?

Four

What had caused her nightmare? Was this going to be a regular occurrence? Was it because she was tired, working too hard? Besides her work, though, what else did she have?

Two A.M., another shower, shampoo, and fresh pj's later, she realized that she was hungry. She remembered she hadn't had any supper. Bundled up in a white terry-cloth robe, with a towel around her still damp hair, she decided an omelet with a couple of slices of crisp bacon would do. Maybe an English muffin with strawberry jam would assuage her hunger and . . . perhaps get her mind back on track. Could be she needed the glucose. Sarah Pritchard, a big-boned Wisconsin girl, her law school classmate, always said so.

"Girlfriend, don't you know you need a sugar lift every now and again? Your little old puny body needs carbohydrates to keep your brain working. Everybody knows that!"

Maybe *that's* why she had the nightmare . . . "carbo-depleted."

She had just taken a bite of her omelet when the quiet was broken. The doorbell rang.

"Miles! When did you get in?"

"Just now. Had a great tailwind from the west. And I couldn't wait to see you, Leese, I've been so far away from you. Come here, love of my life!"

His arms encircled her.

Aware that she wore only her pajamas and robe, she tried to pull back, but Miles was determined and strong.

"God, how I've missed you," he murmured into her ear, and she felt her will waver. She smelled the woodsy, smoky fragrance of the aftershave he wore. The scratchy tingle on her skin came from his mustache. His breath was warm and reassuring. Despite that, however, she shivered. She did not know why, because she was not cold, not really. Her nerves had been so bruised and battered over the last twelve hours, she felt very unlike her usual practical self. She realized, too, that this one time, tonight, at least, she needed stability, and she knew that Miles Kittridge would give her that.

For a brief moment she clung to him, tears flowing unchecked down her cheeks.

"Why am I crying? This isn't like me at all. I'm sorry . . ."

"Don't be, sweetheart. Here, come sit." He led her to the sofa. "Look, I brought you something. I know, I know," he said, forestalling her objections. "I know I promised to hold off on gift-giving, but this . . . well, I couldn't resist."

Aleesa opened the box and carefully unfolded the tissue paper. "What is it?"

"You'll see. I hope you like it. When I saw it, I knew I had to buy it—for you."

She peeled away the folds of paper and her fingers touched the yielding smoothness of silk. Tumbling colors of iridescent orchid, a royal purple, glittering turquoise, a soft, melting rose all bound by a background color of emerald green were woven into a delicate design. Aleesa pulled the cloth from the box.

"It's a kimono! It's beautiful, Miles. I've never seen anything quite like it. But you . . ."

"Never mind the 'I shouldn'ts.' Try it on."

When she returned from her bedroom, she had dried her hair and tied it into a ponytail with a dark blue ribbon. The voluminous folds of the robe gently draped her small body. Miles drew in a deep breath when Aleesa stood in front of him, her hands clasped in obeisance.

"I knew it! Girl, you are just beautiful."

She had a chance to get control of herself. She answered him in her usual feisty manner. "Yeah, right. I bet you say that to all the girls that you bring Japanese robes to."

Miles placed his hand on his chest and gave her a strickened look.

"How can you say such a thing, love of my life?"

"You mean I'm the only one who has received such a magnificent gift?"

Miles raised his right hand in a Boy Scout salute. "Scout's honor," he said.

"Well, then, I guess I can thank you properly." She kissed him gently on the cheek.

He could smell the freshness of her recently shampooed hair, and it took every ounce of strength that he didn't know he had to resist the temptation to hold her close. As if she could read his mind, Aleesa moved away quickly.

"I was just having a bite to eat. That's the reason I'm up so late. Would you like something? Only take me a minute . . ."

"Not really. I did have a snack on the flight."

"Well, how about a glass of sherry or something stronger, gin and tonic, scotch, bourbon?"

"Aleesa, a cold beer would be just fine. I didn't care for the Japanese beer at all."

"A cold beer it is then."

By the time she returned with the beer and a bowl of pretzels, Miles had picked up the tissue paper and box and cleared a space on the table for the tray.

"Here's to you, Miles," she said as she saluted him with her upraised glass of sherry. "To your safe return and all."

"Thanks, Aleesa. It was a long way to travel, but I thought about you every minute. Hey"—he put his beer can on the coffee table—"how did you make out with that case of yours?"

"I won, of course," Aleesa stated, not immodestly.

"Hot damn, I *knew* you would win. Tell me. I want to hear all about it."

He moved to her side on the love seat and took both of her hands in his. The warmth, the secure feeling she sensed, triggered something in her. This man cared. He really did.

She pulled her hands free of his and took another sip of her sherry.

"Well, it was like I said. This was a pro bono case that I was assigned to and I knew that I wanted to do well. So first I went to visit the client in jail."

"In jail? You had to go there?"

"Right. See, he'd been arrested because a police officer found him hanging around the ATM. Then when the robbery occurred and they found his picture, they arrested him. He had given a boarding house address . . . well, not a boarding house exactly, more like a halfway house for the chronically mentally ill."

"Could you tell he was sick when you saw him in the jail?"

"Oh yes, right away. I noticed that it was difficult for him to make eye contact, he pulled on his clothes, and had a very distressing habit of swaying from side to side . . . restless, agitated . . . you know."

"Were you scared of him?" Miles worried.

"At first, a little, but then I began to feel sorry for him. And I knew that if I couldn't help him he was going to be just another brother trampled by the system. Besides, he kept saying that he didn't know what the police were talkin' 'bout. 'Ain't never robbed *nobody*, nevr' min' no *machine*.' "

"Could he tell you anything?"

"He knew the name and address of the halfway house. So I inquired there and the social worker assigned to the house gave me the information I needed to contact the psychiatrist who was monitoring his care."

"And?" Miles was eager to hear the rest of the story.

"And," Aleesa repeated with a wide smile, "that's when we found the conflict in the date the robbery was to have taken place. My client was in the hospital under twenty-four-hour watch because of his diagnosis. His illness had required that he be hospitalized."

"You mean that water intoxication thing?"

"That's right. All the time when I was trying to interview him, he kept asking for water. 'I need a glass of water, ma'am. Please, can I have some water? I'm dying of thirst, ma'am.' It was quite pitiful, Miles."

"I'm sure it was. Couldn't have been easy for you, either." He looked at her with proud admiration. "Made you want to help him even more, I expect."

"It did, Miles. It did."

"So what did you do next?"

"I got him released back to the halfway house in care of the social worker. See, he had been in a state facility, so the judge agreed that the social worker, as an employee of the state, could maintain custody," Aleesa explained.

"So you finally went to court."

"Right, we did, and with Dr. Bissell's testimony—he was the psychiatrist on the case—and the documentation of my client's therapy sessions, the jury had to decide on a not-guilty verdict."

"All right!" Miles whooped. "You go, girl!"

Aleesa smiled at his exuberance.

"There was more, Miles."

"What do you mean, *more?*"

"The guy who robbed the money machine could not have known his picture was being taken. The dummy must have been so happy with the money he was stealing, he looked right into the camera and grinned. Had a big smile with two gold teeth right in front."

"You're kidding!"

"No, I'm not. And Dr. Bissell testified that among my client's various compulsive behaviors was the obsession he had with his teeth."

"What do you mean, obsession with his teeth?"

"This man walked around with toothpaste and a toothbrush in his shirt pocket, like a businessman with pens. The doctor testified that the one thing my client was most proud of was that he had never had a cavity in his life and had all his own teeth!"

"I'll be damned, Aleesa." Miles grinned at her. "How about that!"

Aleesa could see that Miles was delighted and

happy for her. She could see it in his shining eyes and his wide, quirky grin.

He leaned back against the sofa.

"You know, you're some kind of smart young lady, my love, and I'm proud of you. Proud as a peacock," he added.

"I was only doing my job."

"Well, I know, but still and all, doing it for free. A lot of people wouldn't go the extra mile like you did, my dear."

"The extra mile, as you call it, will be if we can sue for wrongful arrest and get some money for the poor man. That is going to be more difficult."

"You can do it. I have every confidence in you."

Aleesa made a mock bow. "Thank you, kind sir."

He smiled at her. "You know you deserve a congratulatory hug, don't you?"

"I guess so."

He opened his arms to her. She knew he wanted to hold her. Was she ready for that? She *had* missed him, and was grateful for his safe return, but did she want more from this man? Her emotions were still jumbled up—the nightmare, Miles's unexpected return in the middle of the night, the turmoil of the trial, the exhilaration of her success—she looked at him. Something in his face assured her that she could respond to him. Something in her own heart told her it was the right thing to do. Was she really, truly falling in love with him . . . as he had prophesied she would?

From her bedroom radio the sounds of Natalie Cole and her father, Nat "King" Cole, drifted into the living room. The soft lyrics of their velvet voices kindled a need in her that she knew had to be satisfied.

Miles heard them, too. "You *are* unforgettable, my love. You know that," he said quietly.

Silently, Aleesa turned toward him. The appeal of his eyes as he reached for her mitigated the reluctance she was experiencing.

Miles understood her hesitancy. He touched her face gently, with the softness of a butterfly's wing. Slowly he lowered his mouth to hers. He had waited so long for this moment. He had been hungry for the touch of his lips on hers, but he knew patience and gentle control would mean a great deal to her . . . and to him. His future with her, the woman he knew he loved, hinged on this moment.

He sensed her vulnerability, but he would not take unfair advantage of her. It took tremendous willpower on his part because every inch, every muscle, every nerve in his body wanted more than life itself to make love to her. But Aleesa was life to him, and he knew he had to control himself. He tore his mouth from her soft, yielding lips and whispered into her ear, "Congratulations, my love."

He saw a bewildered look come into her luminous gray-green eyes, as if imploring him for answers. Her skin glowed from the bewitching tension of the moment and she drew in soft breaths as if she needed air. To Miles she had never looked so appealing, so lovely.

He took a deep breath to allow the moment to dissipate. He looked at his watch.

"It's almost three, Leese, I'd better let you get some rest."

The pause was welcomed by Aleesa because she sensed herself succumbing to Miles's advances. She knew she needed time to sort things out.

"It is late, Miles, and you have had a long day,

what with crossing time zones flying in from wherever."

"No problem, honey, knowing I was coming home
to you." He kissed her lightly on the cheek and was
out the door.

Aleesa closed and bolted the door. She leaned
against it for a moment. She had some serious thinking
to do.

Five

Despite his promise to himself, Miles had a difficult time controlling his urge to call Aleesa every chance he got. He needed to see her, to be with her, to hear her voice, to bask in the delight he felt in her presence. Somehow, though, he had the feeling that, although attracted to him—she'd said as much—Aleesa seemed to be holding back, restraining herself, not allowing her feelings for him to show. Why? he wondered as he drove into his driveway. And that nonsense about not accepting his gifts. What was that all about? He turned off the ignition and sat for a moment, thinking. He had to come up with some plan that would sweep Miss Aleesa Haskins off her feet and knock any reservations she might have about him right out of her head. Already he knew that he loved her, couldn't get her out of his mind.

Weary after another long flight from the Far East where he had dropped off parts to a U.S.-owned athletic shoe plant, Miles needed some rest, but he had to touch base with Aleesa first. It had been two weeks since he'd had dinner at her place.

He entered his apartment and threw his keys on the bedside table. He dropped his overnight bag at the foot of his bed and began to undress as he headed for the bathroom and a much needed hot shower. Maybe once he'd washed away the fatigue and grime from his long flight, he'd be able to think more clearly. He checked his watch when he took it off. Twelve noon, but his body and his brain were still on Hong Kong time, one o'clock the next morning. No wonder he was weary.

After his shower he went straight to bed. Aleesa would be working at her law office, so he decided he might as well get some sleep and call her later that evening.

"Miles, you're back! Have a good trip?"

Aleesa's welcome voice quickened Miles's pulse, and he responded enthusiastically, "Best trip of my life, now that I'm back here in the same place as you. How 'bout dinner tonight?"

"At the Whale's Tale?" she asked.

"Be my pleasure. Your wish is my command," he said.

"Great."

"I'll pick you up at seven."

"I'll be ready," she told him.

That night Miles felt happier than he had in years. He had no long overseas trips scheduled for the next few weeks, only some short daytime flights to nearby cities in the States, and he had accumulated some leave time, so he planned to ask Aleesa to spend some of it with him.

He had also made the big decision to ask Aleesa to marry him. His happiness bubbled up in his chest and he knew he would burst if he waited much longer to ask her. In all of his thirty-something years, he'd never been so certain of his feelings. Aleesa was beautiful, smart, had a sense of self that he admired, and when he was with her his mind told him that this woman made him a complete man in every sense of the word. Love was strange, he thought. Of all the millions of people in the world, there was one person that was meant for you.

As he drove to her apartment that night, he thought about Aleesa's beauty. Not just her enchanting body— slim, lean, with curves in the proper places—but her glorious chestnut-red hair, rosy tan skin, and . . . those emerald green eyes that so bewitched him. He ached to hold her close, to make love to her, to claim her as his own.

"God, you look beautiful," Miles breathed as later that evening he helped Aleesa into his car.

"Thanks, Miles," she grinned at him as she fastened her seatbelt. "How have you been, anyway . . . especially after your overseas trip?"

"Oh, I'm fine, just fine, now that I have you here beside me. You ready for the Whale's Tale?"

"Am I ever!" she exclaimed.

"Bad day at the office?" he asked.

"Nothing that I couldn't handle," she replied.

The waiter, who was familiar with the pair after several visits to the restaurant, led them straight to their favorite harbor-side table. He handed them their menus.

"Sir, would you like something from the bar? Or perhaps wine?" he asked Miles.

Miles raised his eyebrows in question to Aleesa, who shook her head.

"Perhaps later," Miles told the waiter. "Please give us a few more minutes to decide on our orders."

"Very well, sir." He filled their glasses with fresh water and left.

"Well, at last, here we are," Miles said.

"Right, here we are." Aleesa put down the menu. "Tell me about your flight."

He noticed that she had put down the menu. She was apparently ready to order.

"Know already what you're going to have? You're a girl after my own heart . . . know what you want with no hesitation, no 'shilly-shallying'."

"Saves time, Miles."

"Right. And speaking of time, how 'bout if we spend this weekend together?"

"Now who's not 'shilly-shallying'?" she smiled.

Relieved that she had not rejected the idea, Miles figured he'd better press his case. He reached for her hands. They were warm, soft, and smooth. Just touching her made his temperature rise, and he felt deep stirrings in his groin. What power this slip of a girl had over him. Did she realize how she affected him?

"Aleesa, you do know I'm crazy about you. Think I fell in love with you when I met you at that Career Day seminar."

"Yes, and as I remember it," she countered, "you were very bold. Quite forward."

"Couldn't help it. Your beauty took my breath away, and to this day I don't remember how I acted, but please answer my question. Will you spend the week-end with me?"

"What . . . what did you have in mind?" she asked hesitantly.

"I was thinking of a nice, quiet, leisurely drive north to take in the fall foliage. They are expecting great color in the Vermont mountains. We could stay in a nice bed and breakfast inn. I hear they are quite nice up there. What do you say?"

"Maybe. I'll think about it."

"You will?" His eyes widened with pleasure at her response. "That's just great! We'll have a good time. I know we will."

He gave her hands a gentle squeeze, pleased that

she had partially accepted, or at least not turned down his offer.

"Now where's that waiter?" He looked around. "I'm ready to eat, aren't you?" The waiter came right over when Miles beckoned.

"I think so. I'd like the lobster casserole, a small baked potato, and a garden salad with raspberry vinaigrette dressing," she ticked off quickly.

"Sounds good to me. I'll have the same." He retrieved the wine list from the menu folder. He figured it might be a good idea to have some wine to ease the excitement he felt rising within him.

"Would red wine be agreeable with your lobster?"

"It would. Now tell me about your flight to the Far East. I've only been to Hawaii to attend a bar association meeting, and I tell you, Miles, lawyers can be a mighty dull group when they get together."

"It was a routine flight," he explained. "Had to deliver shoe parts for an American footwear company that has their shoe products assembled in shops overseas. Then we had been ordered to load up on computer parts to be returned here."

"Did you see much of the city of Hong Kong?"

"Not much, just enough to know it's extremely crowded and I wouldn't want to live there. Now, about this weekend . . ."

Aleesa knew that Miles was serious about spending the weekend together, but she had reservations about taking such a definitive step in their relationship. She could and did admit to herself that she was deeply attracted to him. He was extremely good-looking, tall, lean, with firm, taut muscles that showed innate strength. His rich brown skin and dark brown eyes with beautifully defined eyebrows formed a face that was one of the handsomest she had ever seen. He was kind, considerate, and had always treated her as if she were the most precious person on earth, and she had responded. She really liked his gallant attention. But a weekend with him, she wondered, was she really ready for such a commitment?

Ambivalence washed over her. She admitted to herself that she had missed Miles when he was away on his overseas flight this past week, but on the other hand she knew she would never marry until she dealt with the dark misgivings that had always hung over her . . . her beginnings. Who had given her her light skin coloring, the emerald green eyes, the chestnut-red hair?

Since she could remember, Carol and Grady Haskins had told her that she was adopted. So she had always known, but would a worldly, sophisticated man like Miles be able to deal with a woman who didn't even know who she was . . . whatever heritage, "baggage" she carried?

She recognized the glow of anticipation and pleasure on Miles's face as he waited for her response. Relief came at that moment when the waiter brought their salads and placed them in front of their places. She needed the time to think. Why had she blithely almost agreed to a weekend? It was not her usual pattern to make quick decisions like that. What had come over her? As a lawyer, she had been trained to think through her options, but tonight she had acted like a needy teenager. God, she had always prided herself on controlling her emotions.

Miles noticed Aleesa's nonresponse to his question. He could almost see the vacillating thoughts flicker across her face.

"Is your salad all right, Aleesa?"

"It's very good, fresh and crisp the way I like it."

He refilled her wine glass. He had to plunge forward, get an answer to his question, because from her manner and the look on her face, he felt she was having second thoughts.

"I want you to enjoy your meal. Now, about this weekend . . ."

A background of comforting murmurs from the other dinner guests in the restaurant and the soft music was pleasantly relaxing to her, even though Aleesa felt her face redden with embarrassment. She had to be honest with Miles and answer him truthfully. Somehow she was in a precarious position. She couldn't make an excuse for not spending the weekend with him. One thing she always insisted on was courage and honesty, both in other people and in herself. And if there was to be a relationship, it would have to be based on honesty.

She looked up to see the waiter approaching with their entrees. She decided the time to answer Miles had come, even though her mind rocketed back and forth and momentarily she felt unstable.

The fragrant, tantalizing smell of the lobster casserole greeted her when the waiter removed the silver domes from their plates. She picked up her fork for the first bite, then replaced it on the table.

"Miles," she said quietly, "I'd really love to spend the weekend with you, but I can't." She stayed his protests with a raised hand. "I know I said I would think about it, and I'd really like to, but I'm not certain this is the right time in our relationship for something like a weekend together. You know I'm fond of you, but are we really, truly at that stage? Aren't we pushing ahead too fast?"

"I don't think so. No, not at all. I know how I feel about you, Aleesa. Since I've met you, you're all I can think about. I believe you already know what you mean to me, don't you?"

She nodded silently, picked up her fork, and began

to eat. She sensed Miles's disappointment, and she was grateful that he seemed to understand.

"Tell you what, honey, let's forget the overnight business . . . I can see you're not ready for that, but I'm going to be patient. I have to be because you are all that matters to me. I don't want you to ever forget that. Nothing can ever change the way I feel about you, my Aleesa. Remember our first date here at the Whale's Tale when I told you I was going to marry you?"

She nodded, her eyes fixed on his face.

"I meant that then and I still mean it. I'll wait, my precious, I'll wait. The day will come and we'll be together for the rest of our lives."

Aleesa's eyes filled with unshed tears at Miles's pronouncement. She lowered her head to hide the moisture in her eyes, glad to be in the dimly lit restaurant. *How will he react when he finds out that the "woman he loves" has no history, no past, doesn't know who her birth parents are or if they are dead or alive? He deserves better than I can give. I want to be with him, accept his love, savor it, hold it close, take strength and pride in being loved by such a wonderful man, but how can I when I can't come to him as an equal with full knowledge of my own heritage? Am I being honest with him by pursuing this relationship when I can't even bring myself to tell him the truth about me?*

Miles was watching her, reading the conflicting thoughts that he suspected Aleesa was experiencing. He glimpsed a shimmer of moisture in her eyes and sensed her subtle distress. He ached to take her in his arms and struggled against the almost overpowering impulse to carry her back to his place and make love to her. He wanted to hold her, protect her from any misgivings or doubts she might have about their relationship. He wanted to kiss her, feel his breath mingle with hers as their lips fused, making their love burst into full flower. But something had come between them, he sensed. Something that created a wedge, a chasm that seemed too perilous to cross.

Miles knew he wanted more than anything to move ahead in their relationship, but in order to do that he'd have to be patient. Slow, steady progress would have to be the pattern to follow.

Silently, they finished their meal. It seemed that each of them was aware that a crossroads had been reached.

Miles put down his knife and fork, pushed his plate to one side, and reached for Aleesa's hand.

"Listen, honey," he began, "you realize that we've got something going here between us, don't you?"

She nodded wordlessly.

"See, my darling, what we have is the oldest story in the world . . ."

"I know, Miles, it's just that . . ."

"Hear me out, Aleesa. Boy meets girl, boy loves girl, boy marries girl, and they live happily ever after."

She gave him a tentative smile.

"You make it sound so simple."

"Well, it is simple. The plain fact is we are attracted to each other. Let's move on from there."

Despite her inner turmoil, Aleesa recognized the truth in Miles's words. She would have to reveal her doubtful beginnings to him sometime, and she made a silent promise to herself to do so at the first decent opportunity. She prayed he would understand when she did so.

She smiled brightly, and with enthusiasm that she hoped didn't sound forced, told Miles what she had decided.

"Let's go to Vermont Saturday for the day . . . and then Sunday I'd like to take you up to Marblehead to meet my parents."

"Sounds like a fantastic weekend to me," Miles exulted. He paid the waiter, giving him a generous tip, and escorted Aleesa to his car when the valet brought it to them. He tipped him, too. All was not lost. He had the promise of more quality time with the woman he loved and . . . she had invited him to meet her folks. *Patience,* he reminded himself, *patience. It will all work out.* And whatever they had to face, they would face together.

"Miles?" Aleesa spoke in the darkened car as Miles drove to her condominium.

"Yes, what's on your mind?"

"Aren't you tired after your flight and the time zone changes?"

"Not really. I seem to be able to set my inner clock to whatever time zone I'm in. I think a lot of pilots do. Those that fly overseas, anyway, and we do get plenty of days off between flights. Why do you ask? Do I seem tired to you?"

"Not really, but I was thinking that perhaps you shouldn't stop up at my place tonight, but instead go straight home."

"Now you know better than that. I'm not about to miss our nightcap together. You know that!"

So they followed their routine. Aleesa made coffee, Miles checked the premises, and they made plans for the foliage trip. It was all Miles could do to control his impulsive urge to hold Aleesa. Every minute that he spent with her made him love her more.

"You know, Leesa, I'm very jealous of that guy."

"What guy?" she stared at him. "Who are you talking about?"

"The guy in India who built that beautiful Taj Mahal for his wife."

Aleesa threw back her head and laughed. "You

dummy," she teased, "that is a mausoleum. She's dead! I'm not *dead !*"

"Thank God, you're not, but I'd love to build a monument like that for you. Only twice as big, to show the world how much I love you."

She touched his face. "You'd better get home and get a really good night's sleep. If I didn't know better, I'd think you were hallucinating."

He held her hand close to his cheek, then kissed her palm. They walked to the door together.

She looked at him and her beautiful emerald green eyes caressed his face. He knew he had to hold her again before he could tear himself away. Willingly, she stepped into his embrace. Desire pounded through his body, and he had to be careful not to let things get out of hand. Her lips were soft and pliant, and he welcomed her arms around his neck, but he controlled his urge to seek more than she was willing to offer at that moment.

He tore his mouth away from hers, kissed her forehead, and pulled her arms away from his neck.

"Be in touch," he murmured as he loped down the corridor away from her door. He hoped she couldn't see the difficulty he was feeling as he left. *Patience, lad*—he repeated the mantra as he got into his car and headed home.

Six

Miles walked out into the still dark night to his parked car. Boston's streets were quiet and dark at that early morning hour. Pools of light reflected from the old-fashioned street lamps onto the cobblestoned sidewalks of the street where Aleesa lived. The South End of Boston, once a rundown neighborhood in Miles's childhood, had been developed into an upscale, desirable place to live. Many old brownstones had been converted into condominiums or apartments, and Aleesa's was a very attractive one. Hardwood floors gleamed throughout, wall sconces glowed softly from the brick-faced walls, and Aleesa's elegant taste in furniture and decorations appealed to him. Serenity, comfort, and discriminating good taste mirrored Aleesa's personality.

But tonight he was perplexed and very concerned. He had seen her emotions range from quick tears to practical common sense when she discussed her recent court case to soft tenderness when he held her in his arms.

He had never considered fragility to be part of her personality. She never seemed capricious or unsure—of herself or anything else. She was strong, a well-educated lawyer, accustomed to handling challenging situations. But what had upset her tonight? Why the sudden rush of tears? As he recalled, her seawater gray-green eyes seemed to implore him for help when the tears started, but then she quickly became her confident self when he asked about her work.

As he had listened, he had become intrigued by her soft, lustrous hair that fell almost to her shoulders, cupping her beautiful face with red-gold strands. Her loveliness stunned him, and he could feel the well of passion rise within his body.

He sat for a moment in the dark quiet of his car. He knew as surely as he knew his own name that more than anything else in this world he wanted to share his future with Aleesa Haskins. It was up to him to find a way to do so.

They took the trip to Vermont on Saturday as planned. It turned out to be a sparkling blue October day. The air, crisp, clean and invigorating, encouraged Miles, and he was certain he and Aleesa were going to have a great day. He was positive of it when he picked her up at her place.

He let out a low whistle when she opened her door. She was wearing a white sweatshirt over a colorful striped blouse. The red and pink tints framed her lovely face. Her jeans tantalized Miles by the way they hugged the gentle curves of her waist and hips. She carried a navy jogging jacket and her stunning hair spilled out from under a baseball cap. She looked like a spunky teenager.

He admired her with a wide grin. "Aleesa, girl, you sure know how to take a man's breath away! Those jeans are sayin' something!"

"Don't look so bad yourself, Miles," she said when he came in. His trousers outlined his sleek contoured muscles and tapered smoothly down his long legs. His navy shirt was open at the neck and she could see silky dark hair seductively curling from his chest, which made her want to touch it. She tore her eyes away and beckoned him inside.

She pointed to a picnic basket by the door. Miles picked it up.

"Thought we might stop and have a bite along the way," she explained.

"Great idea. We may get hungry."

She picked up a tote bag and her purse. "I'm ready."

"What's in *that* bag? Want me to carry it?"

"I can manage it, thanks. It's not heavy. Some cassettes so we can have music as we ride along. Hope you'll like them."

"The cassettes are a good idea, because sometimes the radio fades in and out as we drive through the mountains."

"I thought of that," she said, "that's why I brought them along. I brought one of my favorite saxophonists, some Basie, some of Duke's best, the soundtrack from the movie *The Bridges of Madison County* and some of my *favorite* favorites, Nancy Wilson. What do you think?"

He smiled warmly. "You couldn't have made a better selection. I love 'em all."

Once settled in Miles's car, they drove west out of Boston on Route 2.

"I think the old Mohawk Trail will be perfect about this time of year, and then we'll head north, out of Williamstown, into Vermont. You did bring your camera, didn't you?"

"I did. Right here in my bag," she said as she patted her pocketbook.

"You know, Aleesa, I probably should have offered you a flight to Vermont. Foliage viewed from the air can be quite spectacular, you know, but I selfishly wanted to have you alone, just the two of us, for a whole, uninterrupted day. Maybe another time we can take a quick flight north."

"Is it difficult . . . flying, that is?"

"I believe it's easier than driving a car."

"Really?"

"Yup. And it's less strenuous. At least you don't have to be concerned with traffic problems. As they say, 'The sky's the limit.' Why, Aleesa? You want to learn to fly? Be happy to teach you."

"I've often thought of it. Seems to me there is so much freedom in the air, the sense of space and fluid motion. Maybe that's why I like sailing so much. To be free and unencumbered is such a joy."

Her mind recalled the burden of her own personal identity and she shook her head as if to chase away the thought. Miles, however, noticed her quick movement.

"Are you okay?" he worried.

Aleesa gave him a bright smile. "I'm just fine," she answered.

"I'd be delighted, as I said, to give you lessons."

"Thanks. We'll see."

They drove along past Concord and Lexington, through Ayers and Fort Devens. Both admired the colors of the trees. Aleesa felt herself begin to relax. She decided to try to enjoy herself. Why not, she reckoned.

Miles was an excellent driver, and his car gave them a comfortable ride when they began to climb the Berkshires. As he concentrated on his driving, Aleesa studied him covertly. His handsome features were not to be denied. His hair was close-cropped and slightly curly, and his smile when he gave her an occasional glance was warm and encompassing. His teeth were a glistening white and well shaped.

She already knew his firm lips were extremely kissable. It was comfortably warm in the car and the subtle masculine scent of Miles's aftershave cologne brought to her mind a picture of him standing bare-chested before his mirror, shaving. She felt entranced by the image, and she knew deep down that she was beginning to care for this special man. She forced herself to concentrate on the scenery around them. It was as if they were traveling through a golden maze of trees on either side of the road. Oaks, maples, and birch trees blazed with color.

"I can see why people come from all over the world to see the changing colors, Miles. You almost have to see it to believe it, don't you think?"

"Right. We're lucky we live so close by. How 'bout if we stop soon and tackle that picnic you brought along? We just passed a sign that indicated there's a mountain lookout a few miles ahead."

"Sounds good to me. Could use a stretch about now."

A half hour later they reached the site. There were clean rest rooms and plenty of picnic areas that provided outstanding views of the valley below bursting with yellow, gold and brilliant red foliage.

"Glad we came, Miles," Aleesa said. "This is a beautiful setting."

They enjoyed the tuna salad and roast beef-filled rolls that Aleesa brought. Fresh fruit: grapes, apples and pears, as well as rich brownies appeased their hunger. Cheese and wine completed the meal.

"Did you do all this yourself?" Miles asked as he sipped his wine.

Aleesa laughed. "Not me. I went to my friend at the deli, told him what I wanted and"—she waved her hands in a magician's gesture—"here we are."

"Right. If you can find someone to do the job, why not?" he agreed.

"You've got that right," she said.

They sat side by side in quiet silence, savoring the vista before them. Impulsively, Miles took Aleesa's hand in his. His voice was soft and had an edge of seriousness to it. He went right to what he had been thinking since last night.

"Aleesa, what is it? What's bothering you about us?"

"What do you mean, *about us?*"

"There is something that is keeping you . . . I don't know, but I get the feeling that you don't trust me. You feel apprehensive about our relationship . . . but I feel, too, that you are attracted to me. Is there someone else in your life?"

She was aware of the concern in his eyes, but she knew she couldn't tell him the truth about herself. Maybe tomorrow, after he met her parents. So she spoke as firmly as she could, hoping he would accept her answer.

"There's no one else, Miles. If you sense there's a chasm between us, I don't know what to tell you. I will always be honest with you, as I hope you'll be with me. Can't we let our relationship grow, like I said before?" she pleaded.

He couldn't stop himself. He kissed her then, gently at first. As his lips touched hers, he sensed a palpable hunger from her as if she wanted, needed more. He held her head with both hands, mindful that her baseball cap had fallen to the ground. She fused her mouth to his. What was going on? Was Aleesa denying her reluctance to commit to him, yet still showing that she really cared? What was it? Impatient, needing to know, to love her more, he thrust his tongue forward to taste the inner sweetness of her mouth. She sighed and sought to caress his lips with her own tongue. He welcomed the gesture.

Their table was at a distance from other visitors, but Miles knew if he didn't take control, anything might happen. One thing he did know, was that despite her protests, Aleesa wanted him. He wanted to reassure her.

"No matter what it is, love, you are the only one for me and always will be," he whispered in her ear. "I love you, girl."

Momentarily, they both lost sense of where they were, only that they were in each other's arms. Aleesa quivered when Miles caressed her breast through her clothing and she whimpered from the exquisite sensation when his thumb excited her nipple, which responded involuntarily. Aleesa felt herself acknowledging, accepting the magical sensations that encircled her body. She reached for Miles's head to hold it. She knew she wanted to feel his mouth on her breast, which ached with throbbing desire. She knew, too, that she wanted this man. She could not deny the deep longing, the need she felt for him. She felt like a greedy, hungry child suddenly confronted with a feast. Could she taste it all? Could Miles give her the love, the peace of mind, the belief that maybe she was not flawed? But she couldn't turn off her feelings. She was melting, giving in to the tumultuous longings that were exploding inside her body.

Miles, mindful of where they were, out in the open, sensed that Aleesa was yielding to the momentum of their dynamic wave of desire. But this was not the place—and he knew it. Brusquely, he pulled her hands away from his head.

"Let's get back to the car!" he groaned.

* * *

They had a quiet, sobering ride back to Aleesa's Boston apartment. Each was aware that they had reached a turning point in their relationship. So, unable or unwilling to face that issue, they talked of inconsequential matters. Sports, like the fate of the Red Sox, or the Patriots' upcoming season, the Internet, everything except what was foremost in their minds.

It was very difficult for Miles to control his feelings and thoughts. Especially his feelings. Every fiber, every nerve and muscle in his body cried out for him to hold Aleesa, to kiss her lovely mouth, to make love to her, just to touch her soft, tender skin in a loving way—but he knew the time had not come for him to do so. He would have to allow her, on her own terms, to reach the moment of truth, the truth that she loved him. *That* would come when *she* realized that their love was real and could not be denied. He took his eyes from the road to steal a quick, sidelong glance at her. He could only imagine what it would be like to make love to her. Today's incident at the lookout made him aware of the unleashed passion Aleesa had. He ached to taste it, to share love's ultimate moments with her.

"Still visiting your folks tomorrow?"

She turned to look at him, her hair swinging softly around her shoulders. "You feel up to it? You've done a lot of driving today," she said.

"Oh no, I'm looking forward to it."

When they reached her place, he helped her carry her belongings inside. He made his usual safety checks around the place, and at the door before leaving, he gave her a gentle kiss. "It was some day, hon," he spoke quietly. "Get a good night's rest and

I'll see you in the morning. I love you." He was out the door, closing it gently behind him, leaving a shaken Aleesa on the inside.

Sighing, she undressed and took a shower. She *was* weary after the day-long trip and the serious reactions that *she* had made in response to Miles.

She toweled off and looked at herself in the mirror. Her eyes were innocent but wide-eyed, as if to peer far beyond their normal scope. She brushed her hair, which was streaked light from the summer sun. This face, this look, this body . . . what secrets did it carry from her unknown parents? What genetic material had she inherited that she would pass on to her children? After today's episode at the lookout, Miles was bound to pressure her for a commitment. She sensed that he was aware of her blossoming feelings toward him. Should she go ahead with the plans to have him meet her adopted parents tomorrow? *Aleesa, girl,* she thought, *you'd better come to your senses! You're sending crossed messages.*

She climbed into bed, turned her radio on low to an all-night music station, and waited for sleep. She ran her fingers over her nightgown down her body. What would it be like to have Miles's long, sensitive hands caress her tense, anxious body? She felt her skin flush and her heart throbbed erratically. Could she expect a man like Miles to put up with her juvenile nonsense much longer? She had recognized the depths of his feelings toward her today and knew she would have to make a decision—and soon.

The weather was still beautiful the next day when Aleesa and Miles drove to her parents' home in Marblehead. A breathtakingly blue sky with a gentle breeze that nudged sailboats in Marblehead Harbor created an instant love affair between Miles and the old seaside town.

"What a beautiful spot," he said.

Aleesa agreed and directed him past tree-shaded streets to her parents' home.

"We're here," she told him. Neither of them had mentioned the episode of the previous day.

The small white sign on the front lawn by the driveway simply read HASKINS' WATER'S EDGE.

Miles got out of the car and took a deep breath. "Ah," he said as he stretched. "Smell the ocean! It's so invigorating."

"Come on in, Miles. Look, my folks are on the front porch. Dad, this is Miles."

"Welcome, Miles. First visit to Marblehead?" her father asked.

"Yes, sir, first visit. I'm delighted to be here." Both men exchanged a firm handshake. "I can see why you would want to retire here, sir."

"Nothing like living near the ocean for peace and tranquility." Grady Haskins turned to Aleesa's mother. "May I introduce my better half?" he smiled at Miles. "Mother, this is Aleesa's friend, Miles, Miles Kittridge. Miles, this is Aleesa's mother, Carol Haskins."

Miles shook hands with the woman, who was tall and slender. She was not as tall as her husband, who Miles decided must be well over six feet. She was well groomed, her cocoa-tan, unlined face framed by a well-trimmed haircut. Her mixed gray, close-cropped hairstyle reminded him of a well-known television comedian's wife. She was a stunning woman.

She smiled a warm welcome.

"I'm very happy to meet you, Miles. Welcome to our home, Water's Edge."

"Thank you, Mrs. Haskins. It's wonderful to be here."

Mrs. Haskins turned to her daughter and gave her

a quick hug. "Honey, I've planned to have lunch on the outside patio. It's such a lovely day. That okay with you and Miles?"

"Sounds fine, Mother. Let me freshen up and I'll help you get things out. Dad?" she questioned her father.

He understood her raised eyebrows. "Okay, honey, I'll show Miles around. We'll be ready whenever you ladies are ready for us."

"Don't let Dad talk your ears off, Miles, especially about his favorite team, the Chicago Bulls!" she laughed. The two men walked down the drive toward the back of the house.

"So, you're a Bulls' fan?"

"Oh yes, there's no one like Mike."

"He's one fantastic athlete, that's for sure," Miles agreed.

The Haskins' house was painted white with Nantucket blue-gray wooden shutters, reminding Miles of the houses he had seen in Florida.

"Mr. Haskins, you and your wife have a lovely home. Reminds me of houses I've seen in Key West."

"Thanks, Miles. It should make you think of those Bahama-type houses."

"Really?"

They had reached the lawn beyond the patio. Miles could see that a small inlet of the ocean lapped gently at the sea wall at the edge of the lawn. Mr. Haskins indicated for Miles to have a seat in one of the white Adirondack chairs. They could see the women moving about the patio.

"I expect the women will be calling us soon to eat. But, yes, this house was built in the 1940s by an admirer of Ernest Hemingway. He died, left no heirs, and the place lay fallow, went to rack and ruin. My wife and I were out riding one day, came upon it, and fell in love with it. We made an offer to the trust fund. An offer, I might add, son, that couldn't be refused. No black families had ever owned waterfront property here. Put a lot of blood, sweat, and tears *and* money into this place. But we love it here."

"Have you had any problems . . . with neighbors, I mean?"

"Not really. I believe it's mainly because they were so happy to see the place brought back to life, they didn't care who did it. And *their* property values actually increased. You understand, some of them are still cool to the idea of blacks in the neighborhood, but others are friendly. As for me"—he grinned at his guest—"just let me be and you'll have no trouble with me. I just want to enjoy what Carol and I have worked for all our lives."

Miles nodded in agreement.

"My sentiments exactly, sir. I only want what's mine, not asking anyone to give me anything."

Mr. Haskins responded to a wave from his wife signalling that lunch was ready.

"Okay, Miles, let's go." He stood up. "We've got the word." He clapped his hand on Miles's shoulder, and they walked toward the patio where the women waited.

"Real nice to have you with us, Miles."

"Real nice to be here, sir," Miles said.

"What a great family you have, Aleesa. Got along great with your dad, as if we'd known each other a long time."

"My dad's like that."

"And your mother, so warm and friendly. They're both special people. And anyone can see *you're* the apple of their eyes."

Driving down Route 1 to Boston, Miles thought about the afternoon's visit. He had noticed the affectionate rapport between daughter and parents. He smiled to himself, recalling the lighthearted bantering and teasing that existed in the Haskins family. Such behavior could only be tolerated where there was real love and caring, he thought. Aleesa had a loving, secure family. She was a lucky girl.

Aleesa's voice broke into his thoughts as he eyed the busy evening traffic.

"Mother and Dad were impressed with you, too, Miles. Dad especially, because you are a pilot. And did you notice him teasing me—raising his eyebrows and making subtle glances in your direction? Surely you didn't miss that?"

"That must mean he thinks I'm a good candidate for a future son-in-law," Miles offered.

Aleesa sat up straighter in her seat, turned toward Miles, and waggled her finger at him. "Just a cotton-pickin' minute, here, buster! My folks don't make decisions for me! That's the way they raised me—to be independent and think for myself. If I get married, *when* I get married, and to whom I get married, will have nothing to do with them! It will be *my* decision."

Miles shook his head at her. What brought this on, and after the revealing weekend they had had?

"Sure doesn't take much to get you into an argument, does it?" He gave her a sidelong glance to assess her reaction.

"That's because I'm a lawyer and I react like one," she snapped back.

Still keeping his attention on his driving, Miles saw that the closer they got to Boston the heavier the traffic became. He responded to her feisty comment in a calm tone.

"Look, Leese, I'm not going to pick a fight with you. You know I'm a peaceful, loving man. I don't fight unless there's no alternative out of a situation. I'm a loving man. But you already know I'm not a quitting man, either. I always go after what I want."

Both remained silent for a moment, then Miles spoke, easing the tension.

"Hey, why are we arguing after such a great day?"

Aleesa shrugged.

Miles thought a moment longer.

"Hey, I know! You vixen, you *want* to fight with me because you have to admit you care."

"Oh, all right, Miles. I have to admit I do care . . . wouldn't have taken you to meet my folks otherwise."

"Yes, yes," he teased, "go on."

She threw him a cautious look to measure his response to her answer.

"You're confident, you're thoughtful, fun to be with, have a sense of humor and . . . I hate to tell you this to your face, but you *do* know you are quite good-looking."

"Have to thank my mom and pop for that. Combination of their genes."

"I know," she said quietly.

Intent on getting more of her praiseworthy assessment of him, Miles did not pick up on her dampened mood, but continued with his questions.

"What else?" he insisted.

She took a deep breath before she answered, as if trying to bring herself back to her previous line of thought.

"I do admire, Miles," she said quietly, "your determination to go after what you want, like getting your job with the airlines, along with respect from your peers. I find that admirable."

"You do, huh?"

"Yes, I do. I could never accept cowardice or weakness in anyone, especially in a man."

"I know, my love. We think alike, you and I. You're a woman after my own heart." He leaned over and kissed her cheek. She touched the spot with her fingertips, glad in a way that he hadn't gone further.

Seven

"Like something from the bar, Leese?" Miles rose from his seat after the curtain dropped at the first intermission.

Aleesa also got up from her seat. She shook her head. "No thanks, Miles, nothing for me. Think I'll hop into the ladies' room. Be crowded after the last act."

"Well, meet me at the bar—can stretch our legs until the second act starts."

Together they walked out toward the theater lobby, listening to favorable comments from other audience members. "Great show! Wonderful music!" Miles took Aleesa's arm to guide her through the crowd.

"You like the show, Leese? The star is great, isn't she?"

"Oh, she's talented! And I love the show tunes. I've been hearing how good this musical is. Glad you could get tickets, Miles."

He squeezed her arm as they reached the lobby. "Good connections," he said, smiling down at her. "See you in a bit." He headed for the bar and she found the door to the women's rest room.

"Whatever you have on draft," Miles told the bartender.

He had just reached for the glass of beer when a voice at his shoulder said, "Miles! Miles Kittridge!"

He spun around and seized the young woman smiling at him.

"Lynette! Girl, where did you come from?"

He hugged her fiercely and then stepped back to look her up and down with an evaluating leer in his eyes.

Tall, elegantly dressed in a stunning strapless black dress, her doe-skin brown shoulders gleamed seductively in the subdued lighting of the lobby. Her jet-black hair was groomed smoothly into a French twist. Diamond earrings dangled gently and accentuated her lovely neck. There was no other adornment. Miles decided that she didn't need any. Long, slender legs encased in off-black hosiery and her black satin pumps finished off the picture of an enticing, beautiful young woman.

"Girl, do you look good!"

"So do you, Miles. What you been up to? Still flying?"

"Oh, you know it. Off to Indonesia next week."

"You're lucky, you know. I'm stuck here in Beantown. Lucky if I get to the Vineyard or New York once in a while."

Miles reached for his beer and took a sip. He raised his eyebrows in a question, asking Lynette if she wanted a drink. She shook her head. "Still with the insurance company?" he asked her.

"Yes. I guess I'll be there until they throw me out. Still trying to move up, but all I hear is creaks and cracks—still hitting the glass ceiling."

"Don't sell yourself short, Lynette. Being vice president in human resources isn't bad," he said.

"I know, but you know me, Miles, I want it all. Always have, always will, but then that's me, I guess."

"You know my feelings, girl. Nothing wrong with that. Go after what you want, I always say."

"I've missed you, Miles. You always were a good, decent friend."

Miles saw the somber look that crossed her face.

"I am so sorry to hear your marriage didn't work out. You deserve the best."

She glanced at her slim gold watch. "Thanks, Miles. Well, time to get back to our seats. Good to see you, Miles." She reached for him and he took her face in both hands to give her a gentle kiss.

Aleesa stood in the shadows of the bar. Her eyes widened in the dimly lit area as she witnessed the tenderness Miles showed when he kissed the extremely attractive young woman. She shivered as if a cold blast of frigid air had enveloped her. Her breath came in painful gasps. Who was she? What did she mean to Miles?

Aleesa stepped back into the darkness and leaned against a wall. She tried to pull her thoughts together. When she felt her pulse slow down and her skin return to its normal temperature, she hurried back to her seat. The call lights were blinking theater-goers back into their seats when Miles slipped in beside her.

"Thought you were going to meet me at the bar," he whispered.

"Changed my mind," she whispered back.

Later, as they were driving back to Aleesa's condo, Miles sensed that all was not well with her.

"How come you're so quiet, honey? Didn't you like the show?"

"Oh, it was fine." Tight-lipped, her mouth barely let the words escape.

Miles's receptive antennae came to full attention.

Aleesa's profile in the darkened interior of the car was inscrutable. She stared out the front, fixedly, as if unaware of her surroundings.

Miles knew something was wrong.

"This is not like you, Leese. Tell me what's troubling you."

Slowly turning her head to look directly at him, her voice choked with disappointment. She asked, "That woman tonight that you were kissing in the lobby . . . who is she?"

Miles threw back his head in a great guffaw. "That woman?"

"Yes, that woman, and I don't see anything to laugh at."

"Oh, yes, honey, it's funny. To paraphrase the comedian, 'That was no *woman,* that was my sister.' "

"Don't get flip with me, Miles Kittridge! I know you're an only child and . . . no man kisses his sister the way you . . . all up in each other's arms," she sputtered.

He laughed again at her discomfort. "You should have come over. I'd have introduced you. That was Lynette Jarvis. We grew up together. Our mothers are best friends, and we're about a month apart in age. We've always been in and out of each other's homes . . . raised like brother and sister. Honest. She's an only child, too."

"Didn't look like brother-sister greetings from where I stood."

"To be truthful"—Miles's voice took on a sober tone—"I was happy to see Lynette tonight. She's just getting over a failed marriage. She and Jerry had seemed so perfect together. We were all so happy and had such high hopes . . . the breakup was very painful for all of us, family and friends."

"Too bad."

"Yes, it was too bad. Lynette took the divorce especially hard. I, for one, was truly concerned about her mental state. But she's a trooper and tonight she looked and sounded like the Lynette of old."

"She is extremely attractive."

"Right, she is that, but as far as *I'm* concerned, little lady, she can't hold a candle to you, sweetheart." His voice was calm and earnest. In the quiet interior of the car Aleesa could hear serious intensity in his deep voice. He continued, "You *are* and always *will be* the most beautiful woman in the world to me. I don't want you to ever forget that."

He placed his hand on her knee. "You hear what I'm telling you?"

She nodded. The gentle warmth of his hand on her knee comforted and calmed her. What sensation would she feel, what hunger would be sated if his hands were on other, perhaps naked, more intimate parts of her body?

The erotic thoughts caused the breathless tension to escalate. She felt hot, tremulous, didn't trust herself to speak. She swallowed hard to get past the moment, to regain some composure before she allowed herself to answer Miles.

"I hear," she said.

She handed Miles the key to her brownstone and he unlocked the door. She stepped inside and he followed, returning her key.

"Didn't I hear you say something about going to Indonesia next week?"

"Right. Delivery of computer parts. Seems there's a lot of trade with Asian companies these days."

Following their established routine, Miles checked the condo, drawing the draperies, making sure all was secure, and Aleesa went into the kitchen to prepare coffee. She spoke from the kitchen.

"You better not let any of those Balinese women entice you."

She brought in the coffee tray and placed it on the coffee table.

"Do I see a little green-eyed monster sitting on your shoulder?" he grinned at her.

She shrugged. "Could be I'm just interested in your well-being. Sometimes you can't trust these foreign women. Most of the time all they want is a green card," she bantered.

"Nice to know you care about my well-being, my dear."

"What are friends for?" she asked as she passed him a cup of coffee.

"Friends are fine, you know, but I'm hoping for more, much more, from *our* relationship. But you know that."

Aleesa stood in front of the closed draperies, coffee cup in her hand, and smiled. Miles thought she had never looked lovelier or more appealing than she did at that moment. Her hair was like burnished silk, its red-gold tints adding to the warm blush that suffused her face. She had worn a simple silk navy dress to the theater. Its square neckline was enhanced by a single strand of pearls. Sparkling diamond studs twinkled in her ears when she moved her head. Hoping against hope that he wasn't moving too fast, Miles knew that tonight their relationship had come to a crossroads. He had not forgotten the day at the Vermont lookout.

He was on his way to some destination halfway around the world. Aleesa did care for him, or why else would she have shown interest—no, jealousy—when she'd seen him with Lynette? Tonight was the night for definitive action.

Deliberately, slowly, he placed his cup on the table.

He got up, went to Aleesa, and took her cup from her. He joined her cup with his on the table and returned to her side.

A glittery, feisty gleam sparkled in her eyes as he took both her hands in his.

"Miles! What are you doing?"

"Helping you."

"Helping me do what?"

"Make a decision."

"What makes you think I need help . . . and to make a decision about what?" she bristled.

Miles drew her close, looked down into her lovely upturned face, then nibbled at her ear. "It's time to make a decision about us, counselor . . . and for you to admit that you're in love with me," he whispered.

Her eyes flashed at him.

"Damn you, Miles, you know you're getting next to me! You planned it all along, you and your subtle, wooing manners. I've tried my best not to admit to myself that I care about you, but something happened to me tonight when I saw that . . . that Lynette in your arms." A sudden flush warmed her face.

As if ashamed of her outburst, tears flooded her eyes.

"I, I can't explain the feeling, but it was a physical thing, like I'd lost something that had belonged to me."

"You can't lose me, honey. I'll always belong to you," he tried to reassure her.

"Oh, Miles," her eyes pleaded with him, "can't you see that I've tried my damnedest *not* to fall in love with you? Don't you know that? But you've won! I do love you, God help me, but I do!"

The warmth of her trembling body in his arms was almost more than Miles could stand. He wanted to smother her with kisses, taste the sweet tenderness of her lips, exchange pulsing heartbeats as their bodies came together, somehow make her know how much he loved her. Was she ready to accept him? Did she trust him enough to believe the truth? Then he thought, hadn't she taken him home to visit her parents? Hadn't they spent quality time together, enjoying dinners out, musical concerts, the theater, even discussed Miles's future prospects of owning his own business—a commuter airline between Boston and Portland, or Boston to the Cape and Islands?

Miles sensed a vulnerability in Aleesa tonight. He knew he did not want to take advantage of her, but she had said, albeit reluctantly, that she loved him. Why would he need more assurance than that? A tiny voice told him that now was the right time.

"You're trembling Leese, come sit." He wanted to calm her.

He led her back to the sofa and reached over to extinguish the lamp near the sofa. The living room's only illumination came from the soft glow of a lighted clock on the table.

"Are you cold?" he asked quietly, wanting to allay her fear.

"No, I'm nervous."

"Don't be, honey. You're safe. I love you, Aleesa Haskins."

He kissed her then, first her tear-filled eyes, then her cheeks, and when his lips touched hers, she drew in a quick breath as her lips welcomed his. No words were needed. Her arms tightened around his neck and she clung to him. Desperate now, she needed to ease the aching agony she experienced trying to deny the overwhelming feelings she had for the man in her arms. Her confession of love for him had stunned her, but now it was real—a living truth between them.

"Oh, my own sweet Leese. I've loved you since the moment I laid eyes on you on Career Day." His voice was throaty with emotion. "I saw a beautiful young woman with a serious, intense look on her face. I *had* to speak to you. And when you looked at me with your sparkling jewel eyes, I was overcome. I had to get to know you, to claim you, to love you. Oh, Leese! I was only half a man before I met you. You bring out any good that's in me and I love you for it."

"Miles, I . . . I," she stuttered.

"Sh, sh, my darling. Just let me love you."

Aleesa knew there was no turning back. She felt such a strong need for Miles and his love, she thought she would faint, something she had never done in her life before. She reached for him and held on tight as his kisses burned along her cheeks, her earlobes, her neck, and the hollow of her throat.

With his right hand, Miles kneaded the soft roundness of her breast. She moaned with desire as his thumb brushed across its throbbing peak.

He unzipped the back of her dress and drew it down around shoulders that gleamed seductively in the dim light. He released her bra strap and drank in the beauty of her twin orbs—then drew in a deep breath. "God, you're so beautiful." He accepted her offering with gentle kisses. It was not enough for her. Unaware of what she was doing, she held his head close to the fullness of her breasts. The tiny sibilant sounds that came from her throat excited him even more. She was his, she loved him, she wanted him.

He looked into her eyes, and what he saw validated his next movement. He helped her shed her dress, her silk undergarments, and she helped him strip off his clothing, each pulling frantically at buttons and zippers until they both were free.

Flickering flames of deep, physical need flared be-

tween them. Miles's hands and fingers were gentle and
tender as he explored Aleesa's body. He played and
caressed every inch of her like a musical instrument.
She felt transported to a world she had never imagined. She could only hold on tightly as together they
ascended to such an apex of joy it took her breath
away. She lay spent, tears squeezing out beneath tightly
closed eyelids. Miles could only whisper, "Leese, Leese,
oh Leese, I love you."

They were two lost souls united after years of not
knowing one another, finally where they belonged, in
each other's arms. They were anchored, like a boat,
safe, in from the battering sea.

Eight

"Can't tell you how pleased Aleesa's mom and I feel about this great news, Miles."

Miles had his arm around Aleesa and he brought her close in a warm hug.

"That makes us very happy, sir."

"Well, when's it going to be?"

Miles looked at his fiancée for her input.

"Dad, it's April now and we were thinking in September."

"Yes, you see, sir, I still have to finish out my contract with the airline cargo company. It ends in June, and I'd like to look into starting my own commuter airline business."

"That gives me six months," Aleesa's mother broke in. "Will you be married here at home?"

Aleesa smiled. "I was kinda hoping for that. Will it be okay?"

"Are you kidding?" her mother said. "Always been our dream, right, Dad?"

"You betcha. Nothing's too good for our only child. A September wedding here at Water's Edge, beautiful, beautiful," he said.

"Thanks, Dad," Aleesa said.

"Yes, my thanks to both of you," Miles added.

* * *

Aleesa worked diligently on her client's lawsuit against the city and the police. "I've checked over your brief, Ms. Haskins, and I believe you're handling the case correctly."

"Thanks, Mr. Butterworth. I think we're going to be successful. By the way, the client is a law school graduate. His illness started just after he graduated law school. He still has some fragments of a once-brilliant mind."

"What a pity. It seems sometimes that life is so unfair."

Tell me about it, Aleesa thought. She watched him pat his chest pocket as if to make certain he was still well-put-together and he left her office. *What a secure feeling it must be to know who you really are. No doubt Harrison Butterworth, Esquire, never had any doubts.*

The door to her office was opened again. She looked up, surprised to see Mr. Butterworth's patrician head in the doorway.

"Almost forgot, Ms. Haskins. I hear you are engaged to be married. Congratulations!" And he was gone again before she could respond.

She worked steadily throughout the day, and was pleased with the progress she was making on the case. By four-thirty that afternoon she decided to end her workday.

Miles was due back in a few days from his latest overseas trip, and she planned to take him sailing in Marblehead. She was anxious to share her enjoyment of the sport with him.

"You know, Miles," she had told him, "I believe it is a little like flying, except your craft is moving through water, not air."

"Then I know I'm going to enjoy it."

* * *

Their weekend went well. Miles proved to be an apt student—he said as much to her parents at dinner that night. "It's not that I was a good pupil, but that I had the best teacher in the world."

"He is a quick learner," Aleesa interrupted. "I believe he's sailed before," she teased him.

"Well, I think it's wonderful that you both can enjoy the same thing," her father said. He reached for his wife's hand. "Those that play together, stay together. Right, honey?"

Aleesa didn't miss the loving glances that passed between her parents. *Why did that behavior make her feel excluded?* Her father went on with his conversation.

"Do you think you might take flying lessons, honey?" he asked his daughter.

"I'm thinking about it, Dad. Miles loves it so."

Miles nodded. "I've always told her that flying is the most wonderful, free feeling anyone can experience."

"I'll take your word for it, son, and stay right here on good old terra firma. By the way, you two, how are your wedding plans coming?"

"So far, so good," Aleesa answered. "Mother, we can start looking at wedding invitations soon?" She looked at Miles for confirmation. He nodded his head when she said, "We've set September fourth, at eleven, so we can serve a wedding luncheon here at Water's Edge on . . ."

"My dad has agreed to be my best man," Miles said.

"Sarah Pritchard, you remember, my law school classmate, is going to be my maid of honor," Aleesa announced.

"We certainly should have our 'ducks in a row' by that time. Six months is ample time. I do want to do a little painting, spruce up the place . . . ," Aleesa's father commented.

"Sir, everything looks fine. Wouldn't want to put you to more expense."

"Pshaw. This is my daughter's wedding we're talking 'bout. Everything's got to be first-rate."

Aleesa's mother spoke up. "We are so happy, Miles, that you are going to be a member of our family. We're very proud of you. We just ask you to take good care of her, and there is a 'no questions asked' return policy."

Everyone laughed.

"No chance of *that,*" Miles insisted.

As usual, back in Aleesa's condo, she and Miles went through their late evening routine.

Aleesa brought the coffee tray into the living room just as Miles finished his check of the locks.

"What a great weekend, hon. It's always a delight to be with your folks."

"They're *not* my folks," she blurted out.

Shocked by her comment, Miles stared at her, his coffee cup halfway to his mouth. He stuttered, "Wha— what do you mean *not your folks?*"

"Miles, surely in all this time you must have known that I am an adopted child. You must see that I don't look like anyone else in the Haskins family. Not my parents, my aunts and uncles, my cousins . . ."

"So what? You look like who you are, that's all."

"But that's just it! Who am I? Where did I get this hair, these funny-colored eyes?"

Miles put his cup down and quickly grabbed both of her hands. She tried to withdraw them from his grasp, but he refused to let go of them. He stared at her in disbelief.

"I don't understand at all! I love *you*. Your being adopted doesn't matter to me! *You* matter. Aleesa, don't you love me?" His face was flushed and his voice cracked with bewilderment and confusion.

"Oh, Miles, that's just it! I tried hard not to fall in love with you, you know that. But I do love you."

"Girl, you're not making a bit of sense. We love each other. We belong together. For God's sake, we're planning our wedding!" He threw his head back against the sofa, closed his eyes and clapped his hand to his forehead.

"Maybe we shouldn't be . . ." she murmured softly.

Miles sat straight up. "What are you talking about, *shouldn't be?*"

"Because. Because, Miles, maybe we shouldn't get married until I find out."

"Find out what?"

"What . . . who I am. I've always wanted to know whose genes I carry. What I bring to our marriage."

"For God's sake! What does it matter? What difference does it make? Whatever you bring, we'll deal with it! You're out of your mind to think otherwise."

Aleesa had never seen him so angry. His emotion was so palpable it filled the room. "As a matter of fact, I'll help you. If it matters so much to you, I'll help you search for your birth parents. I'll get right on the Internet."

"Don't need your help. I'm a lawyer, I know what to do. I can search on my own," she protested.

"Oh no, you don't!" Miles got up and paced back and forth. "We're in this together. You're my life, my very heartbeat, and I won't be cheated out of sharing this problem with you." He stopped pacing and glared at her. "What kind of a man do you think I am?"

She remained silent.

"So?" he questioned. "What are you going to do?"

"Get my folks to tell me what they know and I'll take it from there."

Miles's face was dark with worry.

"Suppose you find out that your records are sealed . . . that your birth parents don't want to be found? Have you thought of that? They have rights, too, you know."

When he saw the dispirited look come over Aleesa's face, he softened his tone.

"Come here, sweetheart." He held her in his arms. "Your birth parents, whoever they are, are very special people to have had a child as wonderful as you. Don't fret, hon, we're going to find them, somehow."

"Or there'll be no wedding."

"What!" Miles exploded. "Oh, there'll be a wedding! And *all* your family will be there! Or my name's not Miles Kittridge!"

Determined to speak her mind, she moved out of his arms. Her voice sounded serious when she answered.

"It's okay for you to talk that way, Miles. You know where *you* came from. For me, it's like being flotsam and jetsam, floating aimlessly like a boat lost at sea!" she insisted.

"Don't talk like that, honey! Your folks have given you a great life. You are intelligent, beautiful, well educated, a skillful attorney, and I love you! Doesn't all that count for something?"

"Look, Miles, what you say may be true, but I have a need, a deep need to *know*. I remember once in sociology class the professor was speaking about family. He said, and I'll never forget this, that each of us had two parents and each of them had two parents. So, prior to your parents are four people who contributed to who you are. So, eight great-grandparents, sixteen great-great-grandparents, and so on. You can figure it out. And, Miles, I remember the professor saying that if you figured maybe twenty-five years between generations, and if you went back maybe five hundred years, in all that time, over one million people are in your ancestral chain! I want to know!"

"Leese, that's crazy! I don't know the million people in my—what did you call it?—'ancestral chain,' and I'm not sure I want to know!"

"But *if* you wanted to, you could trace your family back at least two hundred years! I can't even trace mine back five minutes," she insisted. "Why should I be denied?"

"But what does it matter? It's here and now that I care about, and Leese"—his eyes darkened—"right now, this moment, is all we really have."

"I knew you wouldn't understand. Family is what gives the bond of life and I'm determined to find that bond! Maybe, Miles"—she hesitated—"since you can't or won't understand my thoughts on the matter, you better go your way and I'll go mine."

"You can't mean that!" he argued.

"It's the way I feel," she said stubbornly.

Miles stared at her, stunned by her remark.

"What are you talkin' about, 'the way you feel'? I thought you loved me. You said you did . . ."

"But don't you see, Miles, it's because I love you . . ."

"Sure doesn't make sense to me! I don't see what your being adopted and wanting to find your *real* parents has to do with our relationship." He stood in front of the living room windows and continued to stare at her. He ran his hand over his face in a weary gesture and exhaled deeply as if he had just run the high hurdles. Aleesa could see a bulging vein pulsing on his temple. She had never seen him so upset.

"I don't understand your thinking at all," he continued. "Is it foolish of me to try to convince you that *your* past, wherever you came from . . . who your *real* parents were, isn't all that important in our lives? In what we have?" He waited for her answer.

"To me, Miles, it is important," she insisted stubbornly, "and it's not just about being adopted. I love my parents and always will . . ."

"Well, why not leave it at that?"

Aleesa shook her head. By now, despite her resolve not to cry or show any weakness, tears were welling in her eyes.

Reluctantly, she tried to answer Miles's query.

"I don't know why you can't understand how important it is for me, Miles." She blinked away the telltale tears and her emerald eyes seemed to darken with intensity as she tried to press forward with her argument.

"Suppose . . . suppose there's a genetic defect in my DNA that I'm not aware of. Say, like, the sickle-cell trait, or any of many genetic disorders, or even a predisposition to a mental impairment—like my poor client . . ."

"Leese, Leese," impatient now, Miles interrupted her, "now you're grasping at straws! Why do you have to think of such awful things like that? Any problems we have, we'll *share*. Don't you understand?"

He paced back and forth in front of the windows. Aleesa remained seated on the couch.

"Miles, why can't *you* understand? We might . . . we might have children and I . . . I," she stammered, almost unable to continue.

Miles had stopped pacing and stood, his back turned to her as he stared out into the dark night. Traffic was moving up and down the street, people were going about their affairs, possibly going home to their beds, while in this room his future had come to an impasse.

Aleesa sat motionless, watching Miles and wondering how she could get him to understand. Why couldn't he realize how painful it had been for her all these years not knowing who she really was . . . who had given her life? Didn't he understand that it was because she loved him so much, it was even more important now? Couldn't he see that what she wanted for their future was only the best, the finest, the truth, for their future happiness? Finding her birth parents had always been her goal, but now, since finding and falling in love with Miles, it seemed more important than ever. At least to her.

With his back turned to her, Miles stood like a pillar of defiance. She thought, was she going to lose him? She knew he was as strong-willed as she. Perhaps this current crisis was meant to be—to show each of them that they were not compatible, did not belong together at all. Their viewpoints on this matter did not agree. Was she wrong to want to pursue her origins—or was he right to tell her that her past did not matter?

She wanted so much for him to turn around and say he understood. What if he couldn't do that? Where did that leave her? She cleared her throat before she spoke. She would toss down the gauntlet.

"As I said at the outset, Miles, maybe marriage is not for us," she said.

He turned swiftly and glared at her, angry at her pronouncement.

"Like hell! I believe it is! You want to be stubborn about this, that's what is wrong. Every couple has problems, girl," he insisted. "It's how you deal with them that matters. You say you want to find your parents. I say fine, I'll help you do that. But you throw up a barrier and say 'Oh no, I'll do it myself, don't need your help.' Why not, I wonder, if we've decided we love each other? Why shouldn't we share everything, as they say, 'the good, the bad, the ugly'?"

"Don't you see, I don't know *what* I'll find . . . maybe you won't . . ."

Before she could finish the distasteful thought, Miles strode over to her, grabbed her hands and jerked her to her feet. He spoke slowly and directly to her, his dark eyes fastened on hers.

"Whatever you find . . . cross-eyed, pigeon-toed, bank robbers, murderers, won't matter a damn bit to me! It's *you* I love. Go ahead, be stubborn, have it your way. Just remember, I'll always love you."

He kissed her fiercely then, bruising her lips with vehement passion as if branding her as his. He grabbed his suit coat from the chair near the door, and, without a backward glance, left her standing, her hand to her mouth. He slammed the door. Her tears fell then as she heard his footsteps echo down the corridor.

Had the die been cast? she wondered. Was it over between them? Had her long-held 'need to know' cost her the man she loved? She brushed away the tears and went into the bathroom to prepare for bed.

She looked into the mirror. *Where are you? You gave me this hair, these eyes, this stubborn, strong will. Where are you both? Why can't I find you?*

She went to sleep that night, a restless, troubled sleep. *I must find you,* echoed in her mind.

Miles didn't remember the drive to his apartment across the city from Aleesa's South End condominium. His mind was so filled with concern over the unsettling argument with Aleesa, he drove automatically, literally unaware of the journey home.

He pulled up in the driveway beside his apartment building, turned off the ignition, and sat, reliving the distasteful scene. What was wrong with the girl? He should have known she was totally different when she insisted that he stop sending her gifts. That nonsense that he was trying to manipulate her somehow. Most of the women he had known were delighted to receive his gifts. Maybe, he thought as he sat in the darkened car, that was what made her even more attractive to him. She could not be wooed by "things." Evidently she appreciated the lovely gifts he liked to present her with, but it seemed, he thought, that such acceptance diminished her self-identity—in *her* eyes, anyway.

Miles hated to admit it, even to himself, but his admiration for her increased as he thought of her willingness to risk everything, perhaps even losing his love, to press forward to find the answer to her questions about her birth.

How could he deny her the pursuit of her goal? What kind of man was he if he could not respect her strong motivation?

As he sat in the car, he became aware of the night sounds of the city. Traffic had lessened. It was late, but he knew he would not be able to sleep until he had made some decisions.

One thing was certain. He would not give up. He loved Aleesa too much. He decided to speak with her parents. They seemed like wonderful people. He wondered how they felt about Aleesa's search. She didn't say if she'd even spoken to them about it. Their support might even be helpful to him. He would find a way out of this problem. He had to. He couldn't help himself. He loved Aleesa Haskins. He had to work fast. He had several overseas trips scheduled, the first one to Iceland in a few days. He had to put a plan into action . . . and soon.

He got out of the car and walked slowly to his apartment building. He could see faint streaks of light low in the eastern sky. *God,* he prayed silently, *please let the day dawn brighter for me and the woman I love.*

* * *

The very next day Alessa found a private investigator who agreed to take her case.

"Bring me a copy of your birth certificate that was issued when you were adopted and we'll start with that. Sometimes these adoption searches take months, other times, the Internet or a simple phone call . . ." he said.

"I know," Alessa said, hopefully.

Nine

Aleesa drove up to Water's Edge to tell her parents what had happened between her and Miles.

Her mother was visibly upset. Her eyes filled with tears and she went over to where her daughter sat on the sofa and sat down beside her, taking Aleesa's hand.

"I guess you have the right to search. But you know that all Dad and I ever wanted was your happiness. Right, Dad?"

She looked up at her husband, who was standing in front of the fireplace. He nodded his head in agreement.

"Have we made you happy, dear?"

Aleesa gave her mother a quick hug, aware of the bright tears in her mother's eyes.

"Oh, Mother! No one could ever have had better folks than I have with you and Dad." She gave her father a lopsided grin. "That's one reason I never tried to search before . . . didn't want to hurt either of you."

Her father gave her a reassuring smile that let her know he understood.

"Well, how come this searching is so important to you now?" her mother persisted.

"I don't know. There's just this big hole in my heart . . . a space that I can't seem to fill. It's a painful feeling. It's always been with me, but ever since I met Miles and fell in love with him, it's become *so* important to me to know who I am. And I've made up my mind. I'm not going to marry Miles until I find out . . . something."

Her mother spoke up then.

"I always wondered when you would decide you needed to find your family . . . your roots. I remember once when you were about fifteen," her mother continued as she patted her daughter's hand, "a couple of your schoolmates started teasing you about where your hair and eye color came from? I was so glad, so proud of you, when you stood toe to toe with them and answered them so bravely, 'From my folks. The ones who borned me, dummies!' "

Aleesa laughed at the memory.

"I remember that. Susan Mackel and Virginia Ransom, they thought they were so smart, always wanted to start something."

"Well, as I remember it," her mother went on, "they never brought the subject up again. You shut them up! But I wondered then if you would try to search for your birth parents. Your father and I talked about it then and agreed we would never discourage you if ever you wanted to do that. Honey, you've brought us so much happiness—sharing your life with us—we could never deny you. And now that you've found Miles, and we know you love him, we just want you to fulfill your life's dreams with him. He's truly a wonderful young man. We love him, too, don't we, Dad?"

Her husband agreed. "Couldn't have picked a better young man, my dear. Just want you two to be happy."

He came over to where the women were sitting and kissed each of them.

"I know it may be hard, child . . ."

"But, Dad, I have to do it, hard or otherwise. And

God knows what I may find, but I have to take that chance. I can't go forward and marry Miles, as much as I love him, until I find my past."

"In that case," her father said, "come into the den, honey, and let's get started on your search. Your mother and I know how strong-willed and stubborn you can be. We want you and Miles to have that September wedding. I've already spent over two hundred dollars on lawn seed. Surely don't want that to go to waste. Wanted the lawn to be really nice on that day."

"Oh, Dad, you're so good to me. You know I've already contacted a private investigator."

"That's a good idea. Now, let's see," he reached into a lower drawer of his desk and pulled out a folder. "Here we are. This is all we got from the lawyer when we adopted you, honey. It was a private adoption."

Fingers shaking, Aleesa opened the folder. A birth certificate listed Boston Central Medical Center as her place of birth. Mother's name: Svetlana Nevskaya. Birthplace: Ukraine, Russia. Father's name: Boyd Howell. Birthplace: Haverhill, Massachusetts.

"You mean this says my mother was a Russian?"

"Right," her father said. "See, as occupations, both your parents are listed as students. Your father is listed as Negro, as they did in those days."

"I always wondered where my hair and eye color came from . . . why I didn't look more like the family, although you and Mom always said I was adopted."

"And here is a set of my footprints."

"As well as your mother's fingerprint."

"Baby Girl Nevskaya," Aleesa read. "So, my parents weren't married," she mused. "Maybe that's why they gave me up."

"And your mother and I were so thrilled that day when the lawyer called and told us we finally had a baby girl."

"Oh, Dad, thanks. Now I can start my search." She hugged him.

"The lawyer's name is Mordecai Williams. Has an office on Mass. Avenue somewhere. I'd start there if I were you."

"Dad, I've been having nightmares. Didn't want to tell Miles or Mother, but I know I won't have peace of mind until I satisfy my need to know."

"I understand, hon, and no matter how it turns out, you know you're always our daughter and we love you."

"First thing tomorrow morning I'm going sailing. Promises to be a good day and I need to make a plan for my search procedure. And, Dad, thanks for everything. I've had a good life no matter what I find out . . . and I'll always have you and Mom to thank for that."

The next morning turned out to be a sparkling spring day. Aleesa was pleased with her father's information. It gave her a place to start her search. She was satisfied as she drove to the marina where her sailboat waited for her in its slip. Forsythia bushes glowed a glorious yellow along the residential streets. Japanese quince, like white lace, danced delicately in the spring breeze.

Her parents had given her the sailboat as a graduation gift from college.

"This is yours, honey," her father had said, creases of pleasure crinkling round his eyes as he smiled at her.

"Mine? All mine?" Aleesa had stared at the small craft that bobbed at the end of the jetty.

"That's right. She's all yours, a gift from your mother and me. Happy sailing, girl."

She had given her mother a tight squeeze.

"Mom, you always know what I want."

"Mothers are *supposed* to know, my dear. Happy?" she'd asked.

"Oh, I am, I am!"

So *Tismine* for "This is mine" was painted in bright blue on the fantail of the jaunty white boat. A gold streamer flowed under TISMINE, emphasizing the bold blue letters.

When she finally set sail, a stiff breeze came up and caught the mainsail like an unfurled white flag. Aleesa was on her way into the beckoning wings of the harbor. She always found it peaceful to be one with her boat, the sky, the wind, and the water. She knew this was the environment she needed to somehow absorb the past few days' events.

Her thoughts turned to Miles. She steadied the jib and, properly set, the sail responded. Would Miles be patient and tolerant while she tried to find Svetlana Nevskaya and Boyd Howell? How and why did her mother come to America? Why hadn't she and Boyd Howell married? Why was she put up for adoption? As she sailed across the harbor, the questions swirled around in her head. And was Miles right, that maybe her birth parents had good reasons for not wanting to be located? Aleesa was aware of cases in one western state where birth mothers had filed lawsuits against the states for violating their privacy rights. They didn't want to be found, didn't want adoptees to have access to their birth certificates. Was he right in suggesting that she consider their rights?

Grady was not surprised when Miles showed up the next day.

"Mr. Haskins, I had to come. I hope you and Mrs. Haskins don't mind my barging in, but, well, you must know how concerned I am about my relationship with Aleesa."

"Miles, please come in," Grady Haskins said when he opened the front door to find a worried Miles. "I know how upset you must be with Aleesa searching . . ."

"I am, sir. Very upset. We really had quite an argument. Told her it didn't matter to me . . . I love her and I always will. She's my life, sir."

"I know how you feel, son. I totally agree with you. Her mother and I love her, too, and we've tried to show her that love . . . but, well, maybe, I guess there's a deep need in each of us to feel connected to our roots, or something. Perhaps that's what she's looking for."

"She is here, isn't she, sir?" Miles asked anxiously.

"She is here in Marblehead, yes, but she's gone sailing. Left early this morning. But I expect her back before dark."

"I hope so," Miles said. "I do want to see her before I leave. Maybe I should have called," he worried, "but she was so angry with me, it probably wouldn't have mattered."

"What do you mean, *wouldn't have mattered?*"

"I told her I'd be willing to help in her search and she told me to butt out. She would do her own searching. And she even said we would not be getting married until she was satisfied she had done all she could to locate her folks."

"I could tell she was upset, Miles. Probably why she's out sailing in the harbor right now, trying to sort it all out in her mind. She did tell us she'd contacted a private investigator."

"I've got to see her. I have to make a scheduled run to Iceland."

"Iceland, is it?"

"A shipment of medical supplies that have first priority. Have to leave Logan Airport at six A.M. I wish she'd get back."

"Don't worry. She's a fine sailor, has emergency equipment and knows how to use it. And sometimes, if she sails into dusk or decides to stay overnight to sail the next day, she'll put in overnight at a friend's B&B."

"You mean bed and breakfast?"

"Right. Then she'll have a morning sail before she calls it quits. Excuse me a minute." He got up from the chair by the fireplace to retrieve the mail from the front door mailbox. He had seen the postman walk up to deposit it. He put the mail on the sofa table and returned to his seat.

"You know, Miles, it didn't surprise me one bit, her wanting to find her folks. I know she loves you deeply, and only wants the best for you and for the marriage. Leesa was always an intense, driven child. It doesn't seem strange to me that she'd pursue this. Her mother doesn't quite understand, but I do."

"I'm sure it's hard for Mrs. Haskins. As long as Leese knows that I love her, always have and always will, I'm going to try to understand her need to know."

"I may as well tell you, Miles, that I gave her all the information that her mother and I received when we went through the adoption procedure. You know, her mother was a Russian student immigrant and her father was black, a student from Haverhill, not far from here. When their daughter was born, they were not married. I also gave her the name and address of the lawyer who handled the adoption."

"I'm sure that's a start. Did she seem pleased with that?"

Aleesa's father nodded. "She was ecstatic."

"I wish I could stay. I really want to see her. Please

tell her I was here and I'll be in touch as soon as I get back from my flight."

"Will do, son. Don't worry."

"It's very hard for me not to worry, Mr. Haskins. I really do love your daughter."

"We must be confident that everything will come out right," Grady tried to reassure a very worried Miles.

The two men shook hands, then Miles left.

Ten

"I'll be taking a few minutes after my lunch hour to do some investigative work, but if something comes up before I get back, beep me, will you, please? You do have my page number?" Aleesa checked with her secretary, Jen Russel, who was also a part-time paralegal. Aleesa had found her to be an effective worker, although the employee had a tendency to become anxious and tense very easily. There was a nervous quaver in her voice when she asked, "Will you be back for the staff meeting?"

"I expect to be back well before the meeting," she reassured Jen, noting the concern on the young woman's face.

Williams and Williams was located in an old converted brownstone. A florist occupied the first floor. Aleesa was happy to see the storefront window filled to capacity with spring flowers. Did that augur well for her? This venture marked the start of her search, and she was hopeful. The law offices were up a flight of narrow stairs to the second floor.

"I'm here to see a Mr. Mordecai Williams, if I may," she told the receptionist, a middle-aged, brown-skinned woman with a matronly appearance.

The woman looked at Aleesa with a slight smile. "I'm sorry, my dear," she glanced at the card Aleesa had handed her. "I see you're a lawyer. I'm sorry, Mr. Mordecai passed away last year. Is there something I can help you with, or would you care to speak with his son, Mr. Jeffrey Williams?"

"Oh, no, ma'am. I'm sure he has a busy schedule. But perhaps *you* can help me. I was told that my adoption was handled by Mr. Mordecai Williams. Do you think any of my records might still be available?"

"I'll be glad to check." She looked at the card again. "Aleesa Haskins . . ."

"Yes, my adoptive parents were Grady and Carol Haskins."

A few minutes later the secretary returned with a manila folder.

"This is all I could find. Lucky for you the records were not sealed. I'm sorry I can't let you take them, but you're welcome to look the file over. Here"—she waived Aleesa to a chair—"have a seat, take your time."

Aleesa's hands trembled as she held the folder, and she was so nervous she almost forgot to thank the woman.

"Th-th-thank you so much," she stuttered.

She looked through the folder carefully, noting that it contained the same information that her father had shared with her, with the exception that the papers she held in her hand were the originals, and her father's set of papers were duplicates. The only new information she noticed was that both of her parents had the same blood type, AB. That was also her blood type. *Well, there is at least one common thread,* she thought.

* * *

In a way, she was sorry that she had missed Miles last weekend. She had returned from her solitary sailing outing more determined than ever to search for her birth parents. By the time she'd returned to her parents', Miles was back in Boston. Her father reported the gist of the conversation he'd had with Miles.

"He came looking for you, Leese. He's very upset over this search of yours and your refusal to let him help you with it. He said to tell you that he's on his way to Iceland and plans to get in touch with you as soon as he returns—and he told me to tell you how very much he cares about you. He thanked me for the information I shared with him and said he plans to search, whether you want his help or not."

"I know he cares, Dad, and believe me, it's because I care about him that I must do this thing, myself, alone . . ."

"Well, I'm here to help if it gets to be too much, you know that," her father said.

She recalled the last time she and Miles had been together and the acrimonious argument that had created the bitter moment between them.

Miles's face had been dark with anger.

"I don't understand you at all, Leesa," he had thundered at her. "Why won't you let me help you? Why do you have to go it alone? Afraid of what you might find? Well, whatever, I'm in for the long haul, remember that, whatever comes of this search of yours. It's you I love! Remember that! I will always love you." He had fairly spat the words at her. He was so angry.

She didn't know what she was going to do, or how she was going to act when he came back from his trip to Iceland. Perhaps she or the PI would have discovered something about her parents by then. And then, hanging over her head, was the wedding. Would she change her mind and go ahead with the plans no matter what she found out? She would have to make a decision. And perhaps make it soon.

She returned to her office, her mind still on the visit, to find her secretary in an agitated state.

"Mr. Butterworth was just in here, says your case against the city has been moved up on the court calendar to two weeks from today and are you ready?"

Aleesa took in the harried expression on the secretary's face and spoke calmly to allay the girl's fears.

"I'm ready, Jen. Don't worry. Have a few minor details to work out . . . some of the police involved with the case have been on leave, but I'm sure they are available for court appearances by now, or should be in two weeks."

"Mr. Butterworth seemed certain that you might not be prepared," Jen exhaled, her long hair flailing about her shoulders as she threw her head back.

"He should know better than that, Jen. I've always completed my assignments. Just because I'm fairly new to the firm doesn't mean I don't do my work. Don't let it bother you, Jen. Sorry he upset you," Aleesa tried to calm her the best she could.

"It's almost as if he has to monitor *everything* that goes on in this firm," Jen muttered, somewhat mollified.

"I expect when you're a law partner in a firm as old as this one, you tend to feel that way."

"Makes me nervous, every time. I always think he'll find out that I've made some kind of a mistake. He knows I'm a paralegal, just learning . . ."

"Don't fret, kid." Aleesa smiled at her. "We'll do just fine, you and me."

After a dinner of pasta warmed up in her microwave, Aleesa sat down at the computer. She searched for the name Boyd Howell and was rewarded with fifteen Boyd Howells, five of them in Boston and surrounding communities. Excited, she printed out all the telephone numbers.

When she tried her mother's name, Svetlana Nevskaya, she found several with her mother's first name and at least ten last names of Nevskaya, but not the two names, first and surname linked together. She found several families with the last name Nevskaya located in South Boston as well as Brookline and Newton. She printed out the names and numbers.

She sighed deeply and went into the kitchen for a cold drink. She realized that she was procrastinating, but for some reason she felt apprehensive over the next step she was about to undertake. Could Miles be right? Was she afraid of what . . . or who she might uncover?

She steeled herself, reminding herself that this was something she had decided that she *had* to do. She had to make a definite start.

She picked up the telephone and dialed the Brookline number. "This is Rabbi Nevskaya. How may I help you?"

The deep Middle European accent washed over her like a calm blessing.

"I'm sorry, I am looking for a woman named Svetlana Nevskaya."

"Svetlana? I do not know any person by that name, I'm sorry to say."

"I apologize for troubling you, sir."

"No trouble. Good night."

When she replaced the receiver back in its cradle, Aleesa wondered if a bad incident was going to be in her future. But . . . all of her life she had been bothered by the difference in her adoptive parents and herself. They hadn't given her the mahogany-red long hair, the gray-green eyes. Who had? And what else? What other genetic material? What impulses, tendencies flowed in the pattern of the nervous system she had inherited? She had to go on . . . had to find some answers.

She picked up the phone and dialed the Newton number. It was answered after two rings by a woman's breathless voice.

"Brigitte Nevskaya speaking."

"Hello, my name is Aleesa Haskins and I'm trying to locate Svetlana Nevskaya. Is she at this number?"

"No such person by that name here, m'dear. Just me and Lotus, my Siamese cat."

"Can you tell me if you've ever known or heard of a Svetlana Nevskaya?" Aleesa asked hopefully.

"No, I have not. I was married a long time ago to a Peter Nevskaya, but he didn't have anyone in his family by that name. And to tell you the truth, I *can't* ask him. He dropped out of my life after our divorce and I'd just as soon he stayed dropped out, if you get my drift."

"Well, thanks anyway," Aleesa said. "I appreciate your time and consideration."

The woman chuckled on the other end of the line. "You're quite welcome, kiddo. Hope you find whoever it is you're looking for."

The Newton telephone number belonged to a John Nevskaya. His wife answered. No, she did not know anyone by the name of Svetlana, whatever kind of name was that, anyway? She wouldn't disturb her husband to come to the phone. He was sleeping, drove a taxi on the night shift. She told Aleesa that if she really wanted to speak to her husband, she could call between eight and nine in the morning.

Disappointed that her first attempts had proved

fruitless, Aleesa decided perhaps a new start the next day might be better.

After her shower, she stared at her face in the bathroom mirror. She brushed her long hair, staring reflectively at her image. Would this adventure that she had undertaken, against Miles's and her mother's advice, end the way she wanted it to?

She turned her bedside radio on to an all-night music station. She was still tense and knew that sleep might be a long time coming.

It happened again—the same horrible nightmare—a man's face hidden from view, evidently berating a woman who was in tears, her long reddish-brown hair swinging back and forth in some sort of denial.

Aleesa sat straight up in bed, shaking, her nightgown as cold and clammy as if she had been drenched with water. What did this wretched torment mean? What caused her to have this awful nightmare?

Eleven

As she lay sleeping beside him, Boyd Howell looked at his wife Lana with such affection. His mind reeled back to the first time he had ever seen her.

She had been seated down in the front row of the mini-amphitheater classroom used for most of the large freshman class's compulsory courses. The course, Fundamentals of Music Education, was required, and freshman students from at least thirty-five of the fifty states and twelve foreign countries had crowded into the room. New friendships were being formed and already, only one day after the start of the new semester, students were seeking familiar faces or trying to locate a friendly one. However, when the professor entered and took his place at the podium down front, the hub-bub of many voices that rose to an almost hysterical crescendo suddenly ceased, like turning off the spigot of tap water.

It was Lana's glorious chestnut-red hair that Boyd had noticed first. It fell in thick, luxurious curls around her shoulders. He stared at it, almost willing the young woman to turn around so he could see her face. It was hard to pay attention to the speaker at the lectern, but he knew he had to focus on the class at hand. After all, this was what he was here for—to learn all he needed to know to be a well-trained, successful musician.

As soon as the instructor had dismissed the class, Boyd had sought the owner of the red-gold hair. He had been sitting in an aisle seat about halfway up when he had seen her coming up the aisle, her head down because she was checking for something in her book bag. Her face had been hidden by the stunning thick mane. As she'd neared him, she'd raised her head, and Boyd's heart had tripped over itself.

She was beautiful. Honey-toned skin, her features finely chiseled with a soft, smiling mouth that bedazzled him, it had all made Boyd exhale deeply. She must have heard him because she'd stared at him. Her eyes were gleaming emeralds and Boyd Howell had known his life would never be the same. The gods had just dropped the woman in his life that he knew he would love forever.

It had begun with walks to the library to study.

"I can't believe that with all the fine music schools in Europe you'd want to come to America, Lana." Boyd had told her that she was much more beautiful than the movie actress by that name and she should Americanize her first name and her last name, too—so she'd decided, yes, perhaps Lana, but I'll keep my surname, thank you.

"Well, that's understandable, but why come to Boston to study music?"

"My father wanted me to come here."

"Your father?"

"Yes, well, because he was born here, in America, in Georgia."

"Your father is from Georgia?" Boyd could not believe what he was hearing.

"My father," Lana had insisted slowly, "was born in Georgia. He looks like you."

"What do you mean, looks like me?"

"He is colored, like you," she had said simply.

Dumbfounded, he had stared at her. "Girl, you're telling me that your father is colored, a Negro, like me?"

"Like you, only older, with gray hair and more wrinkles." She had smiled.

"Wow! Oh, wow! And your mother . . ."

"Is Ukrainian."

"But how . . . I don't understand," he had stuttered, shocked by her revelation. He could hardly believe what she'd told him about the post-revolution years, the need for industrial growth and development, how her father, a college graduate, could not find employment in the south, how he arrived in the Ukraine as an agricultural specialist and a university professor. How he had helped develop a strain of cotton more suited to the short growing season of the area. She'd told him that it was her father's idea that she study music in his homeland.

"So, I am here," she'd opened both hands in a gesture of submission.

"I'm glad you're here, Lana. But I've never heard such a story before. Wait till I tell my parents. They'll never believe me! You've got to come home with me and tell them yourself."

"That would be all right, to go to your home?"

"Are you kidding? Of course it will be okay. My folks always want me to bring my friends home and . . . you're my friend, aren't you?"

"I am your friend, Boyd Howell." She had grinned back at him.

"I would like to take you home with me, Lana," he'd told her one day after class. "I want you to meet my folks."

"It would be proper for me . . . to meet your parents?" she'd asked him.

"Of course. Didn't you just tell me that you were my friend?" He'd grinned at her.

She'd nodded, wordlessly, but her emerald-green eyes had revealed her excitement at the idea.

"Well, then," Boyd had said, "Sunday morning we will take the bus to Haverhill. Sorry I don't have a car, but I will, someday. Count on it!"

Then came marriage.

"Son, you're in no position to get married, you know that. Thought you've always wanted a career in music."

Boyd had watched his mother move about the kitchen, stirring the beef stew, lowering the gas flame so it could simmer slowly, rolling and cutting out biscuits to place in the oven, all the while talking about his future. He'd known what he had to say next would be upsetting to his mother. He'd plunged ahead, anyway.

"Ma, I know, I know, I do want to finish school, but I love Lana and I want to marry her."

His mother had turned from the oven where she had just placed the biscuits, slammed the oven door closed, and given her son a steady look.

"Want to or have to?"

"Both. I *have* to and I *want* to. Lana is pregnant."

"I figured as much. Well, son, it's your life and I can't tell you how to live it. I could say 'You've made your bed and you got to lie in it,' but I won't say that. All I'm goin' to say is 'God go with you and peace stay behind you' wherever you go and whatever you decide to do."

But the child had come before the wedding could take place.

All that day, between classes, Boyd had tried desperately to find Lana.

He'd finally run into Heather Scott, a classmate from New Hampshire who had been very close to Lana and to him. He knew she was aware of their relationship. He was not certain that she knew about the baby.

"Heather, have you seen Lana? I haven't seen her at all today . . . in any of our classes. Know where she is?"

"No, Boyd, I don't know where she is. But I'm worried. She got sick last night something awful, cramps and . . . stuff like that. I know she went to the infirmary to see the nurse and . . . I don't know what happened after that. She didn't come back to the dorm."

"Oh, thanks, Heather. Thanks so much."

"You'll let me know if you find out anything?" Heather'd sounded worried. "Hope she's okay."

His heart had pounded in his chest, almost choking him. He could scarcely breathe as he raced up the brick stairs. His life, his future, lay somewhere in this bleak, forboding building. Magdalen House, he had been told, was where they had taken Lana. Had she already delivered the baby? He had promised to be with her when her time came. She wasn't due for another two months, so what had happened? If the baby came too early, what would that mean?

At the information desk, he'd blurted out, "Lana . . . Lana Nevskaya." The clerk had taken one look at his panic-stricken face and directed him to a set of doors down the corridor. "Second floor, Room 223," she'd said.

He recalled the anguish, guilt, and dread that had flooded over him as he'd pushed through the stairwell doors. *God*, he remembered thinking then as he mounted the flight of stairs two at a time, *please let her be okay.* His breath had come in jagged gasps as he'd raced down the hall, checking the room numbers.

He'd found it. Room 223. Slowly, he'd pushed the door open. All he could see was a slight form, blanketed and bundled into a fetal position. Her back had faced him, her glorious hair cascading around her slim shoulders.

"Lana," he'd whispered as he crossed the room to her bed.

She'd turned slowly at the sound of his voice. Shocked by the sight of her ravaged, tearstained face, he'd bent over to take her in his arms. As he'd held her close, she'd whimpered his name as if speaking from a distant place. "Oh, Boyd," she'd whispered. "Oh, Boyd, hold me. Please . . . hold me."

He'd held her close. "I know, honey, I know. I'm so sorry . . ."

"I didn't think the baby would come so soon . . . two months early, but then I had such cramps, such pain and . . . and," she'd wailed, "the water came, the pains . . . oh, Boyd . . ."

"It's all right, babe. Don't cry."

"But, Boyd . . . oh, Boyd, the baby! They said the baby died!"

Boyd had stared at the weeping girl.

"Died? How? What happened?"

"I don't know. How could it be? Such strong kicks before she came."

"She? It was a girl?"

"I don't know . . . they said . . . I never . . . I never saw her, Boyd, never saw her." She'd pushed her face back into her pillow as she tried to stifle her cries.

He had been given the same story by a nurse who seemed to be in charge.

"I'm sorry about your loss, sir. But the patient was hysterical, unable to control herself. It was necessary to sedate her. She kept saying the baby's father was colored, 'Like Papa, please, my baby is like Papa!'. We didn't know what she was screaming about. Was she speaking of incest? That her father . . ."

Horrified at the thought, Boyd had slammed his fist on the desk. "I'm the father and I want to know what happened to my baby!"

"The baby was premature, weighed only four pounds, and was stillborn. I'm sorry."

"Where is she?"

"All stillborns are disposed of . . . cremated. Again, I'm sorry."

The words had hit him with such a blow that immediately he'd felt faint.

He had staggered. Someone had pushed him into a chair. Someone else had handed him a glass of water.

Mrs. Howell had recognized her son's pain. His silence as he had struggled through the days after Lana's horrible experience had been deafening. His mother had worried along with her husband about their son's future.

"It's such a terrible thing that happened," she had said to him. "We have to help them get through this. I believe they truly love each other. We can't let this tragedy keep them apart."

Boyd's father had agreed.

"You speak to him, let him know that we'll help him, whatever he wants to do."

"I believe he wants to get married."

"Then that's what he should do, and the sooner the better. Those two kids need to be together after all they've been through."

* * *

"I know it's hard, son, but you've got to go on with your life. You two aren't the first somebodies to lose a child. Just an unfortunate happening."

"But Ma," Boyd's eyes had been red-rimmed from the tears he had shed. "Lana feels guilty about losing the baby, but I keep telling her that I'm the guilty one. Should have married her, not waited for school to be over."

"Now, son, enough of that talk. You two thought it was the right thing to do, we all did, so we are all to blame. Listen to me. You need Lana and she needs you. The love you have for each other will get you through this bad time." She had directed him, "Bring Lana over tonight for supper and afterwards we'll make plans for your wedding. Your father and I will take care of everything. You're our son and we love you. We know you love Lana, and she's in our hearts, too."

"Ma, Ma," Boyd had struggled with his emotions, sorrow mingling with restrained joy as his mother hugged him.

"It's all right, son. Tomorrow you both go to city hall, get your license, and Reverend Rogers says he'll perform the ceremony right after services on Sunday. Go on now, get Lana. Everything is going to be fine."

Boyd would always be grateful to his parents for their encouraging words. He snuggled up against Lana and closed his eyes to sleep.

Twelve

At Magdalen House, now a college dorm, the private investigator had come to a dead end, he told Aleesa. Disappointed, Aleesa discharged him from her case and paid his rather hefty fee.

Frustrated now over her lack of progress in her search, she wondered whether or not she was on a wild goose chase. Her mother thought so. She was positive that her daughter was jeopardizing her future with Miles.

Aleesa turned to her work. A review of her progress in the case had been ordered by Mr. Butterworth. A senior law committee would hear her proposed arguments and offer suggestions and/or opinions.

She explained her planned approach.

"I'm using Article Four of the Constitution as the basis of my case."

"You mean, the right of a person to be secure?" Mr. Butterworth asked.

"Yes, sir." Aleesa looked around the table. She noted that there was only one other person of color present, a female law clerk, who had evidently been included . . . to make Aleesa feel more comfortable? she wondered.

She continued to present her reasoning. "Unreasonable searches and seizures shall not be committed. Just because my client is mentally ill with Self-Induced Water Intoxication Syndrome is no reason for the police to arrest him."

Another lawyer, a rather imposing gray-haired man, spoke up.

"Didn't the police arrest him because he was seen hanging around the ATM and he matched the security camera's photo of the robber?"

Aleesa realized that the man was taking the adversarial position of the police department.

"The police were not thorough in their job. They assumed they had the right man without a complete investigation. True, my client had been seen hanging around the ATM, but isn't this a free country where anyone can move about freely without fear of arrest?" she argued.

Some heads were nodding in agreement.

She continued, "I intend to prove that the police were hasty in their arrest of my client and he is entitled to compensation, as well as punitive damages for his confinement and embarrassment. I also intend to prove that his mental condition was exacerbated by being denied mental health treatment. He was arrested right in the middle of therapy vital to his ongoing condition."

Mr. Butterworth asked, "How much? How much money are we seeking?"

"A half-million, sir."

"Be lucky if we get half that for the client," he said.

Aleesa looked around, brushing her gaze over each person before she answered.

"Don't *you* think it's an important principle that an ordinary man should be treated with respect? And besides, we can't allow the police to willy-nilly arrest someone because he looks like someone else, can we?"

There were more vigorous nods of agreement this

time, as well as a slightly upturned smile from the young law clerk. Aleesa knew she would have to seek her out later and thank her for her silent support. We *always have to hang together,* she thought.

Mr. Butterworth indicated that the meeting was over. He stood up and shook Aleesa's hand.

"Win this case, Ms. Haskins, and I can guarantee you a substantial bonus."

Aleesa gathered up her papers and stuffed them into her briefcase. His words tumbled about in her mind. Success and a bonus would be welcome, but she would rather find her birth parents.

When she got home that night, she felt drained and exhausted. Too tired to cook, she settled for a tuna sandwich and a cup of tea. She went directly to the computer and logged on. She was scrolling down the names of Howells when the telephone rang.

"Aleesa?" It was her mother. "Are you okay?"

"Yes, Mom. I'm fine. A little tired, but I'm all right."

"Good. Honey, have you given any thought to your upcoming wedding plans? You know the wedding invitations should be going out soon, and . . ."

"Mother," she interrupted, "you know I've just started this search—can't think of anything else until I finish. And I'm really busy now with my upcoming court case. I've got a full plate right now," she argued. "You realize that I'm up against a powerful law enforcement agency, the Boston Police Department, as well as the City of Boston. Really, Mother, the wedding is the last thing on my mind. Besides, Miles isn't back yet from his Iceland trip."

She heard her mother's long-suffering sigh come over the phone.

"But . . . but don't you two *love* each other?"

"Mother, love has nothing to do with my search. It's what I need, what I want."

Another long, drawn-out sigh from her mother. Aleesa remained silent.

"Guess there's nothing I can do but wait until you two come to some understanding."

"I'd say that's about it, Mother."

"All right, then. When do you expect Miles to get back?"

"I really don't know, but I'm sure he'll call when he does get back."

"Hope so. Good night, dear. Love you."

"Love you, too, Mother," she answered and hung up the phone.

Her mother's interruption made her thoughts go to Miles. When he did return, what was she going to do about their pending marriage? Would she stick to her original decision not to marry until her search was over? Was she strong enough to persevere? To carry on to reach her goal? Did she have the determination, the will to keep going? Was it truly that important to her?

She called her father later that evening.

"Dad, if I send you a printout of some of the names, addresses, and phone numbers, could you follow up for me by calling them?"

"Sure honey," her father agreed. "I can do that."

"Thanks, Dad. I could use the help. My court case is scheduled to start soon. I'll be so busy . . ."

"Not to worry. Send your list along and I'll get right to work on it." Like her mother, her father was interested in her relationship with Miles.

"Heard from Miles?" he wanted to know.

"No, Dad, not yet. Did think I might by now. I understand it's a four-and-a-half-hour flight from Boston to Keflavik Airport in Iceland."

"Well, he'll call you, I'm sure. Everything is going to be fine."

"I hope so. Thanks, Dad."

"I *know* so. Don't worry. Good night, hon."

"Good night, Dad, and thanks."

She heard from her father a few days later.

"Sorry, hon. Those names and telephone numbers you gave me—dead end. That is, all except one."

"Which one, Dad?" Aleesa asked anxiously.

"The B. B. Howell. Seems there was a family, a Negro one at that, by that name living in South Boston. Couldn't have been easy for them," he commented dryly before he continued. "Anyway, they moved away. I'm going to check to see if any of the neighbors know where they went."

"Be careful, Dad."

"Don't worry. I worked with a couple of guys from Southie. We always got along well. I'm going to look them up. Maybe they can help."

"My court case is on the docket for today," she told him.

"Give it your best shot. Don't worry about a thing. Right will prevail," he reassured her. "Remember that."

Miles's flight engineer, Pete Warren, could hardly contain his enthusiasm.

"Can't wait to get to Iceland, Miles. They say those geysers and hot springs are something else. I've heard that the Blue Lagoon up there is a pool of pure mineral water. Takes every ache and pain right away from your poor, aching body."

"That right? Might need that kind of treatment after a long flight like this one."

"The brochures say this lagoon is right in the middle of a lava field. Over a hundred and fifty thousand visitors go up there for health and relaxation."

"You know we'll only be there overnight," Miles reminded him. "Have to pick up returning cargo to deadhead back into Boston."

"Yeah, sure won't give me much time to try out the hot springs, I guess," his companion said.

Miles's mind was on the trip, but always in the back of it was the problem with Aleesa and the inane search on which she had embarked. What difference could it possibly make who her birth parents were? All that stuff was history. It was the present and their future that was real. And, besides, what mattered to him was how they felt about each other. He knew the love he felt for her would never, ever change. Could he make her see that?

The problem was, the whole situation happened so fast. He had not been prepared to fall in love. His career as a cargo pilot for a well-established express delivery company was satisfying. He was well compensated, liked his work, and was doing the type of work he was prepared to do. He had a substantial stock portfolio with some technical computer company stocks, as well as several well-paying manufacturing stocks, municipal and government bonds, and he had purchased some land on Martha's Vineyard and planned to start building a house there. Everything in his life was going well, but it became perfect when he met and fell in love with Aleesa Haskins.

Besides her good looks and her lovely, sweet body, there was a certain intense depth to her personality and character that appealed to him. When she met anyone she gave all her attention to that person and focused on their needs. She cared, and those who knew her came to understand the depth of her concern for others. Miles had decided that was probably what had directed her to law.

He recalled a story Aleesa's mother had told him about her early years. Aleesa was in her mother's kitchen baking a blueberry buckle—a sort of cake, she told Miles—for dessert that night. He and Mrs. Haskins talked on the patio.

"Aleesa was about ten, Miles, when she began to beg for a pet of her own. Her father and I realized that as an only child she was lonesome at times, although she had lots of friends."

"I'm sure she did," Miles smiled.

"The house was always filled with her playmates, and we encouraged that. But she still kept asking. She wanted a dog. Well, we told her, 'You'll have to take care of the dog if we get one. It will be your responsibility.' "

"So you bought . . ."

"A lovely fawn-and-white boxer pup. We let Aleesa pick him out of the litter when he was five days old. She was so happy. She named him Mister. We picked him up from the kennel when he was weaned, about three months, and brought him home. I wish you could have seen that little girl's face!"

"Knowing my Aleesa, I can imagine how happy she was."

"Happy! She was in seventh heaven! And those two became inseparable. I never worried about her as long as Mister was around. He was her best friend, devoted to her and very protective. If either her father or I raised our voice at her or chastised her, you wouldn't believe the looks Mister would give us. He'd move from wherever he was to go to her and stay by her side as if to say, 'Don't bother my pal.' That dog was some-

thing else. I remember once, Aleesa was sixteen, had
just gotten her driver's license. She was buying gas and
the station attendant started to get a little too fresh
with her. Aleesa told him to stop, but he kept pestering
her. He didn't know Mister was in the back seat until
the dog suddenly rose up and barked at him so furiously the boy almost fainted right there on the spot."
Mrs. Haskins laughed at the memory.

"Served him right," Miles chuckled.

"It sure did. But I never saw anyone grieve more
than Aleesa did when Mister got so sick he had to be
put to sleep. She really loved that dog. I tell you one
thing, Miles. When Aleesa cares, she cares deeply."

"I know," Miles answered thoughtfully.

Varieties of fish products, electrical equipment, and
computer parts were some of the products loaded onto
Miles's plane for transport to Boston.

Preparing for takeoff, Miles struggled to free his
mind of thoughts of Aleesa. He turned to Pete. "So,
you checked out the Blue Lagoon last night?"

"Naw, too far from the hotel. But I did get a chance
to sample the miniature hot springs spa here at the
hotel. Seems these geothermal springs—geysers they
call them—are all over this country."

"So I've heard. Did you like it?"

Pete shook his head. "You know, it was almost too
hot for my taste. A nice cool dip in a swimming pool
or my favorite, the water at Kalmus Beach in Hyannis,
is more to my liking, what I really enjoy."

"I reckon, Pete, it's all in what you're used to."

The word came from the control tower and they tax-
ied down the runway. Miles followed his prescribed
procedure, opening the throttle full power to test the

engine and waiting for permission from the flight tower to take off.

He noticed the rocky terrain surrounding the airfield and planned to take off into the wind. He could hardly wait to get back to Aleesa. He spoke to Pete, "This does seem to be an unusual country, doesn't it? When I first heard of Iceland in elementary school, I thought it was all ice, lots of snow surrounded by icebergs, but it's not. The North Atlantic Drift, a continuation of the Gulf Stream, has something to do with the soft green. Almost like Ireland, I expect."

"Yeah," Pete agreed. "Their tourist slogan is something like 'Iceland might just melt your heart,' something like that. I'd like to come back as a tourist, maybe, someday."

"Gotta get back to that Blue Lagoon one time, eh?" Miles grinned.

"Yeah, well, maybe. What did you do last night? Go shopping, as usual?"

"I did. Bought a few things for the folks back home." He thought of the delicate fine woolen shawl he had purchased for Aleesa, despite her pronouncement of no more gifts. It was as sheer as lace, green and gold, the colors that he knew would match her rose-tan skin tone, as well as her glorious chestnut-red hair.

When the plane in front of them roared off into the wind, it was their turn.

The word came. Miles said, "We're cleared for takeoff. Here we go."

With engines at full throttle, the plane raced down the runway and at the takeoff position Miles brought the stick back to begin the climb into the air. A few minutes later they were in their flight pattern headed for Logan Airport in Boston.

They had just reached cruising altitude when they

heard a loud pop, like a firecracker. Both men stared at each other.

"Damn, what was that?" Miles asked.

"Dunno," Pete said, busily checking the gauges, switches, and dials on the instrument panel as Miles tried to control the plane, which suddenly had started to pitch and yaw. He fought to pull back to gain more altitude, to no avail. Then he saw it. Black smoke curling ominously around the port-side engine. He yelled at Pete, "Shut off fuel to left engine, it's on fire!"

"Oh God," Pete groaned.

Miles radioed to the tower, "WIN flight number 9044 returning to airport. Fire in left engine! Prepare for emergency! Hold on, Pete, we'll make it."

Thick acrid smoke billowed and curled around them in the cockpit. Now, panic-stricken, frozen with fear, neither man saw the ice-blue, snow-clad tundra rise up to meet them.

Thirteen

Aleesa felt exhilarated at the end of her day in court. This judge was a lifetime student of constitutional law and seemed keenly interested in Aleesa's presentation of the facts. She was optimistic that he might rule in her client's favor, but she dare not verbalize those hopes to anyone. She wondered how her father had made out with his trip to South Boston. That part of Boston was notorious for its hostility to blacks. But then she knew her tall, stalwart father could take care of himself.

She was not surprised, when she got into her apartment, to see her answering machine light blinking. She pressed the Play button.

"Aleesa," her father's voice commanded, "call me as soon as you can. It's important!"

She sat down and quickly dialed home.

"Aleesa!" her father answered on the first ring. "I have dreadful news. Have you turned on TV?"

She felt her heart flutter. She could barely speak.

"What is it, what's wrong . . . Mother?"

"No. Miles's plane went down in Iceland."

"Miles? My Miles?"

"I'm almost certain it's Miles. The news said a World International Network plane had left Iceland bound for Boston and had some type of engine trouble.

Something about fire . . . and the plane was returning to the airport when it crashed. They won't give names of the pilot and flight engineer until their families are notified. Do you want to come home? I'll come and get you."

"No, Dad, I can't. I've got to be here for my case. Miles . . . not Miles. I can't believe it. Not Miles!"

"I sure hope it's not him. Maybe it isn't."

She sat immobile, glued to the television set, switching from one news channel to the other for the latest news of the crash. Finally the names were released. Miles Kittridge, thirty-five, pilot, suffered multiple injuries and was hospitalized in Reykjavik. The flight engineer, Pete Warren, thirty-five, was also injured, but less severely, and was released from the hospital after treatment.

Her hands clutched to her mouth, Aleesa stared at the television, unwilling to accept the horrible news.

She picked up the phone on the first ring.

"Hel . . . hello," her voice quavered. "Yes, yes, this is Aleesa. Oh, yes, Mr. Kittridge, I just heard."

"Miles's mother and I are leaving within the hour to go to see about him. The company president"—his voice broke—"the president of World International Network is putting his private jet at our disposal. As soon as we can, I'll be in touch."

"Thank you, Mr. Kittridge. Thank you. I hope and pray that Miles is all right."

"The hospital says his condition is serious, my dear. They . . . they wouldn't be more specific."

"I'll be praying, sir. And, sir, Mr. Kittridge . . . please give him my love."

"Of course, Aleesa."

Aleesa went through her day like someone on automatic pilot. She was physically present at the office, but her mind was in Iceland, a remote place four-and-a-half-hours' flying time away. What had Miles's parents learned when they arrived at the hospital? What was the prognosis? It was evident to her that Miles had not shared with his parents the recent argument he and Aleesa had had.

Aleesa realized that she was grateful for that. It was just like Miles to keep such things private. After all, he was a mature adult. But what about her? This news had shattered her composure, because suddenly she realized that her dumb search—and now that's what it seemed to be, a dumb search—didn't amount to squat. What would her life be like if she *did* find her parents? And what would life be like if she lost Miles? She couldn't compare the two.

Mr. Kittridge's call that night only increased her fears.

"I'm sorry my news isn't much better, my dear."

"How is he? What's his condition?"

"He has a fractured leg that the doctors have treated. He's in a cast. He has several rib fractures, a collapsed lung, bruises all over his body, but"—the man's voice cracked over the phone—"my son is in a coma."

"Oh God, no!"

"Yes, a head injury. They are treating him with medications to reduce the brain swelling."

"I want to come up," Aleesa said firmly, her mind made up.

"No, child. We're going to bring him home to Mass. General, I hope, in a day or two. As soon as he is stabilized. I'll keep you posted."

By the end of the week the verdict came down. The city said it would automatically appeal the ruling, but Aleesa's client was awarded a judgment of three hundred thousand dollars. She accepted the congratulations of her co-workers and peers. Mr. Butterworth was delighted with her success and told her so.

"Good work, Ms. Haskins, good work. As I told you, there'll be a bonus for you. We always appreciate outstanding work here at Carter, Evans and Goode." He glanced out the window. "Why don't you take the afternoon off? Looks like a great day for sailing."

She did not go sailing, however. She went instead to Mass. General Hospital. Miles had been brought in the night before, his father said, and this would be the first time she'd be able to visit him. What would she find? She parked her car in the visitor's parking lot and walked into the lobby on trembling legs.

She stopped at the nurses' station to make inquiries. A middle-aged nurse with a kind smile and a halo of silver-white hair looked up from her desk.

"I'm Aleesa Haskins . . ."

"Oh, yes, Ms. Haskins, you're Mr. Kittridge's fiancée. His parents told us to expect you."

"How is he doing?"

"Not much change. He is still comatose, but his vital signs are within normal range. His collapsed lung has improved. We expect to remove the chest tube in a day or two—but try to prepare yourself. We're pleased with his progress so far, but you are going to think he looks bad."

"Is he on a respirator?"

"For now he is, because his brain tissues are swollen and surrounded by the bony structure of the skull," the nurse explained patiently. "Pressure builds up, which slows the flow of blood that carries oxygen to the brain. So we're giving him oxygen."

"Thank you for the information, Mrs. Grasso." She had read the nurse's name on her name tag. "Are his parents with him now?"

"I believe so. They have been here constantly. Maybe now that you are here they can take a break."

"I'll suggest it. They must be weary by now."

Aleesa walked down the long corridor that seemed endless to her. She passed open doors that revealed patients in various conditions. Some were sleeping, some were moaning in pain, others were sitting, blanketed in chairs, their faces pale with pain and uncertainty. What was she going to find behind the closed door of Room 444 at the end of the corridor?

She took a deep breath and tried to steel herself, tried to will her nerves to be calm. She paused slowly, opening the door to find Mr. Kittridge standing at the foot of the bed. As she pushed the door open wider, she saw Miles's mother sitting beside the bed, holding her son's hand. She was whispering softly to him.

Mr. Kittridge turned as Aleesa came into the room. "Aleesa." He gave her a warm hug.

"How . . . how is he?" she whispered.

" 'Bout the same. Still in a coma."

Aleesa bent to kiss Mrs. Kittridge's cheek, then she dared to look at Miles. She saw the machines, the tubes, the intravenous drip going into his vein. His fractured leg was covered with a cast from his ankle to his hip. His usually handsome face was discolored from bruises, cuts, and scrapes.

"Miles," his mother whispered softly, "wake up, dear. Aleesa's here."

Aleesa bent over the bed's sidebars to kiss Miles's cheek. His skin felt warm and smooth, but she was jolted by the waxy patina to his face. It was expressionless, and that frightened her. She tried to put a good face on, though her voice quavered.

"I'm here, Miles. You're safe. You're going to be all right. Love you, Miles," she whispered.

She squeezed his limp hand, but there was no re-

sponsive squeeze. Her heart dropped. Tears spilled
from her eyes down her cheeks, and she could hardly
breathe. He was so still. She couldn't tear her eyes
from his face—the face of the man she loved. The
oxygen being forced into his lungs by the machine
caused a gentle rise and fall of his chest. It was the
only sound in the room, except for the frequent sighs
from his worried mother.

"What do the doctors say, Mr. Kittridge? How long
will he be like this?"

He shrugged his shoulders. "They say they don't
know. Could be days . . . weeks . . ." His voice trailed
off. He gave a deep sigh and threw up his hands in a
futile gesture. Aleesa knew Miles's father could not verbalize the word *months*—or perhaps . . . She willed herself not to think of the unthinkable. Miles had to live,
he had to, because she loved him. She needed him.
She would have no future without him. And she knew
she had to fight, to will him to return to her and the
life together that he had promised her. She also knew
that her search for her birth parents was of no conse-
quence. They were part of her past. This beautiful,
wonderful, loving man lying so still was her future. She
was scared, and her heart was heavy with fear, but the
path ahead was clear. *Pull yourself together, girl. Start fight-
ing for Miles and his life. Your life!*

She turned to his parents. "Mr. Kittridge, you and
Mrs. Kittridge must be exhausted. I'm free for the rest
of the day. Why don't you two go home?"

"It has been tough on us . . . the trip to Iceland
and back. I'm worried about Miles's mother. It's been
real hard on her."

"I know. Go home, both of you. I'll be here and I'll
call you if there's any change, any at all," she reassured
him.

"Miles, I can't go home!"

Miles Sr. answered her, "Baby, you have to. If only to rest for a little bit. I can't let anything happen to you."

"Please go, Mrs. Kittridge. I promise to stay right here by Miles's side. You know, don't you, how much I love him. He . . . he means the world to me."

"I know, dear." She patted Aleesa's cheek, then kissed her son. "Mama will be right back, son. Try to wake up soon."

Mrs. Grasso, the nurse Aleesa had spoken to before, came in shortly after Miles's folks left.

She checked the IV fluids and added another plastic bag. She took Miles's vital signs and nodded reassuringly to Aleesa when she had finished her tasks.

"He's a strong young man. I think he's going to make it. Except for the head injury, he's healthy."

Aleesa asked, "Is there anything else the doctors can do to reduce the brain swelling?"

"The medication will do that. It's only been a few days since the accident."

The nurse checked the urinary catheter and assessed Miles's urinary output. She seemed satisfied with her findings.

"I'd like to change his position. You feel up to helping me?"

Aleesa jumped up quickly. "Of course, of course, anything! Please let me help."

After they positioned him on his side, Miles appeared to be restless for a few moments. Then his agitation stopped and he slept on.

Mrs. Grasso noticed his behavior and spoke in low, comforting tones.

"Don't be upset, Mr. Kittridge. Everything is okay." She advised Aleesa, "The best thing you can do is talk to him. Does he like music?"

Aleesa nodded. She remembered how much Miles had enjoyed her tapes.

"Well, bring in a tape recorder and some of his favorite music so he can hear it. Anything else, like his favorite shaving cream and aftershave. If we can stimulate the senses, it seems to help. And, of course, touch. That's very important, too."

"Thanks so much for those suggestions. I'll ask his folks to bring in some of his toiletries and cassettes. They'll be coming back tonight."

"I don't want you to think the worst, because no one can be certain of the prognosis in a case like this, but . . ."

"We can fight for him, can't we?"

"Of course. Keep your chin up and think positive."

She turned from the door before she left to ask Aleesa, "Want a cup of coffee or a Coke?"

Aleesa shook her head. "Not right now, thanks."

"Just let me know."

When the nurse left the room, she bent over Miles and whispered in his ear, "You hear that, buster? We're going to fight our damnedest to get you well. You promised me you'd marry me in September and by damn, you're going to! I'm holding you to that promise, my love. Remember, you promised! Forget about that family search business. It's like you said, Miles, it's you and me that's important."

Fourteen

The cassette player on the nightstand was playing Duke Ellington's "Do Nothing Till You Hear from Me." It was tuned to a low soft sound. Aleesa was smoothing shaving lotion on Miles's freshly shaven face. Then she rubbed a creamy hospital lotion on his arms and elbows. She was surprised how comforting it was to her to be touching her lover. Some of the bruises were fading, and the cuts were barely visible. He was beginning to look like his handsome self again. If only he would wake up.

She recalled her earlier telephone conversation with Mr. Butterworth. "Certainly, Ms. Haskins, I understand. Take all the time you need to be with your fiancé. We can assign your work to another lawyer until you get back. I wish you good luck . . . let us know if there's anything . . ."

"I appreciate that, Mr. Butterworth. I'll be in touch with the office."

It had been four days, and Miles's condition had not changed. His parents were there most of the time during the day, and Aleesa relieved them during the afternoon and evening hours.

* * *

Aleesa was having lunch with her parents. They had questions about Miles's condition.

"He hasn't regained consciousness yet, I gather," her father said.

"Not yet, Dad."

"Oh, Leese," her mother said, "that's awful. What do the doctors say?"

Aleesa sighed, combing her fingers through her hair. "That recovery from a brain injury like the one Miles suffered can be very slow."

Her mother frowned when she saw the pain and weariness in her daughter's face. "Can't they give you a more definite prognosis?" her mother questioned.

"Don't believe so, Mother. Wish they could."

Her father concurred. "Medicine is not an exact science, I guess, Carol. Every case is different. We just have to hope and pray that Miles makes a full recovery and soon."

He turned to his daughter. "I know you're not searching now, Aleesa. You've got Miles's health as your greatest concern, but for whatever it's worth, the South Boston lead came to a dead end."

"That's all right, Dad. None of that matters anymore. Don't know whatever made me think that all that stuff was *so* important in my life. I think now that it was very selfish of me to be so overly concerned with *who* I came from rather than *who* I've become—thanks to you and Mother. And I don't want to lose Miles. He is everything to me."

That afternoon, when she went to the hospital, Mrs. Grasso stopped her at the nurses' station.

"Good news, Aleesa! Miles has been taken off the respirator and is breathing great on his own! In fact, I'd say I think his color is a whole lot better."

"Oh, Mrs. Grasso!" They hugged each other. "Thank you! Thank you . . . oh my God, thank you."

"We still have a way to go, honey."

"I know, I know, but every step forward counts, doesn't it?" Aleesa said hopefully.

"You bet. It's step by step."

Aleesa raced down the corridor to Miles's room. She opened the door and stared at an attractive young woman holding Miles's hand and whispering to him. She recognized Lynette Jarvis, the woman he had said was like a sister to him. Her present behavior, as viewed by Aleesa, didn't look "sisterly." The intimacy that she watched from the doorway made her feel as if Lynette were trying to steal someone who belonged to her. Jealous feelings rose up in her like a vengeful ill will, and it was all she could do to restrain herself. After all, she was a lawyer, and a physical attack on Miles's visitor would never do, but she really wanted to slap the girl silly. She couldn't help how she felt.

Instead, she took a deep breath, put on her most dazzling smile, walked into the room, and extended her hand to the young woman. She reached across the bed and they shook hands as if they were adversaries, each claiming the man who lay quietly between them, despite Aleesa's attempt not to be hostile to the visitor.

She smiled.

"I know who you are, Lynette. Miles's friend. He's often spoken of you. How are you?" Aleesa inquired pleasantly.

"Yes, I'm Lynette Jarvis. His mother told me about the accident. This is the first chance I've had to visit."

"Nice you could come. I'm Aleesa, Aleesa Haskins."

"His mother told me that you two are engaged. How terrible to see . . ."

Aleesa, shaking her head no, pressed her forefinger to her lips to shush Lynette. She bent over Miles. "Miles, honey, your friend Lynette is here to see you. Don't you want to say hello? She looks beautiful, too."

She was well aware of her own appearance. Since she had been helping Mrs. Grasso, the other nurses, and physical therapists with Miles's treatment regime, she had come to the hospital wearing jeans, a sweatshirt, and jogging shoes. "We'll turn you into a nurse yet, Aleesa," Mrs. Grasso had teased her.

She was aware that she looked like a nondescript drudge beside the elegantly attired Lynette, who wore a soft, mauve-colored twin sweater set with a pale gray linen skirt. Her only jewelry was a lovely gold chain. Her dark hair had been pulled back in a ponytail. She looked cool, sophisticated, and unflappable. Aleesa felt positively gauche beside her. But she had no time to dwell on the visitor. She drew Lynette away from the bedside.

"I'm glad you came today. He looks a little better since they removed the respirator. I do think he's breathing easier." She studied Miles's face for a brief moment. "Mrs. Grasso, the nurse, is right. He's breathing more normally, and his color is much better."

"I'm glad I didn't see the breathing machine. It just bothers me to see him like this, so . . . so still, so unlike the Miles I've known all my life."

"He said the two of you grew up together."

"Like brother and sister,' " Lynette nodded.

"Well, sister," Aleesa said briskly, "let's get to work."

"Work?"

"Sure, there's lots to do, and the nurses have taught me how to do some simple things that help."

"Show me."

So together they rubbed his back, repositioned him, moistened his lips with cream, moved his uncasted leg in the therapeutic exercises that Aleesa had been taught by the physical therapists, and talked to Miles.

"We know you just *love* this 'brown-skinned service'

you're getting, Miles. You wait, we're sending in our bill and you'll have to pay up!"

"In full," Lynette added as she rubbed lotion on his hands.

The cassette tape was sending soft music into the room as the women worked.

"Listen," Aleesa said, "it's Dinah Washington."

"She's one of Miles's favorite," Lynette said.

"What a Difference a Day Makes"—the sultry voice of the singer floated into the room. It made Aleesa's hostility toward Lynette soften.

"I'm glad you're here today, Lynette. It's true, 'what a difference a day can make.' I feel more optimistic . . ." She stopped speaking. "What was that?"

She stared at Miles's face. "Did you see that?"

"See what?"

"Lynette, I swear I saw his eyeballs move!"

She ran to get Mrs. Grasso, who explained that perhaps, just perhaps, he was starting to come out of the coma.

"It's going to take time. Just keep on talking to him, try to stimulate him gently."

"I've got to let his folks know, Lynette. They have been under such a strain."

But his parents were disappointed. By the time they arrived, there had been no other changes. Except for breathing more easily on his own, and the improvement in his coloring, things were still as they had been.

A decision had been made to transfer Miles to a rehabilitation facility at the other side of the city. As the doctor explained to Aleesa and Miles's parents, he no longer needed intensive care treatment, but needed more concentration on rehabilitation.

Aleesa hated to leave Mrs. Grasso and the quality care she had given to Miles.

"What am I going to do without you, Mrs. G.?"

"You'll do fine. Stay positive and keep on keeping on. I know you can do it. And I promise I will stop in once in a while to see how things are going."

Miles did seem to respond to the change in his environment. His room at the rehab center was on the first floor, a sunny room with a large window which looked out on a lovely wooded area.

A week later, Aleesa thought he seemed tired, and she noticed a quick frown on his face before he relaxed. What did the frown mean? Was something happening to him? Was he in pain? She stared at him. She needed him. She needed his love, she needed to be able to feel again the firm touch of his capable masculine hand cupped gently beneath her elbow as he would proudly escort her into a restaurant for dinner or the theater for a play as if she were the most desirable woman in the world. She needed the warmth of his smile when he greeted her after one of his return flights from overseas, fairly pulling her into his arms. She would give anything, *anything* to see his quirky grin whenever he teased her. She ached to wrap her arms around him. To feel his stalwart heartbeat as she rested her head on the safe haven of his chest. She needed it all, and she needed it now. There would be no future for her without Miles.

A sudden weariness came over her. She was nearing the end of her rope, and was almost at her breaking point. Could she go on?

She stared at him, the man she knew she desperately loved. She spoke softly to him.

"Miles, it's me, Aleesa, I'm here. Miles, please, please come back." His quiet stillness was more than she could bear. She continued, her voice cracking into a sob. "Miles, Miles, please, please," she begged. It had been *so* long and she'd tried *so* hard to bring him back. "Miles, don't, please don't die, don't leave me. I love you so much!"

She could hold back no longer. She rested her head on his chest as a torrent of sobs racked her body.

She was scarcely aware of the movement, her grief was so overwhelming, but somehow she felt it. A hand resting on her back. Stunned, she remained quiet and heard his voice, a coarse whisper, "Don', don' cry, Leese."

She raised up quickly and stared at Miles's face. His eyes were still closed. *Had* something really happened just now? Had she heard his voice? Was she crazy?

She raced out of the room to find a nurse, somebody.

"Tell me I'm not hallucinating!" she said to the nurse after telling her what had happened. "I swear he spoke . . . and he touched me, I swear it!"

The nurse took his vital signs. She shook her head. "It might be a muscle spasm that made you think he touched your back. However, his pulse is up a bit and he seems to be moving his eyeballs, I notice, although his eyes are still closed. We'll keep a close watch on him tonight. Mr. Kittridge," she said to Miles, "Mr. Kittridge, squeeze my hand. Come on, give a good squeeze. You can do it."

There was no response. Nothing.

Fifteen

Dr. Duncan Higginbotham briefed his staff at the regular weekly meeting. He called it Grand Rounds, meaning that all department heads should attend.

"We here at Grafton Hills, I am proud to say, received an excellent rating from the Accreditation Committee when they reviewed us last year. They are due here for another review sometime later next year."

A collective moan went up from the staff, but the Grafton Hills director chose to ignore it.

He continued, "As you are aware, we are a privately funded facility, but we want to be a viable part of the community. The trustees have agreed that we should open our doors so that the community can be more knowledgeable about our work with the brain-injured patient and understand our work in restoring the brain-damaged patient to his fullest potential. So to that end we want to encourage a volunteer staff. Musicians, artists, sculptors, storytellers, pet owners, librarians, schoolteachers, hairdressers, news reporters—anyone who has the time and the experience to share part of their lives with our patients. I'm certain many of you know people who would be willing to do this."

He directed the staff's attention to a young woman seated next to him.

"This is Angela Curran. She will be the coordinator for volunteer services. I know she will be happy to meet with you. Please give her your suggestions and comments. I'm sure she will welcome them."

Angela Curran, a tiny, dark-haired girl, nodded and shared a bright smile as if pleading, *help!*

Aleesa's leave from the law office was over. Miles was making slow progress at Grafton Hills. The slight movement of his non-fractured leg, a twitch of a finger, sometimes even a low moan when he was being turned. But he slept on, and since the night that Aleesa cried over him, there'd been nothing. She still visited as often as she could and helped with his care.

One night Mrs. Grasso stopped in on her way home.

"Aleesa," she observed, "I think you're losing weight, hon. Are you taking care of yourself? You sure don't look it. You won't be a bit of good to Miles if you break down."

"I know, Mrs. G." She asked, "Do *you* see any change?"

"Oh my, yes! I'm encouraged by the tiny changes I see, and you should be, too. Try to get more rest and try to eat regularly. And do take vitamins. You've been under a lot of stress, you know, and that can wreak havoc with your immune system."

"I know," Aleesa answered with a deep sigh. "I know."

It was Miles's mother who was alone at his bedside and witnessed the miracle. His father had just left to get some coffee for them at the hospital's cafeteria.

The petite gray-haired woman stretched her hand between the sidebars to stroke the face of her only child.

Speaking softly, she appealed to him, "Miles? Miles, honey, it's Momma, dear."

Slowly he turned his face toward his mother's touch. She held her breath . . . his voice was weak and strained, as if coming from a faraway place. Slowly his eyelids fluttered, then opened wide as if to focus on his mother's face.

"Hi . . . Mom," he drawled softly.

"Miles! Honey! It's me, Miles, honey! Oh, sweetheart, my baby, you're back. Thank God, you're back!"

"I am?" Frowns of confusion flicked across his face as he tried to orient himself. "You . . . you all right, Momma?"

His mother was frantically ringing the call button for the nurse and tried to stop crying at the same time. She was beside herself with joy. *Where was Miles's father, Miles Lewis, Sr.?*

The nurse rushed into the room, followed by a wild-eyed father who had seen the flashing call light over the door to his son's room.

"What's wrong? What's going on?" the man's voice mirrored his anxiety.

His wife fell sobbing into his arms. "It's Miles, he's awake!"

When Aleesa arrived in the courtroom that morning to defend her client, a college athlete accused of possession of marijuana, the bailiff handed her a note: CALL GRAFTON HILLS IMMEDIATELY.

She looked at Judge Abrams, who had just taken his seat. The bailiff had already called the court to order when Aleesa stood up. Judge Abrams looked at her expectantly.

"Your honor? May I approach?"

"You may."

"Your honor, may I ask the court's indulgence? I've just received an urgent call from the hospital. May I have ten minutes to respond?"

"Yes, counselor, you have the court's permission. This court is in recess for ten minutes," he announced and slammed down the gavel.

"Thank you, your honor."

Aleesa tried to maintain her dignity and not run out of the courtroom. To make matters worse, it seemed that everyone else had urgent needs out of the courtroom. Aleesa had to push her way through to get to a phone in the corridor.

With shaking fingers, she dialed Miles's room. On the first ring his father's voice boomed joyously over the line. "Yes, yes, Aleesa! Miles is out of the coma! Awake *and* talking! When can you get here? He's been asking for you!"

"Be there as soon as I finish this hearing. Just as soon as possible. I've got to get back to the courtroom. Mr. Kittridge?"

"Yes?"

"Tell Miles . . . tell him I love him, and I'm on my way."

Her eyes widened with delight when she got to Miles's room and saw him sitting up in a lounge chair, his cast leg stretched out on the extender. He was wearing a wine-colored velour robe. When he saw Aleesa, his familiar engaging grin brightened his face.

"Hi there," he said, as if this was an ordinary day.

Aleesa thought her heart would burst right out of

her body. Miles opened his arms and she collapsed beside the chair, her head cradled on his chest. Tears mingled with broken sobs.

"Oh, Miles, I was *so* scared. So scared of losing you."

He stroked her hair to comfort her and murmured, "Don't cry, baby, don't cry."

She raised her head.

"You said that to me before, do you remember?"

He shook his head slowly. "Can't say that I do, honey. Can't remember much except that we were in some kind of trouble. We crashed, didn't we?"

He looked at his parents who hovered nearby, a question in his eyes. "Pete? Pete Warren? Is he . . . what happened to him?"

His father answered. "Walked away from the crash with a broken arm, some bumps and bruises. He's been in to see you several times. I'll get in touch with him. Let him know . . ."

"Good, I'm glad he's okay . . ."

Aleesa broke in, "When can Miles go home? What do the doctors say?"

Mr. Kittridge understood Aleesa's questions.

"They are going to have a staff meeting later today or first thing tomorrow morning to discuss his case."

"I want to take him home right now!' " his mother said.

"I know, Mother," her husband agreed, "but I guess certain arrangements have to be made before he can be discharged. For one thing, I guess he's going to have to be able to walk with crutches, that sort of thing. Got to build up his muscle strength, you know."

The three of them agreed that it made sense to be cautious. Certainly having come this far, no one wanted a relapse. It made sense to be patient a little longer.

Sixteen

"I enjoy my volunteer work at Grafton Hills, I really do," Lana explained to her family one night at dinner. She passed the dish of lasagna to her daughter. "You did a great job with this lasagna, Staci, and the salad is real nice."

"Thanks, Mom. What do you have to do at the hospital?"

"Have you seen any sick, dying people, Mom?" her teenaged son, Brendan, asked, shoveling his food into his mouth.

"Brendan! Don't eat so fast, you'll choke! The boy's always shoveled his food into his mouth."

"No, I won't."

"Yes, you will, if you're not careful. But to answer your questions, I haven't seen any really sick patients. Mostly the ones I see are up and about, able to walk or use a wheelchair. They come to me, to my music room. The hospital provides some instruments and CDs, as well as disc players, music, that sort of thing. What I try to do is involve the patients in music in some way. Singing in a group, playing an instrument, whatever the patient wants to do. Some just want to listen to their favorite records, and we have a small area just for listening. It seems like good therapy."

Her husband stopped eating and smiled at her. "So, you like being a volunteer."

His wife smiled back at him.

"I love it. I put on my peach-colored smock the hospital gives each of us to wear, such a cheerful change from the black that Tim Gregory insists we wear, pin my name tag on, and I'm 'ready to rumble'!" She laughed.

"I don't know why you want to do it, Mom. You don't get paid. Should think you'd have enough, working with the symphony and all," Staci insisted.

"It's different, gives me a good feeling that I'm sharing something of myself. I think it's because I'm happy." She shared a knowing look with her husband. "I'm lucky to have a wonderful family, and I know it. So if I can help someone else, I want to do so."

From the responsive looks on her children's faces, she knew they understood. She continued, "Just today a new patient came to the music therapy room— wanted to know if we had any Duke Ellington, Coleman Hawkins, Count Basie records."

"He wanted to listen to those old guys?" Brendan asked.

"What's wrong with them, son?" his father asked. "In case you don't know it, they were masters of jazz."

"I did ask him," Brendan's mother said, "and he said he had grown up listening to their music. Probably reminds him of happy times."

"How come he's at that place, Grafton Hills?"

"He's a pilot. Injured when his plane crashed in Iceland."

"Wow! A pilot!"

"I was told that he's just come out of a coma . . . still has a broken leg, but gets around real well on crutches."

"Wow, a pilot," Brendan repeated. "Sure like to meet him."

"Maybe you can. We'll see."

Boyd Howell felt relaxed and happy. He smiled at his wife and lifted his glass of ginger ale to her in a mock toast. She responded with a smile, acknowledging his salute.

Their daughter, Staci, saw the exchange. Her parents were *so* loony about each other, and since the family had moved to Calderton, their lives had been much happier.

The move to the small town had been everything that the Howell family wanted and needed. The children were good students and Staci received a full college scholarship as valedictorian of her high school graduating class. Now, four years later, she was completing her senior year at college, and Brendan, an excellent football player, cocaptain of the team, was ready to start college. Both parents encouraged their children and would not let their race cause limitations. Subsequently, the family was well thought of by the townspeople.

Miles had made steady progress. He was walking well with crutches and had gained some weight, but he was not sleeping well. He was worried about the future, his and Aleesa's.

Aleesa visited each day after her work at the law office.

"Miles, have the doctors said anything about discharge?"

"They said something on rounds this morning about a discharge conference soon. I'd like to go back to my own apartment."

"Think you can manage by yourself?"

"Yes, I can. There's some talk of giving me a lighter walking cast. So that would be good . . . wouldn't need the crutches."

"It's good that you have an elevator in your building. Stairs would be rough."

They were having their dinner in Miles's room. If requested in advance, the hospital chef would prepare a dinner tray for a patient's guest. Aleesa looked forward to sharing the meal with Miles. Tonight it was an excellently prepared steak with baked potato, steaming hot, a salad with a light dressing, and fresh strawberry shortcake.

Miles cleared his throat.

"Aleesa, honey . . ."

"Um-m?" She looked at him.

"I've been meaning to tell you that . . . that you don't need to visit me everyday."

"What you talkin' 'bout, Miles? Why not? Don't you want to see me?"

"It's not that. Of course I want to see you . . . but . . ."

"But what?" she demanded.

"You . . . you have been under a lot of strain, your work, worrying over me, taking care of me. I don't want you to get sick . . ."

His voice trailed off. He could see right away that he had messed up—pushed the wrong button with her.

Aleesa dropped her fork on the tray, wiped her mouth with her napkin and glared at him.

Miles's face took on a perplexed look, and immediately Aleesa saw the indecision in his face. She frowned.

"Miles! You're having second thoughts!"

"No, Aleesa, that's not it, not it at all."

"Well, what is it?"

"I . . . I've been called to report to the main office

of World International for an examination. This damn cast"—he clunked the rock-hard cast with his fist—"as soon as it's taken off and I'm ambulatory, I have to meet with their doctors to see if I'm fit to fly."

"Of course you're fit to fly! What nonsense!" she insisted.

"But after a head injury, the NSTB, National Safety Transportation Board, and the FAA, they have their rules, and I have to go by whatever they decide. There's a battery of tests that I'll have to pass, and . . . I can't think about our future until I know."

"I know!" Aleesa broke in. She saw the concern in his eyes and understood his anxiety over his future.

She went to him, pushed his tray table aside, and put her arms around him.

"Listen to me, Miles. It seems like a lifetime ago, but you told me once that you were going to help me find my birth parents whether I wanted you to or not, and that you were in it for the long haul. You said no matter what or who I found. So now, Miles Lewis Kittridge, I have something I want to say. I've decided that I don't *need* to find any birth parents. My future is with you, and for better or for worse, I'm in it for the long haul. You better remember that! And you're going to pass those tests, all of them! You promised me, and I'm holding you to those promises. One, to marry me in September at Water's Edge, and two, to teach me to fly."

Miles kissed her then, a sweet, satisfying gesture that comforted each of them.

He smiled at her and tweaked her cheek.

"Your mother was right. When you care, you *care!*"

"Mothers are always right. Didn't you know that?"

"Know it now," he answered. "Would you mind passing me my strawberry shortcake?"

"If you say please, buster, and apologize for your foolish nonsense."

"Please . . . and I apologize."

"See that it doesn't happen again," she grinned.

Miles kept his misgivings to himself. Shouldn't he have been able to land his plane safely, even with one engine? He remembered pulling the throttle back and yelling at Pete to cut the fuel to that smoking engine. *Will the review board consider it pilot error on my part? If I lose my license, how will I be able to make a living if I can't fly? What will all of this mean for our future?*

Seventeen

"Mr. Kittridge, I've been able to get hold of some Duke Ellington recordings for you."

"Oh, thank you, Ms. Miller." Lana's professional name, Lana Miller, her maiden name, was visible on her name tag.

"I also came across a biography of his collaborator, Billy Strayhorn, who composed many of Duke's tunes, like 'Satin Doll' and 'Take the A Train.'"

"One of my favorites."

"I thought you might enjoy reading about him."

"I certainly will. Thanks so much."

"You are welcome, Mr. Kittridge. Enjoy."

"Ms. Miller?" Miles stopped walking and leaned forward on his crutches. "Did anyone ever tell you how glorious and beautiful your hair is? I don't mean to take liberties, but the coloring is so unusual."

"Just something I inherited, I guess, Mr. Kittridge." She smiled.

She watched him clump away on his crutches. She thought, *Neither of my children inherited my hair coloring. I wonder if . . .* She pushed the thought of her dead daughter into a dark recess of her mind and slammed a door closed after it.

She turned to greet a wheelchair patient. With a

genuine smile, she asked him, "What music would you like to hear today?"

The thought of her daughter bubbled up again later that day. Annaliese would have been thirty-two years old had she lived. After that dreadful day at the hospital, she and Boyd had never spoken of the child, but her birthday was approaching. She and Boyd would follow the tradition they had always observed over the years—slip away from their two other children, go to the beach at Nantasket and release a balloon in memory of the baby neither of them ever saw.

"Love you, Annaliese," Lana would whisper as Boyd released the pink balloon.

"How do you feel, Miles?"

"Great, honey! I really feel great. To tell you the truth, the past few months seem like a bad dream. We're on our way, Leese. Get through these tests and start living again!"

"Right." She grabbed his arm and rested her head on his shoulder.

"Real nice to be flying to New York in first-class seats, isn't it, Miles?"

"Sure is. One of the perks of the company."

"And, remember, Miles, you are going to come through with flying colors. No pun intended!" she said.

"I'm real optimistic, hon, and even if I don't make it, the world's not going to come to an end. I have you, the light of my life."

"We're going to have a great time in New York, the Big Apple!"

"And I really feel like taking a nibble or two," he teased as he nipped her ear.

They both decided to have room service for their

evening meal so that Miles could get a good night's rest before facing the next day's battery of tests.

"Tomorrow, instead of staying alone here in the room, Leese, why don't you go out and do some shopping while I'm going through my tests?"

She waved a slip of paper at him from the table where she was sitting.

"Got my list right here, my man!"

"Good." He took some money from his wallet and handed it to her. She tried not to accept it, saying, "Don't need your money, Miles, I have money . . ."

"I know you have, but I want you to have some of mine. Please take it."

"In for a penny, in for a pound," she sighed. "I'm sharing this room . . ."

"You're sharing my life and don't you forget it," he insisted.

After a light meal of sandwiches, salad, and potato chips, ginger ale for Aleesa and a Coke for Miles, they decided to watch television. There was nothing on of interest to either of them.

"May as well shut it off, Miles. It's boring. I think I'll work on our invitation list. My mother has been hounding me to get it to her ASAP now that we've ordered the invitations."

"Think I'll shower and chill out. Tomorrow's going to be a long day."

"I know. That's a good idea."

When he had finished his shower, he found Aleesa still working on her list.

"You smell good, my man," she grinned at him. "Here, right here." She indicated that he put his head near her face. She sniffed loudly and said, "Ah, you smell delicious!"

Miles laughed at her antics. He loved this woman.

"I'm trying to keep the list to two hundred, Miles, a hundred for each family."

"I only have a few first cousins," he admitted.

"But you have lots of friends, Miles, that I know. We could have wallpapered your room at the hospital with all the cards you got. Never saw so many. You're a very popular guy. That's why I love you . . . you know everybody!"

He sat quietly for a while watching her work, her silky hair falling forward as she bent to her task. He was reminded suddenly of Lana Miller, whose chest-nut-red mane reminded him of Aleesa's hair.

"Leese, you never met Ms. Miller, the music volunteer. Beautiful woman, has hair almost the same color as yours . . . of course with a few gray strands here and there. But she was very nice to me. Very thoughtful, really. She went out of her way to bring me tapes, CDs, books . . . helped me get through those last few tedious weeks at Grafton Hills."

"Maybe we should invite her to the wedding," Aleesa suggested.

"I'd like that. Think from what little she said she has a husband and children. Don't know where she lives, though."

"No problem. We could sent it care of volunteer services at Grafton Hills."

They were both silent for a moment, each thinking about their future. Aleesa broke the silence. "Miles, I'd like to invite Mrs. Grasso, too. She is an awfully nice person. She took such good care of you and was very, very supportive. Don't know how we'd have managed those first days of horror and worry we had without her help."

"By all means, send her an invitation. You know, it's really scary to realize that your life was in the hands of others."

"I know, but thank God they were good, capable hands and gentle, caring hearts that took care of you. I'll be forever grateful."

He reached for her and gathered her in his arms. "Come here, close to me." Her lovely hair swirled around her shoulders as she stood beside him. They looked out the window at the city below. He took her face in his hands and bent to kiss her. Her striking eyes darkened with intense feeling as she looked up at him.

"I've waited so long, Leese. It's only a few months before our big day, when you'll be mine forever. It's going to be so wonderful. I just wish you had been able to find your birth parents."

She snuggled closer to him. The woodsy cologne he wore heightened her sense of security. She was safe in this man's arms, and that was all she needed.

"Miles," she confessed, "I've put that nonsense behind me. When you were in that coma and I thought I might lose you, I knew I had been a fool . . . looking back to what had been when I should have been planning ahead for a future with you, the man I love."

At that moment the flame between them that had long been smoldering during the days and nights of Miles's incapacitation flickered around the edges of their hearts, and each knew that their love was about to burst into a roaring fire, one that neither of them wanted to extinguish.

Miles pulled Aleesa close. When he touched her silky soft face, his blood rushed white-hot and he could wait no longer. The king-sized bed beckoned—a nest, a harbor, a secure haven for them.

He held her face with both hands. Her eyes sparked with emotion. He saw it all in her eyes—fear, hope, promise? He saw only love.

He nibbled at her ear. "Trust me, honey, trust me.

I promise everything will be all right. It's been so long for us, too long, so much . . . happened to us . . . like a bad dream, but it's over now."

He kissed her then. Her eyes were closed in contentment. He kissed her nose, the lids of her closed eyes, the enchanting hollow of her throat. Aleesa moaned as Miles's lips touched her.

"Let me touch you all over, babe," Miles said as he removed her blouse and skirt. He helped her free herself from her restraining bra and undergarments. He took her to the bed. His eyes never left hers as he shrugged off his robe and pajamas.

She was fascinated by the sight of his magnificent bronze body. Sleek, lean, with supple muscles that spoke of hidden strength, she did what her mind and heart told her to do. She opened her arms. She felt his warm breath as he sighed deeply. She saw soft beads of moisture on his skin. The healthy sheen excited her and she clung to him.

He kissed her mouth and opened it with his probing, insistent tongue. She reacted breathlessly, receiving the intimate caress and responding with her own.

Both were gasping, but hungry to explore their passion to fruition.

"Oh, Leese, Leese, I want you so much, I need you. Love me, babe, love me!" He wound his fingers into her tousled hair, staring into her eyes. "Say you love me, precious, please, say it!"

"I love you, Miles, with all my heart. I love you."

She was reminded of how very close she had come to losing Miles. How could she ever have lived without him? Her so-called desperate need to locate her birth parents seemed so mindless to her now. The importance of what she had in loving this man pushed that silly notion from her head. What was real was the here and now. She repeated her words. "I do love you, Miles."

Hungrily, he pulled her close. He knew he'd never get enough of her. Again he kissed her eyes, her cheeks, and the hollow of her neck before he sought her mouth to sear it with his own. His hands moved seductively over her slim body, and beneath him he heard her breath quicken as he palmed his hand over the inside of her velvety soft thighs. He groaned her name, "Aleesa, Aleesa," as he sought to savor first one rose-colored peak of her breast and then the other. She was on fire, she thought. "Miles, please, please . . ." Her voice was low and throaty with emotion.

"I know, my sweet one, I know," he murmured. "God, baby, how I want you, need you, love you. It's been so long."

The flaming passion unleashed between them, plus the heat of their bodies, caused an aura of magic to envelop them. Both knew there was no world outside that mattered to them, only this moment was real.

Miles kissed her repeatedly, as if starving for the taste of her exquisite body. He sought the cradle of her femininity, and when he touched her she arched her body in response.

There was no turning back. Aleesa could not stop touching, exploring, reveling in this precious love ballet with Miles. Every kiss, every touch moved each of them with certainty to the moment for which they had longed. Neither was prepared for the rocketing, stunning, shattering waves that shook them.

Breathless, unable to speak, Aleesa lay quietly in Miles's arms. Silent tears of joyful peace slid from beneath her closed eyelids. Never had she dreamed she would share such a volatile experience. Miles saw the

tears and knew that Aleesa had been deeply affected.
He kissed the moisture from her eyes.

"This love is ours forever, Leesa. No one, *nothing* on
this earth will take it from us."

Eighteen

She smiled at him across the breakfast table. Her heart pounded in her chest at the memory of what they had shared the night before. She knew, too, that last night's episode was only a glimpse of the sheer joy that awaited her with the man she loved.

His eyes were clear and alert. His beautiful face shone with robust good health, and she saw aggressive energy ready to surge as he faced the future. She was proud of him.

"You know, Miles, the way you look, and the way you walk, carry yourself, no one would ever know you'd been in a coma. You're going to knock the socks off that review board. Trust me."

She was delighted when she saw the familiar lopsided grin he gave her.

"Oh, I trust you, babe. I trust you."

Lana Miller had received the wedding invitation. So, her former patient was getting married. How wonderful, she thought, happy to think perhaps she had helped a little in his recovery. He was such a wonderful young man, he deserved to be happy after all he had been through.

The invitation was elegant, with simple gold lettering

on heavy, off-white fine quality paper that Lana recognized as vellum.

> *Mr. and Mrs. Grady S. Haskins*
> *request your presence at the marriage*
> *of their daughter*
> *Aleesa Grace*
> *to*
> *Miles Lewis Kittridge, Jr.*

Lana saw that the wedding would be held in Marblehead at Water's Edge, the bride's home. The time was twelve noon, with a luncheon reception to follow.

"You mean, we're all invited?" Brendan asked.

His mother recognized her son's eagerness at the news. She showed him the envelope that had been sent to her care of volunteer services at Grafton Hills.

"See, it says Ms. Lana Miller and family."

"Are we going?"

"You want to?"

"Well, sure. Chance to be at a real pilot's wedding! And get fed, too. Why not?"

"How 'bout you, Staci? Want to go?"

Her daughter shrugged her shoulders, unimpressed.

"Guess so. Be somethin' to do."

Lana turned to her husband, Boyd.

"Sure, my dear. We were all invited. I think we should all go," he said.

Aleesa found her wedding dress at the Saks Fifth Avenue store. She tried on several, finally settling on an off-the-shoulder ivory taffeta that had a fitted waist with a slightly flared skirt. The salesperson oohed and aahed over Aleesa's hair and insisted that bare shoulders would be very dramatic with her extraordinary hair cascading down her back.

"I've never seen such coloring! Goes so well with your ivory tan skin and your eyes. Sure you're not a model?"

"Not hardly," Aleesa admitted. "I'm a defense lawyer."

"Well, I know one thing," the salesperson said as she carefully wrapped the gown in tissue paper and encased it in a plastic cover, "I'm sure, with your looks, you knock the jury dead!"

Aleesa laughed. "It's not that easy!"

She returned to the hotel and secreted the gown in a traveling garment bag she had bought just for the purpose of being sure Miles would not get a glimpse of her purchase.

She took a quick shower and decided on her tan light wool slacks. A soft green silk blouse with a large, floppy bow at the neckline framed her face. The color accented her skin tone and eyes. She twisted her hair up into a topknot, and fastened gold and pearl earrings into her pierced ears. She wore dark brown flats and selected a matching bag. She placed the bag at the foot of the bed next to her jacket. She sat down to wait for Miles's return. She said a quick, silent prayer. *Oh, God, please let it be good news for Miles. Please, let him be happy. You'll have no more trouble with me, God, as long as Miles is happy.*

She heard him at the door. She looked up expectantly as he came into the room.

"Ta-dah!" He stood, arms opened wide with a grin as big as all outdoors.

Aleesa raced into his arms.

"You passed! You passed!"

"With flying colors, my love. With flying colors! Just like you said."

"Tell me what happened . . ."

"Well, they went over my medical records with a fine-toothed comb. The doctors back home said they felt I was fit to fly. The company's doctors said maybe so, but they would like to wait a year, then have me reexamined to certify my license to fly their jets."

"But you didn't lose your pilot's license?"

"No, only the license to fly jets was suspended for a year."

"Miles, I'm so glad for you. Now what?"

"I left the review board, honey, and went over to the WIN corporate office. I talked to personnel. Aleesa"—his eyes sparkled with joy—"I can retire with six months' severance pay, keep my company stock, my paid-up life insurance policy, and, honey, there's no reason why I can't start up my commuter airline from the Cape and surrounding islands to Boston!"

He blew out his cheeks and exhaled deeply. "What a morning!"

Aleesa sat beside him on the bed. He pulled her into his arms and kissed her hungrily.

"Right," she echoed, "What a morning!"

Silently, she thought, *Thank you, God.*

Lana's response that she mailed back to the Haskins home revealed that a Ms. Lana Miller and her family of four accepted the invitation to Aleesa and Miles's wedding.

Miller, Aleesa's mother thought, *not from* our *wedding guest list—must be one of Miles's friends.*

The RSVPs were coming in—the wedding was about six weeks away. Carol Haskins was happy about that. Her organizational skills were about to go into high gear. Planning and organizing an event was an enjoyable activity for her. She had taught her daughter the importance of planning and organizing, particularly of time and effort. She figured those techniques had always helped her daughter do well in school. From her father the child had learned the importance of hard work and the resulting rewards it could bring. But Carol often wondered if her child's obstinacy and tenacity had been bequeathed to her by her birth parents.

Aleesa seemed to have dropped the search for her parents, but Carol knew her child. The importance of Miles's recovery and their impending wedding had taken top priority in Aleesa's life, but something she let slip alerted her mother. They were going over the wedding guest list.

Aleesa sighed.

"What's the matter, honey?" her mother asked.

"I was just thinking, it would have been nice if . . ." her voice trailed off.

"If what, honey?"

"Oh, nothing."

"You wish you had found your birth parents, don't you? This is such a big day in your life."

"Mother, it's all right, really. I've got you and Dad and Miles. What more could I ask for?"

Only your roots, her mother thought.

She thought she would mention this episode to her husband. She remembered that Aleesa had given him a list of names before. Was there anyone still on that list that hadn't been contacted?

She spoke to her husband that night about Aleesa's offhanded comment. They had just finished dinner, put the dishes into the dishwasher, and tidied up the kitchen.

They went into the den, a small, comfortable room

with Grady's desk and chair, a lounge chair that Grady liked when he read, and a love seat that Carol favored. She could spread her quilting material all over it with no fear it would be disturbed. She was working on a wedding quilt for Miles and Aleesa. The late afternoon sun reflected across the water into the clerestory window that Carol had insisted upon when the room was remodeled. It was a cozy, serene room—one in which many a family problem had been solved.

"Grady?" Carol questioned her husband.

"Yes, hon, what is it?" He looked up from his reading.

"It's about Leesa."

He lowered his paper to look at her.

"What about Leesa? What's wrong?"

"Well, I don't know that anything is, really. It's something she let slip that has me wondering . . ."

"About what, dear?"

"Well, you know, since Miles's accident, she has insisted that she's given up the idea of searching . . . but I wonder if she really has."

"Why do you wonder?"

"We were going over the guest list and she said that 'it would have been nice if . . .' and then she stopped speaking. So I asked her, 'You wish you'd found your birth parents, don't you?' "

"What did she say to that?"

"Shrugged it off, saying that she had us and Miles, what more could she want? Something along those lines. Grady, have you contacted *all* the names on the list she gave you?"

"Yes, I have . . . I think. Why? You think I should go over it again? I'm not sure she wants me to now."

"Right. You're right . . . better not interfere. Grady,

have you ever thought what we would do, how we would feel or act, if she did find her birth parents?"

"Carol," her husband sighed, "you know me. I believe we'd have to deal with it, whatever happens. Legally, remember, she is our child."

Carol looked out the window at the peaceful water.

"You're right. She's been ours for thirty-two years. No one can take that away from us."

Nineteen

Lana was playing the piano for a wheelchair-bound patient who was scratching unearthly sounds from a violin. Her long hair bounced on her shoulders as she kept the beat, nodded encouragement to the handicapped man whose tremulous smiles indicated he knew how awful he sounded.

Miles watched from the doorway of the music therapy room. He admired the woman's patience and the manner with which she motivated the patient to persevere.

"Mr. Raines, I really think you have come a long way with your violin lesson."

She was rewarded with a lopsided smile. "You think so, Ms. Miller?"

"Indeed I do think so," she smiled at him.

She looked up and spotted Miles.

"Mr. Kittridge, how nice to see you . . ."

"I'm not interrupting?"

"Not at all. Mr. Raines was about to leave." She turned to the patient. "I'll put the violin away, sir, and I'll expect to see you next week."

She placed the instrument in the case and put it in a nearby closet. The patient wheeled himself out. Miles noted that he propelled himself with his left foot and left arm. He gave Lana a weak wave of his right hand.

She explained to Miles, "His major weakness is on his right side. He is determined to regain some use of his right hand." She added, "He was a violinist once, a long time ago, before his accident."

"You certainly are patient with him."

"I try to do what I can," she said simply. "And how about you? You look wonderful! I must tell you, my family and I are very excited about your upcoming wedding."

"That is great. You were always so kind to me, I told my fiancée that I wanted to invite you to our wedding."

"We are delighted that you wish to share such an important day with us. I hope you don't mind, but I told my son that you were a pilot. He can't wait to meet you and I suspect by now he's bragging about knowing an airline pilot to all of his friends."

"No problem at all."

Then Miles remembered why he had come to the hospital.

"I brought some new cassettes and CDs for the patients, Ms. Miller. You were so nice to me when I was here, I wanted to show my appreciation."

"Thank you, this will add to our music library."

"You are most welcome. I look forward to seeing you at the wedding."

"*We* look forward to coming."

She walked him out of the music room to the sunlit lobby in the front of the hospital. She wore gold earrings, and for the first time in the brilliant sunshine, Miles noticed her emerald-green eyes. He thought, *she is a very attractive woman. Why do I feel as if I know her?*

"Thanks again, Mr. Kittridge." She shook hands and walked back to her music room.

There's something about her, Miles insisted to himself. *She has a slight accent. Could be I've met her before . . . in my travels? I wonder.*

* * *

"I'm so happy things turned out as they did for you, Miles," Grady Haskins said to his prospective son-in-law.

"Thanks, sir. I'm very pleased, too."

"Understand you'll be receiving a substantial amount of money as part of your severance package. You're satisfied with that?" the older man inquired gently.

"Oh, yes, I am satisfied. And I'm retaining my shares of company stock."

"Going to try to regain your jet pilot's license?"

"Don't know 'bout that yet. Have to decide if I want to fly commercially or not."

"Hm-m-m. It is something to consider later down the road, I guess."

"I *can* tell you, sir, right now I'm looking forward to marrying your lovely daughter, applying to the Department of Transportation for a license for a commuter airline between Boston and Portland, Maine, and Boston to the Cape and the islands."

"You know I wish you the best, son."

"Thank you, sir. Thank you very much."

Miles looked toward the back of the house to the kitchen area. He drew in deep, appreciative breaths, enjoying the cooking odors coming from that part of the house. "Wonder what the women are cooking up? Sure smells good."

"Knowing my daughter, it'll be something special. That girl loves to cook. If she hadn't decided to go to law school, she might have been a chef with her own restaurant by now."

"I know that, sir. How lucky can I get? I'm marrying a beautiful, talented young woman who loves me and I'm going to be my own boss. Wow!"

"Been through a lot, Miles. You and Leese deserve the best."

The dinner that Aleesa and her mother prepared was declared "outstanding" by both men.

"Aleesa," Miles asked, "what did you do to this chicken? It's great!"

"Like it?" She smiled and offered him another portion. "What makes it so good is a special glaze that I basted it with."

"If you haven't already, you should patent that recipe. Could make money on that, that's for sure."

"More vegetables, Miles?" Aleesa's mother asked.

"Another spoonful of the peas and rice, ma'am, with a little more gravy, please."

"You could stand to put on a few more pounds, Miles," Carol said.

"I don't think so, Mrs. Haskins. I want to be able to fit into the tux I've ordered for the big day." He leaned over and kissed Aleesa on her cheek. "Right, my dear?"

"Right you are, sir," she answered brightly. "And if the tux doesn't fit, put on any old thing, just be here at Water's Edge, ready to tie the knot. Got that, buster?"

"Got it!"

Everyone laughed.

Miles completed the therapy exercises he had been instructed to do, then sat down at his desk to go through the application forms from the Department of Transportation. The ring of the telephone interrupted him.

"Miles, sorry to bother you. This is Grady Haskins."

"Yes, sir, Mr. Haskins. What's up?"

"Miles, I don't want you to think that I'm interfering . . ."

"Not at all, sir. What can I do for you?"

"Well, Aleesa's mother and I were talking last night before you two arrived, about how happy you both were and how happy *we* are, and Carol said that she feels that as much as she denies it, in the back of her mind Leesa is still fretting over her inability to locate her birth parents. Carol said it was something she let slip. I think planning for the wedding and all, her anxiety level is high, although she would never admit it. My wife said that Leesa insisted that everything was okay—she had both of us, and, of course, she has you—so all is well. What do you think, Miles? Think you and I should try to see what we can do?"

"More than anything in this world, sir, I want Leese to be happy. But you do know that the one big argument between us came when I said I wanted to help her in her search and she told me to butt out. But"—Miles drew in a deep breath—"she wouldn't *dare* be mad with us, if we worked together, would she? I say, let's go for it! I especially want to ease her mind. I think she's ready for whatever we find. You agree?"

"Yes, son. I think so. Tell you what. Let's work together, see what we come up with. I'm going back to South Boston. That was my last lead. I'll be in touch."

"Great, and please let me know about anything I can do."

"Sure thing."

Grady Haskins drove to South Boston, found a parking spot on Dorchester Avenue, locked his car, and, after feeding the meter, started out on foot. He had decided, perhaps, some of the shopkeepers might remember a black family named Howell.

He stopped at a Dunkin' Donuts shop, glad that he had worn an old windbreaker and a pair of jeans. It would not have been wise to overdress in this blue-collar neighborhood.

He sat at a table near a window, nursed his coffee and munched on a bagel with cream cheese. He watched the heavy pedestrian traffic on the sidewalk. Mothers pushing strollers, sometimes with one, often with two toddlers and/or a skirt-hanging-on toddler trailing behind. There were quite a few senior citizens, too, some coming into the shop for coffee and donuts. "Don't forget, senior discount," he heard more than one say to the teenaged clerk at the counter. He thought how fortunate he and Carol would be to be comfortable in their senior years.

He pushed his chair back, placed his paper cup and plate into the designated waste area, and went out onto the sidewalk, dodging a kid on a bicycle as he did so.

He stopped at a drug store next, but the clerk did not know any black family named Howell. He walked across the street to a vegetable and fruit stand where the answer was no. At a dry cleaner's he received another negative response.

Next he stopped at a garage. There were two pumps outside and some used cars for sale in a side yard. The garage had two bays in it, and one had a car raised upon the hydraulic car lift.

A young black man who was working on the car heard Grady and turned to speak to him. He wiped his hands on a rag.

"Can I help you, sir?"

"I hope so. Did you ever know a black family named Howell here?"

"Howell, Howell, yeah, believe I do. Ain't too many of us 'round here, but, yes, there was a family. Man's wife looked near white, had two children, boy and a girl. Didn't know 'em too well. Used to stop for gas sometimes. Seemed like nice people . . ."

"Know where they moved to?"

"Let's see. I believe he told me they were buying a house in Calderton, up on the north shore. Lucked up on something, I guess."

"Thanks for the information."

"No problem, brother. Have a good day."

"Thanks, you, too."

Grady smiled to himself. Maybe he had struck pay dirt.

Twenty

Calderton, Grady thought as he drove back home. *It's not far from Marblehead. Horse country,* as he remembered. *How did a black family fit in there?* he wondered. Maybe he and Carol could take a ride up there after lunch and look around.

He found his wife in the kitchen. She smiled as he came in.

"You're right on time, Grady. How does a chicken sandwich sound?"

"Great!" He kissed her.

"Think I've got a lead on the Howell family," he reported to her.

"Really? I hope we're doing the right thing, following up this search," she worried.

"I'll do anything to give Aleesa peace of mind, you know that, Carol."

"I know." She patted his cheek. "Sit down. Want iced coffee or tea?"

"Neither, hon. Ginger ale would be fine."

He told her what he had learned that morning and that he wanted to poke around Calderton later that afternoon.

"Well, after I clean up I'll change into something more suitable for the 'money' town of Calderton." His wife laughed.

"Think I'll look at the paper while you get ready," her husband said.

The words and the picture jumped out at him when he turned to the sports page. *HIGH SCHOOL SENIOR ATHLETE OF THE YEAR* was the by-line. The picture showed a fresh, open-faced young man with a football clutched under his right arm and his left in a defensive position. His name was Brendan Howell. Listed were the names of his parents, Lana and Boyd, his sister, Staci, as well as his likes and dislikes. Favorite food, fried chicken; favorite musician, Babyface Edmonds; favorite hobby, chess; favorite subject in school; languages. He already spoke French and Russian and was studying Japanese. His ambition was to be a foreign service officer. He had been accepted at a nearby college. Grady could hardly believe what he was reading. He dropped the paper on the floor and ran to the hall to yell upstairs to his wife.

"Carol, Carol, get down here! Quick!"

"What's the matter, Grady? What are you yelling about?"

She rushed into the living room, still fastening her wristwatch.

"What is it?"

"Here, here, right in the paper!"

"What? What?"

"The Howell family." He picked up the paper and began to read, "Student Athlete—Brendan Howell, mother—Lana Howell, father—Boyd Howell! Honey, those are the names on the birth certificate. The couple wasn't married, but those were the names, Svetlana—Lana—and Boyd! Still think we should go up to Calderton and see what we find?"

Stunned by his news, his wife sat down on the couch and looked at him. Indecision spread across her face.

"Gosh, now, Grady, I don't know. Should we?"

He saw the hesitant look in her eyes.

"Maybe we should wait, ask Miles, see what he wants to do. Yeah," he continued, "might be wise to cool our jets, not rush headlong into something."

"I agree, Grady. Could be it's *not* the family we're looking for."

"Right," he agreed, "but somehow I think it is. Got a feeling." He got up and went to the telephone in the den. "Calling Miles to see what he wants to do," he explained. He reached Miles at his apartment and informed him what he'd discovered.

"Oh my God, Mr. Haskins!" Miles excitedly answered. "Do you think they could be Aleesa's birth folks?"

"Dunno. But I wanted to get your okay to go ahead. What do you think?"

Miles hesitated for a moment. He spoke slowly. "I think we should go slow, sir. It wouldn't be right, perhaps, to have people show up on your doorstep with, 'Yoo hoo! Guess what!' "

"You're right, Miles. After all, it's been thirty-two years. Wouldn't be too pleasant, be very disturbing in fact, to have your past come barreling right up in your face."

"Mr. Haskins," Miles broke in, "why not send a letter, ask if they ever had a daughter put up for adoption?"

"Sounds like a good idea. And, as her adopted father, I could send them a copy of her birth certificate."

"Right," Miles agreed. "That will give them time to think things over. It's bound to come as a surprise. Unless, of course, *they* have been searching."

Brendan brought in the mail.

"Here you are, Dad. Here's your mail."

Boyd Howell looked at the packet of mail that his son kept in his hand as he handed the rest to his father. He shook his head, his pride in his son evident in his voice. "Still getting fan mail, eh, son?"

"Sure am, Dad." Brendan grinned sheepishly. "Some colleges are interested, too."

"Well, take it in stride. Don't let it go to your head. But your mother and I are very proud of you and your sister, too. We're blessed to have two great kids."

He looked through the mail his son had handed him. The usual junk mail, catalogues, flyers, advertisements, the regular household bills, and a business-sized envelope addressed to Mr. and Mrs. Boyd Howell. Boyd looked at the return address and saw that it was from a G. Haskins, Water's Edge, Marblehead, Massachusetts, 01945.

He opened the envelope slowly, thoughtfully. Why did he have this feeling of apprehension, as if maybe the news in the letter might upset the equilibrium he enjoyed with his family? He read the typed letter.

Dear Mr. and Mrs. Howell,

My name is Grady Haskins. I am writing to you to inquire if you ever had a daughter who was put up for adoption. My wife and I adopted our daughter, who was born April 27, 1967 at Magdalen House in Boston. I am inquiring because our daughter has been searching for her birth parents for some time.

Enclosed please find a copy of our daughter's birth certificate.

Very truly yours,
Grady Haskins

A formal-looking document had been stapled to the letter.

Boyd sat in his favorite lounge chair, stunned. What

did this all mean? His child had died at birth. Neither he nor Lana had ever seen the baby, or even held their child. Now this, from out of the blue. He suddenly had plenty of questions, but where were the answers? What would Lana say when he told her about the letter? She'd be home in another half hour. He'd have to decide what to tell her and how to tell her.

Carefully he replaced the letter and the birth certificate in the envelope, folded it, and stuffed it into his back pocket. He also made a decision. He would not tell his wife about this news, not just yet. Tomorrow, when he got to his small office at the VA Hospital, he would respond to the shattering news.

Dear Mr. Haskins,

I received your letter with your questions. I am sorry to inform you that our daughter, born April 27, 1967, died at birth. My wife and I never saw her.

I have not spoken to my wife about your letter. It would be very upsetting to her. I hope your daughter has good luck in finding her birth parents.

Sincerely,
Boyd Howell

Several days had passed when Grady received this letter.

"Now what, Miles? What should we do?" he asked.

"Go back to the beginning, I guess, sir."

"Back to . . ."

"Magdalen House in Boston."

Grady Haskins found the small brick two-story building not far from one of the many boarding houses located near Kenmore Square. A young woman, probably the same age as his daughter, answered the door.

Her long blond hair hung like a curtain, and she kept brushing it away from her eyes. She was polite and friendly. She answered Grady's questions pleasantly.

"I was told this used to be a place where girls, students mostly, came to have their babies," she said. "But that was years ago. Now it's a dorm for students. I'm Stephanie and I'm a student intern in social work."

She led him into a small office and indicated that he take a seat.

"Mostly I just do office work, pass out keys and mail," she told him.

He looked around the office. There was the usual office equipment, a computer and printer, telephone, file cabinets and some diplomas on the wall. Grady couldn't make out all the names from where he sat, but he thought someone qualified must use this office whenever Stephanie was not around. There were piles of folders and papers on the desk. Perhaps Stephanie had been working on them.

She noticed his glance toward the work pile. She laughed. "Always some scut work for the student intern to do." She pushed the pile to one side as if glad of the reprieve from working on it.

"I'm not sure you can help me. My name is Grady Haskins. My adopted daughter was born here at this facility. I'm trying to help her locate her natural parents."

"What year was your daughter born, Mr. Haskins?"

He handed her a copy of the birth certificate. "Here it is, see, April 27, 1967."

"Oh, oh." Her eyes widened and she flung her long hair back.

"What do you mean, oh, oh?"

"It was way before my time, sir. In fact, I wasn't even born then."

"What happened?"

"From what I've been told, plenty! It's not a pretty picture, but I guess a lot of bad things happened back then. You know, before women's lib an' stuff."

Twenty-one

"Miles, I couldn't believe my ears. This girl was telling me that between 1959 and 1967, any girl who was foreign-born or unwed, or Chinese or Latin American or black, if she delivered her baby at Magdalen House, nine times out of ten she'd go home without a baby and be told her baby was dead."

"My God, how terrible."

The two men were in Miles's apartment. They had decided to try to figure out their next course of action.

"This social worker student told me the whole thing was all over the papers at the time. I went to the *Boston Globe,* and went through the files. These are copies of what I've found." He gave Miles some news clippings.

"Now, Mr. Howell said that he and his wife were told their daughter had died shortly after birth," Miles said, looking at the news clippings, "but according to these news items, this crazy nurse who ran the delivery room would take the newborns away immediately. She had an accomplice that would get them eventually to a lawyer for adoption."

"Is that what happened when you adopted Leese?" Miles wanted to know.

"I don't know, Miles. I really don't know. Mordecai

Williams was a lodge brother. I trusted him, and he had known for years that Carol and I wanted to adopt. As I recall, he said her parents had signed for her adoption, that she was legally free for adoption. I had no reason to doubt him. He was a well-known professional."

"How old was Aleesa?"

"We brought her home on May second. So she was five days old. We loved her from the start.

"This student, Stephanie Lamott, said that by the time they found out what this crazy woman was doing—it went on for almost eight years—quite a number of babies had already been stolen and placed in new adoptive families."

"What became of the damn witch?" Miles asked angrily.

"She was found guilty, sentenced to state's prison, and eventually died there," Grady told him.

"According to the newspaper stories, she thought she was doing the 'right' thing to get these babies into 'better' homes than their unwed mothers could provide," he continued.

"Played God and felt she was entitled to do so." Miles's face was flushed with anger. "Mr. Haskins, would you like something to drink? I'm real hot under the collar myself right now. I've never heard of such a dastardly deed."

"Yes, you have, Miles," Grady reminded him. "There's crazies all over the world. Look at that woman who drowned her two little boys. Yes, I would like something cold. Beer, if you have it."

"No problem. Coming right up."

He returned with two cans of beer, gave one to his guest, popped the lid of his own can, and took a satisfying swallow. He walked over to the window, stared out for a moment, then turned to take his seat across from Grady Haskins.

Each man was quiet, both thinking about the horrible information they had just learned and what it might mean to someone they both loved.

Finally Miles, turning the beer can around in his hand, spoke.

"I think we have to let the Howells know that there is a possibility their daughter may be alive and . . . we certainly have to let Aleesa know, as soon as possible."

"I agree," her father said.

"I'm taking her out for dinner tonight at the Whale's Tale, down on Bankhead Harbor. It's one of our favorite places. I'll tell her what we've found out."

"Good. Think I should contact the Howells?" he asked Miles.

"Sure. You have already made contact with the first letter."

Grady wondered aloud. "Don't think I'll send the clippings from the newspapers. But I will tell him they are on file."

"That gives him some control on what he wants to do next."

"You're very quiet tonight, Miles. Feeling all right?" Aleesa's face showed her concern for her fiancé.

"I'm fine, Aleesa."

"Something *is* on your mind, I can tell."

She had noticed that he seemed restless, picking at his broiled swordfish that he had ordered and usually relished with gusto. He seemed ill at ease, not at all like the assured Miles Kittridge that she loved.

"What is it?" she prodded. She took a sip of her wine, wiped her mouth with her napkin, and waited for his answer.

Miles Kittridge knew that his next few words could alter the future he had planned for himself and Aleesa. She looked so lovely. Her hair sparkled with lively tints of reddish-gold mingled with the deeper chestnut color, from being in the sun, he suspected. She wore a deep coral silk knit sweater with matching skirt. Each time he saw her, he marveled at her delicate beauty. Soon, God willing, she would be his wife. He imagined her standing beside him in a beautiful white gown as they pledged their vows.

He breathed a silent prayer. *Please God, help her understand that I love her, want her to have peace of mind, and I want to provide her with tranquillity in the knowledge of who she is.*

He took a deep breath and answered her question.

"I think I've found your parents."

"You what?" Her face froze, eyebrows raised, her eyes widened in disbelief. "Miles, I told you *not* to interfere, that I'd given up on all that. In my heart, I'm satisfied . . . I don't need . . . what do you mean, *found my parents?*"

"Now just hold on, honey." Miles tried to placate her with a smooth, calming tone of voice. "Leese, I understand how you feel, and I love and respect you for that feeling. Let me try to explain."

She sat back in her seat. When she spoke, her voice was cold and matter-of-fact. "Please do."

"First off, I'm not blaming your father. I take my share of responsibility . . ."

"What's my dad got to do with this?"

Miles took a deep breath, reached for her hands again.

"When you and I returned from New York," he began, "remember we had dinner at your folks'? Well, anyway, your dad called me the next day to see how I felt about pursuing 'the search.' We both discussed the matter, knowing how strongly you felt about it, but we also felt that if there was a chance of discovery, it would ease your mind, bring some closure and peace of mind to you. Something you said to your mother. Your dad had this lead in South Boston. He followed up on it and discovered a Howell family, the same name on your birth certificate. The family had lived there, but had moved to a town named Calderton on the North Shore."

"Calderton? Isn't that the 'horsey-set' place?" She leaned forward now, eager to know more.

"That's the one. How a black family got to live there is beyond me. But you know your father . . ."

"Like a hound dog. Will run a lead right in the ground."

Miles smiled at her, relieved that some of the tension had been lessened.

"Go on."

"Your father told me later that he and your mother . . ."

"Mom is in on this, too?"

"Honey, we just want to make you happy. Yes, your mom is in on it. Anyway, they were going to ride around Calderton, see if they could locate the Howells. But before they could do that your dad happened to pick up the paper. On the sports page there was a profile of the student athlete of the year, one Brendan Howell."

"You're kidding!"

"No, I'm not. I couldn't believe it myself when your father called and told me. We talked it over and figured the best thing to do was write a letter and let the Howells know that we were searching for the birth parents of Aleesa Haskins."

"Then what happened?"

"Mr. Howell wrote back to your dad saying yes, he

and his wife had a daughter born April 27, 1967, but she died at birth. They never saw her or even held her. So, he said he doubted that Mr. Haskins's adopted daughter—you—could be *his* daughter."

"Miles, this is interesting. I had no idea . . ." She saw something flicker across his face, a pained, distressed look.

"What? Miles, what?"

"Aleesa, honey, you were stolen, kidnapped from your parents."

"What? I don't understand. How could something like that happen?"

"God bless your dad, honey. He went to the newspapers after he got information from Magdalen House, where you were born, and he found the whole story."

"Which is?"

"Some crazy old nurse was making decisions about the lives of others. It seems that if a young woman, immigrant, student, or an ethnic minority, unwed, didn't seem to matter much, she'd make certain they were heavily sedated and, of course, you know if the mothers are sedated, the babies are, too. A mother never heard her baby's cry. So, the nurse would tell the mothers that their babies had died and she would, with the help of an accomplice, put the baby up for adoption. That's what happened to you, most likely."

"What happened to the bitch?"

"She was sentenced to prison for life and died there."

Aleesa sat quietly, twirling the stem of her wineglass. Miles watched her, his heart aching for her. What a devastating set of facts he had exposed her to. He knew her mind was reeling from the onslaught. He wanted to comfort her.

"Hang on to this thought, honey. If these Howells

turn out to be your family, they did not *give* you away. You were *stolen* from them! *Stolen!* They did not give you up!"

"Now what?" she asked, tears flooding her eyes.

"Your dad plans to write Mr. Howell again, tell him about the crime, let him know the news clippings are on file and let him decide what he wants to do. I told your dad that you and I were having dinner tonight and that I'd tell you and you could decide what *you* want to do. I know it's a lot for you to take in all at once, but it's whatever you want to do. It's your decision."

Aleesa looked out the window at the harbor. It was a dark night. A few boats bobbed at their anchors. She thought of *Tismine,* her own little sailboat. How many times had she sailed around Marblehead Harbor, hoping and wishing that someday, someone would smile and say, "Yes, my dear, I *am* your birth mother."

The thought that she had been stolen away from her young parents, that they did not give her away, lifted a great burden from her heart. She *had* been loved, *had* been wanted. She remembered the nightmares of the woman with long hair, crying as if from a broken heart. Had her subconscious mind presented that past to her?

Twenty-two

Boyd Howell picked up the news clippings from the newspaper office. Back in his tiny office in the therapy department of the hospital, he closed the door. He would not be interrupted. It was his lunch hour, and both patients and associates recognized the closed door meant *do not disturb*.

His mind whirled as he read over the clippings. He felt a pain strike the pit of his stomach, his palms grow sweaty, and he felt his heart race so rapidly, he thought he would choke.

How could he tell Lana? There had been so many nights of tears and misplaced guilt and blame. So many.

We should have married sooner. Boyd always blamed himself for that delay. *But who knew the baby could come early,* Lana would say. She blamed herself for not having been able to explain her situation. *My English not good enough. I try to explain . . .*

Neither of them had ever forgotten their first child, the manifestation of their love. They both adored and were proud of their other children, but the ache in their hearts for the loss of their firstborn had never left them.

Boyd stuffed the clippings back into the brown envelope. He had to go home now.

He cleared some leave time with his supervisor. "A small emergency situation," he explained, then he called home.

"Lana, I'm coming home."

"Something is wrong?" she answered anxiously.

"Not really, my dear. It's a lovely afternoon and I decided I wanted to spend it with my wife."

She laughed. "Boyd, you are such a romantic! I see you soon, eh?"

"Soon, my dear."

But first he decided to stop at the hospital laboratory.

The house that he and Lana were able to buy was on a winding road that had once been farmland that produced fruits and vegetables, some of which were sold from farm stands. Today there were new homes with acre-sized lots. The Howells were happy to have the moderate cape that the disgruntled widow had sold to them. The good-sized lot had space in a side yard for a small garden. When Boyd drove up, he was not surprised to see Lana, a wide-brimmed hat shading her face from the sun, a loose, long-sleeved blouse protecting her skin as she worked in the garden.

When he got out of the car, she turned and greeted him with a cheerful wave. She pulled off her gardening gloves as she walked toward him. They kissed each other.

"So, you play hooky today?"

"Anytime I can be with you . . ." he teased as they walked arm-in-arm into their home.

"Lana, my dearest," Boyd began. He put his arm around her as they sat side-by-side on the sofa in their living room.

With no preface, he plunged ahead with his news, still holding her close.

"What if we could find out what really happened to our baby?"

Her face blanched with disbelief and horror. She fell back against the sofa.

"They . . . they said she died!"

"I know," her husband said quietly, "but suppose they lied to us?"

He held her close for a moment. Then he told her, showed her the clippings, and explained what he had been told by Grady Haskins. He showed her the copy of the birth certificate. Lana clutched it to her breast, tears streaming down her face.

"I'm glad the children are in school."

"They'll be home at three," his wife gulped through her tears.

"That's why I came home early. I wanted to talk about this alone, just the two of us. We can tell the children later. But now, my dearest, what do you want to do?"

"Do? I want to call this Mr. Haskins . . . Boyd!" Her eyes widened. She drew in a deep breath.

"What's wrong?" he winced at her excitement. "What's the matter?"

"Haskins, Haskins! Boyd, that's the name on the wedding invitation! I'm certain of it! Wait!"

She ran into the kitchen. The invitation had been pinned to the family bulletin board. She snatched it and ran to her husband. "Aleesa Grace Haskins!" she read, her voice rising with excitement. "Boyd! Maybe this is our daughter, getting married and . . . and to Miles Kittridge, my favorite patient. Oh, Boyd! We *must* call!"

"I guess so."

"Why do you say 'you guess so'?"

"Lana, it's been thirty-two years. I don't want you to be hurt if . . ."

"I need to *know*, Boyd. I must know," she insisted.

"All right, sweetheart, I'll call Haskins. But first I want to get your fingerprints checked against the ones on this birth certificate. And second, the guy at the lab that I spoke with this morning said that there is a DNA test that can prove a mother-daughter relationship. You don't mind . . ."

"No, no, anything to prove! Oh, Boyd, husband of mine, could such a miracle be possible?" Her tears almost choked her.

He held her, and she curled into his body for solace and comfort. They both cried.

"Dad." Aleesa's voice quavered over the phone. "Miles told me tonight . . ."

"Isn't it something, honey?" he broke in. "You're not mad at us for searching?"

"I couldn't be, Dad. I know that all of you, my family and Miles, want me to be happy. I'm grateful and I love you for it. Have you heard from . . . from"—she hesitated briefly—"from the Howells?"

He made his voice as positive, as reassuring as he could.

"Not yet, but perhaps today. Do you want to talk with him? Want me to do it?"

"Dad, why don't you and then let me know? I have some preliminary work that I have to complete for a client I'm defending. I'll call you tonight after work, okay?"

"Do that and we'll go from there."

"Dad, what does Mother say about all this?"

"She's so excited, she can hardly stand it. She wants her only child to be happy, that's all."

He put down the receiver. His hand was still resting on it when it rang again.

"Hello. Yes, this is Grady Haskins. How may I help you?" He did not recognize the man's voice as a familiar one. "Yes, yes, Mr. Howell! You received my letter."

On the other end of the line, Boyd explained that he and his wife would like to follow through to investigate the possibility that Aleesa might be their daughter. He mentioned that the circumstances as revealed in the newspaper clippings matched the experience they had been through when their daughter was born.

"Mr. Howell, what you and your wife went through was criminal and unforgivable," he said to the caller.

"It was almost more than that, sir. It almost drove us apart, but thank God, we survived."

He continued to explain to Grady that he was having his wife's fingerprints verified and that there was a DNA test that could possibly prove that Aleesa was their daughter.

"Do you think, sir, she'd be willing to have the test done?"

"Mr. Howell, I'm proud to say that my daughter, Aleesa, is a defense lawyer, and a very good one. And I'm sure she would be agreeable."

"Good. Just one more thing, Mr. Haskins. This may seem to make very little sense to you, but can you tell me, does your daughter have long second toes, that is, her second toes are longer than her big toes."

"Oh, yes, she sure does!" he laughed. "Her mother and I used to call her 'Miss Long Toes'!"

There was silence on the line. Then a quiet voice came, "Mr. Haskins, there's a possibility that your daughter is my daughter, too."

* * *

Back in her apartment, Aleesa knew she had to do something in the kitchen, something to keep her hands busy while her mind was occupied by the staggering news Miles had given her.

She pulled out her breadmaking machine. She measured flour, sugar, yeast, and water into the container. She added raisins and cinnamon. The smell of baking bread would be comforting, she knew.

Once the bread was baking, she decided to prepare a beef dish. Miles would be coming over, and she could always reheat the beef carbonnade.

She took a pound of cubed beef from the refrigerator, placed it in her heavy Dutch oven, and seared the cubes until they were brown. She removed the meat from the Dutch oven, placed one cup of chopped onions, a little sugar and flour, as well as a bay leaf into the pot, and browned those ingredients. She returned the meat to the pot, added one six-ounce can of beer, and placed the heavy lid on the pot. She turned the heat down to simmer.

Her mind raced along, fragments of Miles's news flicking through her mind. *Howell,* her real last name. *Boyd and Lana,* her parents' names. Students, music school, young, unmarried . . .

Surrounded by the comforting smells of baking bread and simmering meat helped to ease her tormented mind a little, but she needed more relief.

She needed *her* family. *Where is the family that created me, who reflect who I am, who gave me the bond of life, the corkscrew of DNA strands that I received from two people named Boyd and Lana?* Her distracting thoughts demanded answers and shook her to the core.

The pain she felt in her heart, the heaviness she had

borne all of her life, suddenly overwhelmed her. She had to have relief, she *had* to know.

She dialed information.

"What city, please?" the operator asked.

"Calderton, Massachusetts."

"What listing, please?"

"Howell, Boyd Howell."

"Thank you, one moment, please."

Aleesa knew it would take only a moment, but it seemed like hours before the operator came back on.

"The number you requested"—and she gave the number which Aleesa scribbled down—"may be automatically dialed for an additional charge of thirty-five cents by saying yes at the tone."

"Yes, yes," Aleesa breathed.

"One moment while we connect you," the operator said.

Connect. I'm being connected. When I was born I was disconnected. Now I'm being connected . . . reborn?

She did not hear the telephone ring, instead a man's voice answered, "Howell residence."

"This is Aleesa Haskins."

"Aleesa Haskins? Aleesa?"

"Yes, Aleesa Haskins. Is this Mr. Boyd Howell?"

"Yes." The voice sounded positive and firm to Aleesa. "I'm Boyd Howell. Are you the Aleesa Haskins adopted by Grady and Carol Haskins?"

She held tightly to the telephone as the man's voice continued.

"I've been contacted by your . . . your father, and I believe you could be our daughter. Has he spoken to you about that possibility?"

Aleesa heard a tremor in the man's voice as he called out to someone. "Lana! It's her!"

"Hello," a woman's voice quavered softly.

My mother!

She heard a deep intake of breath, then the woman's voice trembled over the line. "Oh, my baby, are you my baby?"

"I . . . I think so. My . . . my father and my fiancé have been searching . . ."

"Miles Kittridge . . . he invited us to your wedding! When, when can we see you? When can you come? Are you happy, safe? Oh, when can we see you?" her voice broke. Then Aleesa heard Boyd Howell's voice come on the line.

"We have been so shocked to find out that maybe our child is alive. We were told that you had died at birth. So you can understand . . ."

"I do understand, Mr. Howell. It has been a shock to me as well, especially when I learned of the crime."

"Your father told me that you are a lawyer. That's wonderful. Your father did not show us any pictures of you, but tell me, what do you look like?"

"Well, reddish-chestnut thick hair . . ."

"Like your mother," he interrupted.

"My eyes are gray-green . . ."

"So, like your mother's . . ."

"I'm about five-foot-six, and I guess I weigh . . ."

"If you're like your mother, you weigh about one-hundred-twenty pounds," he laughed.

"I wish," Aleesa confessed, "more like one-hundred-twenty-five."

He laughed, then his voice sobered. "Your mother and I wanted to name you Annaliese, her mother's name, and we have always called you by that name. So to find out that you were named Aleesa, a form of Alice, which you know is from Greek origin meaning truth, means a great deal to us."

Aleesa heard him say, "Yes, dear, here you are." He must have transferred the phone.

Lana's concern made her voice tremulous, as she

inquired, "Lunch tomorrow? You come, you must come tomorrow. My husband will give you directions. Your brother and sister can't wait to see you."

"Brother, sister? I have a real brother and sister?" Aleesa's voice squeaked.

"Staci is twenty-two and Brendan is eighteen."

"Oh my God, I never expected . . . oh my God," she repeated. "I can't believe this! After all this time I really have a family!" She started to cry. The weight, the burden of not knowing who she was for all of her life, thirty-two long years, seemed to leave her body. She felt as if she could fly. She felt light, free, unfettered.

She wrote down the directions Boyd gave her with a promise to get to Calderton in time for lunch.

The loaf of bread turned out beautifully. It would be, she decided, her first gift to the Howells, along with the album of pictures that her mother had put together.

She called Miles with the news.

"Miles, they sounded so wonderful, like regular people. Will you go with me tomorrow to meet them? I'm so nervous I don't think I could drive up there alone."

"Are you kidding? Of course I'll take you. Now, try to relax, have a nice relaxing shower, and get a good night's rest."

"I'll try, but I know I won't sleep a wink."

Before she could get ready for bed, she knew she had to share her staggering news with her parents. Her mother answered when she called.

"Mother! I called them!" she blurted over the phone.

"Called who, dear?"

"The Howells! Mother, I couldn't wait. I had to call.

They sounded so wonderful! Invited me to lunch tomorrow. Miles is going to drive me up. And mother—there's more!''

"More? What?" Carol could hear the bright happiness in her daughter's voice. She listened as her only child's voice bubbled over the telephone.

"Mother, I have a brother and a sister!"

Something Grady and I were never able to give her, Carol thought. *Had to settle for a boxer pup.*

"Honey," she answered as truthfully as she could, "you know Dad and I will be very happy if it turns out that you've found your folks. We know what it means to you."

Twenty-three

He arrived at her apartment early the next morning, not surprised at all to find her still excited.

"Miles, you're sure you don't mind going with me?" She needed his support, although she was reluctant to admit it.

"Wouldn't have it any other way." He grinned at her, his charming smile, as always, tugging at her heart. "Honey, this is going to be some day."

"I know. I can hardly wait. Mother and Dad think it's a good idea for me to have time alone with the Howells, but I need . . . I want you with me."

She put her head in her hands for a moment, then looked up at Miles. "Did I tell you that the fingerprints match and the DNA blood samples match, too? I think my heart is going to jump right out of my body. After I spoke with them on the phone . . . it all seems like a dream, Miles. Oh, Miles, I feel as if I'm about to fall into a pool of love!"

"Don't worry, everything is going to be fine. I'll be with you every step of the way."

Her voice sober, she confessed to him, "I owe you and Dad so much. You both kept searching even though I said I didn't want you to. Honestly, Miles, all I wanted was for you to come out of that coma, to come back to me, to be well and healthy. I couldn't think of anything else. Nothing else mattered because you are the most important person on this earth to me. But now"—tears flooded her eyes, her voice cracked—"now I do have a family of my own. I'm so . . . so lucky, so lucky."

He opened his arms and, sobbing openly, she sought sanctuary in them.

"Don't cry, babe." He bent his head to kiss her. She clung to him. Suddenly he realized how vulnerable she must feel. This was the young woman who was always so gutsy, so sure of herself she would take on the toughest prosecutor in any court. But the present situation—meeting her parents for the first time—had really overwhelmed her.

He breathed words of reassurance into her ear. "Sweetheart, trust me, everything is going to be fine. You'll be fine." When he kissed her this time, he increased the pressure on her lips, to which she responded with throaty sounds that only increased his desire to comfort her.

They left Boston at eleven that morning to be in Calderton in time for lunch. Miles placed the written directions under the visor, but he figured he pretty much knew how to get to the town.

Aleesa had changed into a sea-green pantsuit, and it seemed some of her anxieties had lessened. She looked lovely to him, her eyes, as usual when she was excited, sparkling emerald-green with hope and optimism.

They drove up Route 1A, past Salem and its history of witches, into a country area of long-held family farms, acres of apple orchards, and burgeoning vineyards. Occasionally they caught glimpses of rocky beaches as they passed through towns the settlers had named for the English villages they had left: Ipswich, Essex, and others.

It was a clear, bright, sun-lit morning. Cheerful forsythia branches waved delicately as if beckoning good fortune, Aleesa thought. Magnolia trees crowned with waxy pink petals cheered her, but misgivings filtered through her mind the closer they got to Calderton. *Suppose they don't like me—feel that I'm an intruder in their lives?*

She glanced at Miles. He was concentrating on his driving. She saw strength in his large, capable hands . . . hands that could control a 747 cargo plane with confidence, hands that could caress her so tenderly that she feared her skin would melt. His long, lean body, his graceful muscles made her insides quiver as she recalled the intimate, shared moments of love she had known with him.

She cleared her throat. Miles took his eyes off the road to give her a quick glance.

"You all right, hon?"

"Yes, I'm okay, Miles. I have to tell you . . ."

"What?"

"That I don't know what I would have done without you . . . in my life. You give me such strength . . . such support."

He smiled back at her, placed his hand on her knee, and squeezed it gently.

"Don't worry for one moment. I'm in for the duration. No matter what we find at the end of this trip. You and I are an item. *Capice?*"

"I understand." She leaned over and gave him a quick peck on the cheek.

"Look, Miles," she said, pointing to a road sign. WELCOME TO CALDERTON. ESTABLISHED 1755.

"Won't be long now, honey."

"I know. I'm scared *and* excited!"

"How do you feel knowing you have a brother and sister?" he wanted to know, an only child himself.

"I couldn't believe it! When I made *the* call, spoke with . . . Mrs. Howell, she has an accent, you know. Well, when she told me, I couldn't believe I was hearing her correctly. Staci, my sister, is twenty-two, ten years younger than me. And Brendan is eighteen, starts college in the fall."

"Leese," Miles interrupted, "check the directions again, please."

Aleesa unfolded the paper he handed to her. "I think this may be the exit. Says to look for Greylock's Horse Farm." She pointed to the right. They left the black ribbon of the highway for a single-lane road. On either side were wide pastures, some with cows, some with golden-colored palominos, chestnuts whose muscles rippled in the sun, and Aleesa recognized an appaloosa or two.

"Miles, this is really country out here. I love it!"

"I do, too." He rolled down his window. The smell of freshly cut grass, and fresh air undiluted by noxious, industrial fumes billowed into the car. Both Aleesa and Miles drew in deep, satisfying breaths.

"Aleesa! I see a pink ribbon on the tree over there."

"And there's another one!" she pointed excitedly.

"Oh, honey, your family is welcoming you!"

Pink ribbons tied in big fat bows fluttered from every tree along the winding road that led to the Howells'.

Miles turned into the driveway. On the front door a huge sign read, WELCOME HOME, ALEESA.

When they got out of the car, before they could close the doors, people came rushing from the house.

Miles stared at the woman whose chestnut-red hair

blended with her daughter's hair coloring as both women clung together, sobbing with joy.

"My God, it's Mrs. Miller!" He recognized the volunteer from Grafton Hills.

Boyd Howell reached for his child, tears streaming down his burnished brown face. "Baby," he choked. He held her with one arm around her and the other around his wife. Three heads were bowed onto each other's shoulders as the moment that they were robbed of thirty-two years ago became a reality.

Miles watched the drama unfold, then recognized the other two onlookers.

"You must be Staci." He shook hands with a young woman who looked like Aleesa. Her hair was dark brown and quite curly, and her eyes were sable brown. She shook his hand. "Yes, I'm Staci, and this is my brother, Brendan."

"Miles Kittridge, and I am happy to meet you both."

Aleesa's father turned a wet face to his children and said, "This is your sister, Aleesa. Aleesa, your sister, Staci, and your brother, Brendan."

Then there was another threesome hug between Aleesa and her siblings. Tears continued to flow.

Mr. Howell finally, in a gesture of taking charge, dried his tears, wiped his hands with a handkerchief, and extended his hand to Miles.

"Welcome, sir, and thanks for bringing Aleesa home."

"My pleasure, sir."

The father looked at the man who would become his son-in-law.

"And," he continued, "welcome to our family." He waved Miles toward the front door. Everyone moved inside, except Lana and her daughter, who lagged behind, arms around each other.

The question came up that had tormented Aleesa all of her life.

"Are you my birth mother?" she said softly. She knew the answer but she had to hear it from the only person who could give her a true answer.

In her calm, slightly accented voice, her mother said, "Yes, my dear child, I am your birth mother."

Twenty-four

Lunch was an exciting affair. After Boyd Howell said grace with a special prayer of thanks—*Oh God, we thank thee that thou has seen fit to make our family whole*—to which everyone echoed Amen, everyone seemed to talk at once.

"So, you're a lawyer?" Staci asked Aleesa.

"Yes, I am. What was your major?"

Their father interrupted, "Your sister wants to be a doctor." Aleesa heard the parental pride in his voice. "She's already been accepted at Boston University Medical School."

"Great! And you?" She turned to Brendan.

"Probably college, most likely here in New England."

Aleesa nodded. She looked from one face to the other, overwhelmed by the thought of family. *Mine,* she thought, *my family.* She could hardly believe what she was seeing. The emerald-green eyes of her mother, whose chestnut, russet hair was so like her own, the sleek, dark brown hair of her father, whose handsome, bark-toned flawless skin charmed her, her sister and brother who, like her, shared the same high forehead that Miles always said indicated intelligence. Aleesa was stunned by the enormity of it all.

She heard Miles speak to Lana Howell. Wonderful

Miles! Because of him and her father, she knew who
she was. He must have known that she didn't want to
leave this world without knowing who she came from.

"Mrs. Howell?"

Aleesa's mother turned to him with a warm smile.
"Yes, Miles?"

"I had no idea that you were Aleesa's mother. But
I always felt somehow that I *knew* you . . . had met you
before. Now I realize it was the resemblance to my
love, Aleesa."

He put his arm around Aleesa's shoulders and
hugged her.

"Miles, there must have been a reason that you and
I were drawn together," Lana said. "Boyd and I are
truly blessed. We have our firstborn, and soon . . . we
have a new son."

Her husband agreed with an expansive smile. "And
the wedding is?"

"Next month," Miles and Aleesa answered simultaneously.

Everyone laughed. The emotional tension was sub-
siding.

"I brought a photo album. My . . . my mom put it
together. She and Dad always took pictures, birthdays,
special occasions, that sort of thing. She thought you
might like to have it."

Lana's face brightened and she answered with eager
enthusiasm.

"Oh, yes, we would like to have pictures."

Miles jumped up.

"I'll get it from the car. Anything else, Leese, that
you want me to bring in?"

"Yes, please, there's a shopping bag," she explained.
"A few gifts."

Her mother's eyes glittered with tears.

"Gifts we don't need. We have you, our beloved

child, at last." She reached over to take Aleesa's hand. Nothing more needed to be said.

They looked at the pictures, Aleesa in her baby carriage, as a Brownie, then Girl Scouts, summer camp, high school graduation.

"You were valedictorian?" Brendan asked.

"Right."

"Wow! Some smarts in this family."

"Don't sell yourself short, Brendan," Staci defended him. "There's nothing wrong with your brains, you know."

Aleesa recognized the support Staci was offering her sibling. She assumed Staci had always championed her brother. Aleesa admired that. How often during her growing-up years she had wanted a sister or brother to be on her side. A thought occurred to her.

"Miles, could we have Staci and Brendan in our wedding?"

"I think that would be a wonderful idea!" he answered.

A dark look stole over Staci's face. Brendan, however, was excited about the prospect.

"I'd get to wear a tux?" he exclaimed.

"Sure would," Miles answered the young man.

Aleesa, however, had seen the hesitation on Staci's face. She tried to appease her sister by explaining, "I have a friend from law school who is going to be my maid of honor. I didn't know I had a sister, but now that I know I have, I would like to have you in my . . . our wedding as a bridesmaid."

Both parents looked expectantly at their daughter who had been thrust into the position as middle child, demoted as it were. They both knew their daughter, recognized her reluctance.

Aleesa understood.

"We can talk about it later, Staci. You don't have to

make up your mind right now. It's a bit much, I know, coming along with everything else. You can always let me know."

Lana explained it to Staci later that night. She sat on her daughter's bed. Staci sat in a big wing chair in the room, her favorite chair for reading. Feet tucked underneath, she listened intently.

"When I came to this country it was like coming to another planet. There was so much I didn't know. My father, your grandfather, you know, is a black man. And even though he told me a lot about this country, I didn't know much at all."

"So that's when you met Dad, at the music school, here?"

"That's right, my darling. Maybe he reminded me of my beloved father, I don't know, but we fell in love. At the . . . place where your sister was born, I couldn't make myself understood, so . . ."

"They took the baby away from you."

"They lied, said she was dead. And I never heard her cry, so I didn't know."

"Mother, how awful for you."

"We had a very hard time, your father and me," Lana confessed to her daughter. "We loved each other desperately, but it seemed our love was doomed. We could not seem to make another baby. We . . . I cried many, many nights, my arms and my heart empty. Then, it seemed like after a lifetime, you came."

Lana got up from the bed, walked over to where Staci sat, and kneeled in front of her child. She opened her arms, and Staci allowed herself to be held.

"Staci, darling child, when you were born it was as if heaven itself opened up, smiled at us, and said, 'You have suffered enough, my children. Be happy.' And we were. My dear child, you brought us glorious happiness. You have had us as your parents all of your life," she brushed back the hair that had fallen over her child's bended head. "Your sister, Aleesa, I know is a stranger to us, in a way, although she never left my heart. But now she has had *her* birth parents for only a short while. She and Miles, a wonderful young man, I believe, will be getting married soon, and there is one gift only *you* can give your older sister."

"I know," Staci said quietly.

"Only you can give her the love and support of one sister to another. Is that not true, my darling?"

"Yes, Momma."

"You will give that support?"

"Yes, Momma, I will."

"Darling child, I love you and I knew you would understand." Her mother hugged her, relieved that the impasse between her two daughters had been resolved. She prayed that in time they would grow to love each other as sisters.

Twenty-five

Miles and Aleesa were working at the kitchen table at her apartment. They were reviewing their wedding plans. The original plan was to come up with the personal wedding vows they would exchange. They had decided that each would write whatever vows seemed appropriate, then they would compare and make a decision as to the final vows.

The table was littered with pieces of paper as they worked in silence, discarding, scribbling, rewriting. Aleesa had told Miles that their vows had to be perfect and reflect how they felt. He had agreed.

"Miles," Aleesa spoke. He looked up. "Staci has finally agreed to be in our wedding. You remember I had asked her, but I sensed some hesitation on her part. She called me last night, and so, Saturday we are going over to Bloomingdale's to pick out a gown for her. I'm so glad she decided that she would be my bridesmaid. Makes me believe that she's accepted me into the family."

"Great, honey! She's very attractive, and smart, too. I'm glad she's willing to be part of our big day. Does she have an ongoing relationship?"

"I don't know," she said thoughtfully. "She did say that she's not thinking of marrying anybody until she gets her M.D. degree."

Miles tossed his head in Aleesa's direction and grinned at her. "Stubborn, strong-willed, like her big sister, eh?"

"Now look here, buster," she bantered, "you know you wouldn't have it any other way. You *like* your women strong and stubborn. I know you, Miles Kittridge!"

"So . . . is that what you're going to say when we take our vows?" he teased. "I, Aleesa Grace, strong and stubborn, take you, Miles . . ."

Impulsively, she threw a pencil across the table at him. He ducked, laughing at her poor aim.

"I'm tellin' you, Miles," she said, "I won't say it out loud, but when I put the ring on *your* finger, you're goin' to know who's 'strong and stubborn.' "

Soberly, Miles reached across the table where they had been working, reached for her hands, and pulled her forward to kiss her.

"I will take you any way I can get you, my love. No questions asked. For richer or poorer, in sickness or in health, 'til death us do part," he said solemnly as he planted a light kiss on her nose.

"Sounds fine to me. Make sure you're at Water's Edge on time, that's all."

"Speaking of time, honey, we'd really better write out those vows for the preacher man. We are going to make them simple, right?"

"Right. We don't want to be standing up there in front of our guests too long."

Miles said, "Let's just say the words as quickly as possible, then, as the man says, 'let's get it on!' " Miles raised his hand in a high-five salute, and Aleesa laughed as her hand met his to return the gesture.

They resumed their tasks, finally settling on: "I take thee (name) to be my lawful wedded (husband, wife). I promise before God and this company to be true and faithful to you, to love you and honor you, to respect you and trust you, all the days of my life until death do us part."

Aleesa put her pencil down after they were satisfied with the result of their work.

"Miles, I've been thinking. I don't know what to do about who is to give me away."

He looked at her and saw the earnest look on her face. "Hm-m-m, you do have a problem there. You can't slight either of your fathers."

"I know. I don't want to hurt anyone."

They were both quiet for a moment, reflecting on the problem.

Miles spoke up. "What could be wrong with having them both?" he asked.

"Right." Then Aleesa brightened as another idea struck her.

"Why not have all four? Mothers *and* fathers give me away?"

"Why not? Sounds perfect to me. Besides, it's our wedding and we can do what we want. When the minister asks, 'Who gives this woman to be married?' they can answer in unison, 'We, her parents.' "

"Miles, I think that would please everybody."

Boyd Howell drove into the driveway beside his house. He sat for a moment in the car and looked about. He thought how lucky he was. He had a beautiful, loving wife, smart, healthy children, and the terrible nightmare that had almost destroyed him and his beloved Lana thirty-two years ago had come to a magical conclusion. He had a dream come true. He thought he had lost his child, but God was good. She had been returned.

He got out of the car, noticed how lovely Lana's

garden appeared, noted the house that bloomed and flowered under her care, realized how happy Staci and Brendan were with their lives and promising futures. *How fortunate can one man be,* he thought. He felt tears of joy prickle in his eyes and he wiped them away briskly as he went into his house.

He found his wife in the kitchen, checking a lamb roast in the oven. The pungent, hearty aroma of garlic smelled enticing.

"What's up, honey?" he asked as he kissed his wife, her face flushed from the oven's heat. "Why roast lamb for dinner tonight?"

Lana brushed her thick hair away from her face before she answered.

"Aleesa and Miles want to come to see us. They called earlier to see if we'd be home, said they wanted to talk to us about their wedding. So I said yes, come to dinner. I knew you wouldn't mind." She reached into the refrigerator and took out a pitcher.

"Want some lemonade?" she asked her husband. "It's so hot out."

"Thanks, sounds good. It's real nice of them to include us in their plans."

Lana concurred with a nod as she handed him a glass of the frosty drink.

"It really shows just how considerate they both are and how much they think of us."

"We're lucky, Lana, to have found our child after all these years and to find out that she's turned out to be such a lovely, smart young woman. We could never ask for more. Grady and Carol have been perfect parents, I think. Now"—he drank most of the lemonade before he put his glass down—"is there anything you want me to do to help with dinner?"

His wife stirred a pot of rice she was preparing to go with the lamb.

"I don't think so. Maybe set the table in the dining room. I have everything set out that I plan to use, the Battenburg tablecloth and napkins and the Lenox china. I want everything to look real nice."

"Will do. What else are we having tonight?"

"Plum rolls. You think they will like my plum rolls?"

"Everyone likes your plum rolls. What else?"

"I thought a wilted spinach salad with a vinaigrette dressing would go well with the roast lamb. Of course, I have mint sauce, and I'm also making a light gravy to serve."

"Sounds great," Boyd told her. Then he asked, "Will Brendan be home for dinner?"

"No, he won't be home till later."

"That's right," his father remembered. "I forgot he has a track meet this afternoon, in Lowell. Isn't that what he said?"

"Yes, and you know the team usually stops somewhere to eat after the meet, but I'll put up a plate for him to heat up in the microwave when he comes home."

"I believe he said he's running the four-forty individual race and the relays. Sure hope he does well."

"He seems to think he will," she told him.

Aleesa and Miles arrived at about half-past six. Boyd and Lana welcomed them into their home.

A slight reservation, some understandable reticence was apparent as they went into the living room to have drinks before dinner. Each of them felt the awkwardness as they jockeyed for seats.

"Sit anywhere you want. Make yourselves at home. We want you to feel welcome, you know," Boyd told his guests.

"Thank you, sir," Miles said as he and Aleesa sat on

a floral-upholstered sofa. The delicate soft greens and mauves provided an attractive focal point for the room.

"You have a lovely home, Mrs. Howell," Miles said, indicating the fresh flowers in the various vases around the cheerful room.

"Thank you, Miles, and please call me Lana."

Miles laughed. "I'm used to thinking of you as Mrs. Miller, my music therapist," he admitted.

"That's right," Aleesa said. "Miles, do you know you've known my birth mother longer than *I* have!"

Then everyone laughed and the chill was broken. There were smiles all around.

"I think *you* should call us Lana and Boyd, too, Aleesa," Lana suggested. "It would be easier for you. Carol and Grady are legally your parents, you know. But as a lawyer, I'm sure you're aware of that."

"I am, and I . . . we, Miles and I, have talked about this wonderful set of circumstances that have brought us together."

"I, for one, never believed it would happen. To be told your child was dead," Boyd choked, "it was the most devastating thing . . ."

Lana interrupted him. "Your folks were wonderful though, Boyd. We had a brief wedding, your folks helped us with that . . . and we tried to go on with our lives. It wasn't easy," she confessed. "I had a lot of crying spells and Boyd tried so hard to comfort me."

Aleesa broke in. "Would you believe it? I had nightmares, too. Dreams, something like that. I dreamed of a woman with long, reddish-brown hair, I never saw her face, crying her eyes out while a man hovered over her telling her not to cry!"

"I felt so guilty over that," Boyd said. "So sorry that our plans to get married were delayed, but we thought we had time . . . the baby wasn't due for two months.

I blamed myself for a great deal of what happened,"
Boyd added.

"Things were different then," Aleesa said.

Boyd got up then from his chair and went to a table
where a temporary bar had been set up. Evidently he
wanted to move past the painful memories.

"Miles, Aleesa, what would you like to drink? Scotch,
bourbon, gin, or would you prefer wine?"

"We'll be having wine with dinner, hon," Lana said
as she rose to go into the kitchen.

"I'll have gin and tonic," Aleesa said. "Can I help
you with anything?" she asked quickly, as if remembering her manners.

"Oh no. Sit and have your drink. I'll be right back."

"Scotch on the rocks sounds good to me, sir," Miles
said as he passed Aleesa her drink.

"So," Boyd said as he took his drink and sat down.
Lana came back from the kitchen. "Honey, your drink
is on the table there beside you," he pointed out to
her.

"Thank you, my dear," she said.

"So," Boyd began again, "how are your wedding
plans coming?"

Aleesa looked at Miles and he responded to her cue.
He offered the explanation for their visit.

"Aleesa is very happy that Staci and Brendan will be
in our wedding, and we wanted to ask if you two would
agree to give Aleesa away, along with her parents."

Lana gave a loud gasp and Boyd shook his head as
if he couldn't believe what he was hearing.

"You . . . really . . . want . . . us . . . to help give
you away? Can we do that, with . . . your folks . . . they
don't mind?" Boyd asked.

"They're all for it. Think it's a great idea," Aleesa
answered. "As for me," her voice grew quiet as her
emotions rose, "I never, ever dreamed I'd find you,

and now I want to share this special day with you. Some day soon, perhaps after the wedding, I want to hear more about my 'roots,' who I really am."

Lana got up and went to where Aleesa was sitting. She bent over to kiss her long-lost daughter.

"You've made us very happy with your invitation to be a part of your wedding. Isn't that so, Boyd?" She looked at her husband.

"It certainly is a remarkable gesture on your part," he told Aleesa.

"Come, dinner is ready. Let's eat and I will try to tell you a little about your grandparents in the Ukraine," Lana said.

The dinner was a great success. The roast lamb really delighted Miles. He spoke up.

"Leese, now I know where you get your culinary skills."

Aleesa then explained to Boyd and Lana that she always loved to cook, that she was always happy in her kitchen.

"I've meant to tell you, my dear," Lana said, "the loaf of bread that you brought that first day when you came to meet us was wonderful."

"Thank you. I love making bread and giving loaves away as gifts."

"Nothing wrong with these plum rolls, either," Miles said as he reached for another one. "Do hope you'll give the recipe to Aleesa."

"They are easy to make. An Old World recipe from my mother," Lana explained. "She was Ukrainian, you know." Her voice grew quiet.

"My mother-in-law died last year," Boyd said. "I was sorry that we were not able to visit before she died."

"But your father, my grandfather, is still alive, still living in the Ukraine?"

"Oh, yes, my dear. He has retired from the university."

"Did you say he is a Soviet citizen?"

Aleesa was anxious to hear more about her maternal grandfather.

"My father was so upset by the treatment he received in Georgia when he and my mother visited there that he became a Russian citizen. I was an infant, so of course I don't remember any of that."

"But when you were born you were an American, right?" Aleesa said.

"That's correct, my dear. Even though I was born in Russia, my father was an American citizen at that time, so I had American citizenship."

"But on *my* birth certificate, you, my mother, are identified as Russian."

"They asked for my birthplace and I said, 'Russia,' so they assumed, I guess, that I was Russian."

"And, the night you were born, Aleesa, I didn't know where Lana was. She was alone in a difficult situation and clearly was taken advantage of. It's easy to see now how she was terrorized, and ultimately we were both lied to about you. It was a horrible nightmare. I don't know how we got through it except we loved each other so much. It was our love that saw us through."

"Love can do that, you know," Miles said. "Aleesa and I hope to share that kind of love, don't we, sweetheart?"

"Yes, we do," she said.

The look that passed between them confirmed their thoughts.

Boyd and Lana looked at each other and smiled. Then Aleesa asked again about her grandfather.

"From what you tell me, Lana, my grandfather was a proud, determined man."

"He still is. Proud that he was able to contribute as a black man. He had a talent and skill to give to others, even if they were Communists. He was never very interested in politics. I have not seen my father for over thirty years, but when I talk to him, by phone and only rarely, he sounds as strong and determined as ever."

"I hope some day I can meet him," Aleesa said.

"Someday we will," Miles promised.

Twenty-six

The wedding day dawned breathtakingly beautiful. The air was calm, cool, and crisp. A soft rain the evening before seemed to have cleansed the air of all pollutants and insects.

Water's Edge lived up to its name. Placid, brilliant blue water lapped serenely against the stone retaining wall. The grass seed that Grady had used to re-seed the lawn had grown into a thick, velvety carpet. White folding chairs for the one hundred and fifty expected wedding guests had been placed in rows forming a wide semicircle. The focus for everyone's eyes was the white gazebo where the couple would take their vows. Fresh flowers had been intertwined in the lattice work, and a lovely floral bower was the result. The vibrant colors danced against the background of the water. Large white wooden baskets filled with golden chrysanthemums created the aisle down which the wedding party would proceed. In planning the wedding for her only child, Carol Haskins had left no stone unturned. She talked with her daughter the day before the event.

"I'm so happy, Leese, that you were finally able to find your folks, and I'm even happier to know what a wonderful family they turned out to be. Course, they'd have to be special to have produced you!"

"I'm so lucky," Aleesa said.

"Honey," her mother insisted, "your dad and I are the lucky ones! We've had you all to ourselves for thirty-two years, so . . ." She choked back a sob. She brushed away her unshed tears to continue discussing the details for the wedding.

"The caterers have set up a large tent for the reception, and the receiving line will be outside as the guests move into the tent."

"Mother, you've planned everything so beautifully," Aleesa said. "But, then, you always do, and Mother . . ." She kissed her mother.

Her mother accepted the kiss her daughter placed on her cheek. "Mother, I want to thank you and Dad for everything, I'm really glad that you both agreed that the Howells could join you and Dad in giving me away. You're . . . you're both the greatest . . . the best parents a girl could have!"

"We love you, baby, always have, always will."

At eleven-thirty, a small group of musicians took their place on the left side of the gazebo. The music floated out over the water as familiar show tunes were offered for the guests' listening pleasure.

At five minutes to the noon hour, Miles, his father as best man, and a beaming Brendan as a groomsman stepped up to the gazebo entrance.

White paper was rolled out down the aisle of chysan-themums, and the musicians played the wedding march.

Staci Howell, slender as a willow, walked serenely down the aisle. Her dark brown cap of curls framed her face as she walked toward the wedding bower. Her bridesmaid's gown of dark green taffeta rustled softly as she took her place. Sarah Pritchard followed Staci.

Her gown was also dark green taffeta with an overskirt of sheer silk of the same color. They each carried a bouquet of yellow roses.

Miles's face beamed when he saw his bride. Her wedding gown of ivory taffeta, with a fitted waist that fell slightly, then flared in a full-length skirt, took his breath away. Her glorious hair swept over her bare shoulders. She wore a Juliet cap of seeded pearls with a chin-length veil. She carried several elegant sprays of calla lilies.

Carol and Grady walked down the aisle on either side of their daughter. Lana and her husband, Boyd, followed. When her minister asked "Who gives this woman to be married to this man?" the answer came in unison, "We, her parents."

Aleesa turned and kissed each one, first Carol, then Grady, Boyd, and lastly Lana, who held her daughter tightly for a brief moment.

There were murmurs in the crowd as guests whispered, "She's just found her real parents." The words went swiftly from one to another. "Her real mother." The intimacy of the moment was not lost on all who witnessed it. Many eyes filled with tears at the sight of the poignant moment between mother and child.

Miles stepped forward to shake hands with each father and kiss each of Aleesa's mothers. He tucked her hand into his elbow as they took the last step together to face the minister.

"Didn't I promise you your whole family would be here?"

She nodded, tears shining in her yes. "Let's get it on," she quipped.

"Let's," he answered.

The minister greeted them with a smile. "Ready?"

"Yes, sir, we are," Miles whispered.

The ceremony took only a few minutes. There was

hearty applause from their families and wedding guests when the married couple turned to face them and walk down the aisle as Mr. and Mrs. Miles Kittridge, Jr.

Miles and his bride continued to walk over to the stone wall embankment near the ocean's edge. Two white ornate cages had been placed there. Inside each cage was a dove. The wedding party and the guests stood around in a semicircle and watched as the bride and groom simultaneously opened the cages to release the birds.

Applause echoed from the crowd amid oohs and aahs as the birds immediately took flight and, side-by-side, soared into the heavens. The symbolic gesture was apparent to all who observed it. More than a few tears were shed.

Miles and Aleesa stood, their arms around each other as they watched the birds take flight.

Aleesa had tears of joy in her eyes as her new husband kissed her.

"Happy, darling?" he asked.

"Unbelievably," she answered.

Then they walked across the lawn to the green and white tent to receive their guests and accept their good wishes.

During the reception, Grady Haskins found Boyd Howell speaking with some of the guests. Everyone, it seemed, wanted to hear the story of Aleesa's newly found family.

"Boyd, one moment, please," Grady whispered.

Boyd excused himself from the group with whom he had been talking to follow Grady into the house.

"What is it, Grady? Something wrong?" he asked anxiously.

"No, I don't think so. Depends . . ."

"Depends on what?"

"On you."

"On me?"

"Yes. There's a reporter here who has heard about your story and he wants to interview you. Maybe the family, too."

"I don't know about that, Grady. We are a private family."

"I know. I feel the same way. The reporter said reuniting adopted children and their parents is big news right now. Said he knew for a fact that the national news media, *Time, Newsweek, USA Today,* are interested, and that he'd even approached *60 Minutes* about doing a piece."

"Grady, tell him no. My family and I have been through enough as it is."

"Well, he said your story, if told properly, would give hope to others who thought their child had died, only to find the baby had been stolen."

Boyd was quiet for a moment. Then he spoke. "Have him leave his card with you, would you please, Grady? Tell him I'll get back to him. I'm not going to spoil this day for Aleesa and Miles, not for any news reporter!"

"I agree entirely."

"Happy?"

"Miles, I didn't know I could be this happy."

"You're beautiful, you know?" He smiled. The familiar quirky smile that had endeared him to her made her heart do flip-flops as Miles flew the small plane to their honeymoon destination of Martha's Vineyard.

"Wait till you see the piece of land we're going to build our dream house on," he told her.

"Do you have plans drawn up?"

"I have some ideas, but you have to come up with some ideas, too."

"Is it near the water?"

"Not very far from the water, but we have deeded rights to a nearby beach. How does that sound?"

"Sounds fine to me. So, where are we going today?" she wanted to know.

"One of my pilot friends has given us as a wedding gift the use of his summer place. I think you're going to like it. We will have the whole house to ourselves."

They picked up a rental car at the airport and arrived at a lovely beach cottage. There were blue hydrangeas nestled close to the gray wooden Cape Cod cottage. They walked through a glassed-in porch into a living room with a fireplace and comfortable furniture. Two bedrooms were on the other end of the house, separated by the full bath and kitchen. Aleesa thought it was delightful and told her new husband she liked everything.

"I *love* this kitchen, Miles." She admired the utensils, the butcher block island, and the gleaming stove.

"Don't think you're going to spend time in the kitchen," Miles warned her. "We'll be eating out a lot because I have other ideas of how to spend our time. Come with me, my love."

He led her into the master bedroom. A queen-sized bed with a white comforter laden with blue and white nautical printed pillows on it was in the center of the room. Large windows looked out over the backyard with maple and birch trees. A table with chairs and an umbrella, comfortable lounge chairs, and a hammock that swung between two smaller trees looked extremely inviting. And it was all very private.

"It's really nice, Miles. So peaceful."

"After all you've been through, my dear, you deserve a little peace. Come with me, there's something else I want to show you."

He took her outside. Behind the attached garage

was a fenced-in swimming pool. "My friend, Roger, said that even though he had rights to the ocean, he liked privacy, so he built the pool. Inside the cabana is a dressing room, a half-bath, and . . . a hot tub!"

"A hot tub!"

"Ready and waiting. What do you say, my love?" He started undressing. "Last one in the pool is a monkey's uncle!"

"Oh no, you don't!" Aleesa shouted as she stripped off her summer shorts and shirt. Clad in only her underwear, she dove into the pool.

"Not fair!" Miles jumped in and bubbled up in the water beside her. Her hair streamed from her wet, upturned face like a banner of glorious fire as Miles reached for her. She scampered away.

"You took advantage of a poor cripple," he teased her. "And I had on long chinos. You only had on shorts!" he complained.

"What cripple? Haven't seen one limp from you all day, Mr. Kittridge!" she teased back.

He dove under the water and came up on the other side of her. She turned in surprise as he grabbed her. She let out a long breath as his hands circled her waist. She shivered, not from cold but from excitement.

He helped her out of the pool and into the cabana where they found towels. He dried her hair and toweled off her body. No words were exchanged as they walked together, wrapped only in the huge thick towels.

Aleesa knew that this moment, this night with her husband, would be a night she would never forget. She loved him, she trusted him. She would give him her love, her life, because he gave her strength and courage to face life, and, as he promised, he would take whatever came because he loved her.

The late afternoon sun filtered in through the bedroom windows, but Miles drew the drapes, enveloping them in their own private retreat. He tossed the pillows on the floor and pulled down the comforter, with Aleesa helping on her side. Giggling like two mischievous children, they dropped their towels and scrambled under the bedcovers.

Still in a playful mood, Miles took her in his arms. "Mrs. Kittridge, I presume?"

"Damn straight, Mr. Kittridge!" Aleesa shot back. He laughed and kissed the tip of her nose.

He breathed in the smell of her still damp hair that clung in tendrils, curled about her face. His hands sought to test the silky softness of her body as they explored the wonder of it.

"Are you cold?" he murmured.

She put her arms around him, her soft, delicate mounded breasts nestled close to his strong body. She shook her head no as the searing heat from him inflamed her. She knew she was where she was supposed to be, curled safely next to the security of his strong, sleek, firm masculine body.

"You're so beautiful, wife of mine." He teased the raised pebble of her breast as it firmed itself against his fingers. She gasped when his lips closed over it. She had never known such exquisite torture. She yearned for more. She moved, undulating her body as Miles's delicate hands and sensuous kisses drove her almost to distraction.

"Please, Miles, oh, please," she begged as he pulled her closer. He kissed her all over as her body writhed in ecstasy, her breath coming in ragged gasps. Her breasts, her navel, the inside of her thighs, her legs, even her feet—his lips touched each spot. As he did so, she flung her head from side to side and reached for him. She wanted him, she needed him, and she felt her body grow hot with yearning for release.

Finally, he bent to her mouth and took charge of it with a long, searching kiss. Instinctively, she arched against him, offering herself. She trusted him, he knew, and he was as gentle as he could be, moving slowly against her until he worried that the flame sparking within would consume them both. But there could be no turning back, no retreat, only the magnificence of the triumphant consummation of their love. It was a powerful moment as exquisite pulsations claimed Aleesa. She felt changed, free, as if floating.

She watched her husband as his breathing slowed to normal. He looked into her mesmerizing emerald eyes, heightened by the excitement they had just experienced.

He kissed her, his hands threading through her hair.

"I love you, beautiful wife."

"I love you, Miles, and I've made a decision."

"What's that, my love?"

"My decision is I don't need flying lessons. You've shown me how to fly."

Snuggled secure in his arms, she knew she was right. She would let him be her pilot, *always*.

Twenty-seven

The next morning Aleesa woke, stretched languidly, and for a moment did not know where she was. Then she remembered it was in this room, in this bed that she had experienced the most unbelievable, soaring moments of happiness. She realized that she felt refreshed with a new husband, a new life, a new family. She closed her eyes in a brief moment of prayer. Not that she was all that religious, but it couldn't hurt to let God know how very grateful she was for his loving kindness.

She smelled fresh coffee brewing and bacon frying. *Miles, bless his heart, he wants me to know he can cook.* She smiled to herself.

"Good morning, princess!" Miles, with a breakfast tray, a kitchen towel flung over his arm, entered the room.

He looked like a Greek god to her. Dressed in white pajamas and a white terry-cloth robe, he was *so* handsome, and her heart quickened. Embarrassed that she was naked, she quickly pulled the bed covers up to her chin. He laughed at her, placed the tray on the table and threw her a terry-cloth robe that matched the one he was wearing. He made a big show of averting his eyes as she put on her robe. She padded barefoot over to the small table in front of the windows. Miles bowed forward at the waist. "Breakfast is served, Mrs. Kittridge."

He pulled back the chair and seated her.

"Such service." She smiled up at him.

He kissed her. "Continued service guaranteed with payment like this," he teased.

After breakfast, they showered together, then, wrapped only in large towels, rushed to the secluded pool to swim, naked as newborns.

Lunch was crackers, some cheese, and cold cuts they had scrounged from their host's larder. Still wrapped in beach towels, they ate quickly as their hunger for each other grew. Their love knew no bounds. Their minds were free and unencumbered. Their bodies were finally tuned to each other's needs.

"Come," Miles said quietly. Aleesa took his hand and he led her into their bedroom sanctuary.

"My beautiful wife," Miles nuzzled her ear. Hungrily, she responded to him as she curled spoon-fashion into his body. His hands roamed over her body lovingly as she drew in quick gasps of ecstasy. He throbbed against her. In the darkened room, in the erotic cocoon of their bed, Aleesa smiled that she could bring such happiness to the man she loved.

When she woke, the room was dark. The afternoon sun had receded deep under the ocean's edge. Miles slept on. They had spent the whole afternoon in each other's arms. She looked over at him, sleeping serenely, quietly. *Please, God, don't let anything happen to him. He's my life,* she prayed.

She slipped out of bed. It was her turn to provide nourishment. She dressed quickly, closed the door softly behind her, and went into the kitchen.

It didn't take her long, even in an unfamiliar kitchen, to find what she needed. A can of tuna, frozen peas, and a can of mushroom soup for a casserole, tomatoes and lettuce from the fridge for a salad, and a bag of Cape Cod Potato Chips. Iced tea was easy to prepare and store in the refrigerator. In the freezer she found some rolls to thaw and bake. Fresh cookies and ice cream would do for dessert. She hummed happily as she worked, preparing the food. They would eat outside under the delicate stand of white birch trees.

She had just finished setting the table with white place mats, blue and white china, and cobalt blue glasses, when Miles appeared.

"Lovely, lovely," he said as he greeted her. He was freshly shaven, and his face shone with good health and vigor. Long gone was the faded pallor from his hospital stay.

He wore dark blue jeans and a white V-neck sweater that set off his good looks, his bronze-toned skin.

"Sit, my lord," she gestured.

When she brought out the food, Miles's eyes widened in surprise.

"How did you ever get all *this* ready?"

"Magic, sire." She bowed to him.

"The magic came the day we met as volunteers at the junior high school, my love."

She poured iced tea into their glasses and handed one to him.

"May the magic never leave us." She raised her glass to him.

"Amen to that, my love."

They relished the meal she had prepared. Miles handed compliments to her right and left until finally she said, "These sweet words will get you nowhere. You still have to do the dishes."

He groaned. "Remind me to buy paper plates and cups tomorrow when I go to the store. Got no time for washing dishes, got other things on my mind."

As soon as they had cleaned up, Aleesa said she'd help this one time. Miles told her they had a date in the living room.

"A date?"

"Right. Found a movie we can watch on the VCR."

"That's great."

They sat down side-by-side on the sofa facing the television. Miles had turned the lights off, so only the flickering screen threw light into the room. Miles operated the remote and the movie began.

"Happy?" Miles asked as the credits for the movie, a 1955 film, *Love Is a Many-Splendored Thing*, starring Jennifer Jones, began.

"Um-m-m. Very happy," she whispered.

"Me, too. And our wedding . . ."

"Miles, it was everything I had ever hoped for. Thanks to you and Dad, I have everything I'd ever dreamed of. A whole family, my own family that I've known and loved for thirty-two years, and you, my one true love. I wouldn't know how to handle any more happiness."

His lips found hers, and his caress was gentle and loving. "You deserve all the happiness in the world, and I'm going to do everything I can to see that you have it. Trust me."

His fingers curled around her soft breast as they kissed each other. She moaned perceptively, and her response to his touch mounted. He cradled her tenderly against his strong body. The movie was forgotten—their need for each other was much too great to be denied.

The decision was made to buy a house that would be close to everyone. They found a nice house in Peabody.

"I can commute to the office easily," Aleesa explained to her parents, "and Miles can get to Logan without too much difficulty. He plans to get started on his commuter airline soon. He's already filed some applications," she told them proudly.

Both sets of parents were pleased that everything was going well. When they heard the news of the location, Miles's parents were delighted. Peabody was nothing at all compared to their only child's peregrinations all over the world.

"Now I can reach my son by telephone if I want to," his mother said.

"You bet, Mother, anytime," Miles hugged her. She smiled up at him.

They were able to pass papers on the new house and move in a month after their wedding. Furniture from both apartments blended well together. The only new items they needed were a refrigerator and a new alarm system. They were very happy. Each day seemed to bring more newness to their lives.

Aleesa had noticed that when she hurried or rushed about, she seemed to feel short of breath. She noticed, too, that her ankles seemed a little puffy. Due for an annual physical, she said nothing to Miles. She'd see what her doctor had to say. In the meantime, she made a conscious effort to eliminate salt from her diet. Happily, she noted it seemed to help. Some of the ankle swelling subsided. Even the shortness of breath did not seem to occur as frequently. She decided to see her primary physician and made an appointment to do so.

Dr. Stackworth came in to the examining room with a cheerful grin and a warm handshake.

"So, how is married life?"

"Wonderful! I highly recommend it," Aleesa responded. She liked Dr. Stackworth. He had been her primary physician since she'd graduated from law school. She was pleased, too, because his office was not too far from the law office of Carter, Evans and Goode. She could keep appointments, sometimes, during her noon hour.

"Well, how are you feeling?"

"I'm fine, mostly . . ."

"What do you mean, mostly?"

"Last month, just before my period, I noticed some swelling in my ankles and I had some shortness of breath, especially if I rushed."

"Shortness of breath, eh? Let me take a look." He placed the stethoscope on her chest.

"I'm not supposed to get sick! I'm as healthy as a horse. You know that, doctor!"

"Just check you out anyway. Run some tests . . ."

He probed and prodded, but his facial expressions gave Aleesa no sign of what he may have found.

"Okay," he said finally. "You can get dressed and I'll see you in my office."

She dressed quickly, and when she got to the office the doctor was on the telephone. He motioned for her to have a seat.

"Well, young lady." He turned to face her, some requisition sheets on his desk. He scribbled orders on several of them.

Aleesa liked her doctor. She liked his warm, friendly, low-key personality. He was an excellent listener, never seemed hurried. He was a tall man with smooth honey-brown skin. Balding, a fringe of jet-black hair framed his head like a monk's tonsure.

"Here's what I would like you to do for me so we can get to the bottom of this little problem. I want you to wear a monitor, a device that will tell us how your heart is behaving. You'll wear it for twenty-four hours."

He pushed some other papers around on his desk, took off his glasses, and smiled at her. "Don't worry, we'll check everything out. I want you to have an electrocardiogram, some lab work, and I'll see you back here in one week, okay?"

"Yes. Doctor Stackworth, could this be serious?"

"Don't know yet, my dear, but anytime we're concerned about the heart . . ."

"Should I be worried?" she wondered.

"Not yet. Not until we complete the workup. However, you should discuss it with your husband. You know, tell him that I have a concern about your health. He will want to know why you're wearing the monitor. Before you leave, a technician will wire up the device. Don't take it off, and return tomorrow at this time and it will be removed by the technician."

"What will the monitor tell you?"

"How your heart acts during various activities. Eating, driving a car, sleeping, and so forth."

"I really do feel fine, even the swelling has gone down, and I've been breathing . . ."

"I know you don't want to believe anything could be wrong, but . . ."

"Don't want to worry Miles needlessly. He's starting a commuter airline, has a lot on his mind right now."

"My dear." Dr. Stackworth's face flushed with intensity. His manner was serious, but calm. Obviously he wanted to let her know how important this matter was to her health, but he did not want to alarm her. He got up and walked her to the door.

"Aleesa, it has always been my experience, for whatever it's worth, that it's important to share information with one's spouse."

"Oh, I'll tell him. After the tests and we know for sure what's wrong . . . if anything turns up, promise."

She wondered, would she be able to hide the device

from Miles? She certainly didn't want to worry him needlessly. Everything had been going so well. They were so happy. She didn't want anything to spoil the wonderful life they shared.

Twenty-eight

Thank God, Aleesa thought as she prepared for bed, *the monitoring device is small, only the size of a cigarette case.* Maybe she could hide it from Miles's eyes if she wore flannel pajamas, not her usual lovely silk nightgown. But if she slept in his arms as she did most every night, he would be certain to discover the monitor anchored to her waist with a strap.

He was already in bed, reading some flight material. He looked up, surprised by the thick flannel pajamas that hung loosely from her small frame.

"PJs, honey? Are you cold?"

"It's been getting colder every night, Miles. It's November, you know. But that's not why I'm wearing these."

"Oh?"

Here comes my first lie to my husband, she thought. *I hope that there won't be many more.*

"I thought I should sleep in the guest room tonight," she ventured. She was not surprised at the strange look he gave her.

"Why would you want to do that?" He did not understand.

"It's . . . it's, well, it's my period. It's very heavy and I know I'm going to be getting up and down all night. The first twenty-four hours are always like that. I don't want to disturb you."

"You could never do that, my love. But I don't want you off by your lonesome in the guest room, not at all, especially if you're not feeling well."

"Do you think"—she hesitated, watching his face for a reaction—"do you think you could promise not to . . . to touch me?"

"What do you mean, not touch you? Why shouldn't I touch you?"

"Your touch, you know, Miles, does have an effect on my body. My body temperature rises and . . . I flow even more when that happens." She spoke quietly, embarrassed by the whole farce.

"I promise not to touch you. It will be hard, but I'll keep to my side of the bed." He grinned at her. "Tell you what, since we have a king-sized bed, we'll put the big bolster between us. How's that?"

"I'm so embarrassed," she murmured.

"Don't be, my love. Adjustments always have to be made in life, especially married life."

He put the large bolster from the head of the bed down the middle.

"Honey, if this pillow is all that ever comes between us, I won't complain. I just want to have you with me, all the time."

Dr. Stackworth greeted her with a warm smile when she arrived at his office. Her stomach was roiling with fear, her pulse was racing. She wiped her sweaty palms with a tissue. She waited for his diagnosis. She was scared.

Her apprehension grew as she watched him shuffle

the papers in her folder. Finally he retrieved whatever it was that he was looking for. He went right to the point.

"Here's what we know. You have an enlarged heart."

"What do you mean, enlarged?"

"Your heart muscle is bigger than it should be. The heart is a muscle, you know, and for some reason it's gone flabby, doesn't pump as effectively as it should."

He watched the emotions of fear and disbelief flick across his patient's face, but he continued to try to explain what was happening in her body.

"That's why the venous stasis, the blood pooling in your ankles, and your shortness of breath sometimes."

She stared at him, could hardly speak. *Am I going to die? How can I tell Miles?*

"But I'm not supposed to get sick! I'm as healthy as a horse!" she protested, her eyes swimming in tears.

All she could think of was Miles. She should have told him about her symptoms when she first noted them.

And what about her parents, Grady and Carol? How would they react? Boyd and Lana, whom she was just getting to know? They'd have to be told. Crazy thoughts whirled madly in her mind.

The doctor's voice broke through her jumbled thoughts. He was saying something about immediate hospitalization, something about surgery.

She stared at him, willing him to make sense. She trembled as his words penetrated into her brain. "You said surgery, on my heart?"

"I did. There's a procedure in which a wedge is cut out of the heart muscle and the muscle is sewed back together to remove any slack and thus tighten the muscle. You'll be as good as new."

"And you say I should be admitted to the hospital right *now?*" Her voice cracked. "My family, my husband doesn't even know . . . we've only been married a few months."

"There's a bed available in the cardiac unit right now. I want you to have it. I'm going to send you by ambulance and I will get in touch with your husband, explain everything to him, and have him meet you at the hospital."

"I don't believe this. It's all happening so fast . . . like a dream."

"I know it's a shock, my dear, but there's something you can do for me."

Aleesa stared at him. "Do for you? What can I do for you?"

"Stay optimistic. And please, get a second opinion. I want you to be comfortable with my diagnosis. I'm sure I'm correct in my assessment, but I want your mind to be at ease. It's important."

By the time she got to the hospital, went through the admission procedure, had more blood work done, and finally got to her assigned room, Miles was there. He jumped up from the chair where he had been sitting and hurried to Aleesa, who was being pushed in a wheelchair. He was breathless, his eyes wide with fear and anxiety.

"Aleesa, honey, what is going on? Why are you here? Why didn't you tell me you were sick! I almost called Dr. Stackworth a liar when he told me."

She started to cry. The nurse helped her into bed, handed her a box of tissues, and promised to be back soon.

"I'm so sorry, Miles, I should have told you, but I didn't know . . . didn't know it could be serious. I . . . I didn't believe it myself."

"We'll get everything straightened out."

"But Dr. Stackworth wants me to have a *heart* operation. Oh, Miles, Miles!"

Her tears fell freely as Miles held her. "You stood by me, Leese, and I'm not leaving your side. I've always told you, we're in this life together, no matter what!"

"Miles," she sobbed, "I'm so scared, and I should have told you, but I just didn't feel that sick. Just my ankles were puffy and . . ."

He scolded softly, "You *should* have shared it with me, Leese. You know that, don't you? You know you're my world. Now we'll see what the second opinion turns out to be."

Dr. Stackworth came into Aleesa's hospital room, accompanied by another physician.

"Mr. and Mrs. Kittridge, I'd like to introduce Dr. Mario Guitterez to you. He is a world-renowned cardiac surgeon whom I'm happy to recommend to you."

Miles rose quickly from his seat to shake hands with the new doctor, a deeply bronzed man, who looked as if he had lived in a sunny climate. Miles noted that his grasp was firm, yet friendly. His dark eyes studied Miles's face as the two men shook hands. He bowed slightly as he acknowledged Miles. "I am very pleased to meet you, sir," he said in a voice with a hint of a Latino accent.

His nationality was confirmed when Dr. Stackworth explained, "And this is our patient, Mrs. Aleesa Kittridge. Dr. Guitterez is from Brazil, Aleesa."

"Madame"—again the slight bow as the foreign-born doctor took Aleesa's offered hand—"I am sorry to learn of your misfortune. I have reviewed your record with Dr. Stackworth, and there is a new surgical procedure, new to this country, I might add, but nonetheless one that I believe can help you."

Miles shook his head as he stared in disbelief from one doctor to the other.

"Oh no, sir, that is simply out of the question. Dr. Stackworth, you must be out of your mind to even propose such an idea. Whatever made you think that I would agree to an operation on my wife by a foreign doctor, no offense intended, doctor . . ."

Dr. Guitterez nodded. "None taken, sir."

". . . in a new procedure not even used yet in this country! This is my *wife* we're talking about!"

Dr. Guitterez stepped back a few paces as Miles confronted Aleesa's doctor, as if putting space between himself and the two adversaries.

Aleesa said nothing, but fear pushed itself into her throat. She couldn't speak even if she had wanted to. Did all this mean she was going to die? She and Miles had been so happy.

Dr. Stackworth raised his hand in a conciliatory gesture. He tried to ease Miles's fears.

"I understand, Mr. Kittridge, just how you feel about this sudden change in your wife's health condition. That's why I urged you to get a second opinion. Now, Guitterez here *is* a board-certified cardiac surgeon. All of his medical education was received here in the U.S. Please allow him to speak. He can inform you about the surgery."

"As my esteemed colleague has said," the doctor said, "I am a native of Brazil. All I ever wanted to be was a doctor. I left home at a young age and attended Northfield-Mount Hermon School in Massachusetts. After graduating from there I studied at Harvard and received my medical degree from Yale

University. My internship and residency were completed at Bellevue Hospital in New York."

"You've been around the block," Miles conceded grudgingly.

"I have heard that expression before, and I expect you are right. Almost every human medical condition that could exist was found at Bellevue."

"But my wife's condition," Miles interrupted.

"It's not rare at all, but up until now, as recently as the past five years, little could be done to treat it . . . surgically, that is."

"And that's what you think," Miles ventured.

"Yes. Imagine my surprise when I returned home to Brazil to start my practice in cardiac surgery and learned of a procedure to correct an enlarged heart, perfected by a Brazilian surgeon!"

"Has it been done in this country?" Miles wanted to know.

"Yes. Very successfully, I must say. Sixty-five percent of the cases have been quite successful, and the patients restored to good health. Your wife is young, and the heart enlargement is moderate."

"If you don't operate?" Aleesa asked.

"Possibly the enlargement will only continue and subsequently you would become an invalid," Dr. Stackworth said. "That's why I want you to have the surgery, Aleesa. Of course there is a risk, but if we do nothing, the risk is greater. The quality of your life would be diminished, and I know you don't want that. I, for one, want you to have a happy, fulfilling future."

Miles saw the wistful look on Aleesa's face. His own mind was in such a turmoil over the impending news of a heart operation on his wife that he could hardly think. His beloved wife's life hung in the balance. The hospital room was quiet. Miles could hear hospital noises outside the door, life going on as usual, he thought, while for him his world stood still.

"What caused this condition, anyway?" he asked.

"We're not sure, Mr. Kittridge. A virus perhaps that has weakened the heart—it became flabby and so it's difficult for the heart to pump blood. But if we decrease the size of the heart—it *is* a muscle, you know—then the muscle works much more effectively."

Dr. Guitterez continued to explain the procedure. "The patient is placed on a heart-lung bypass machine and a slice of the muscle is removed. The valve is repaired and the procedure is complete."

"How long?"

"Oh, about four hours, Mr. Kittridge—and if your wife's recovery goes well, as I believe it will, she will be out of the hospital in less than ten days."

"Dr. Stackworth, Dr. Guitterez"—Miles stood and shook each man's hand—"my wife and I will discuss this with each other, and with our families, and make a decision. Thank you for your consideration and advice."

Aleesa nodded her head. She was so relieved to have her husband taking responsibility for her. Used to making her own decisions, it seemed only right now to have someone else to share the burden.

Within the next hour, her hospital room was crowded. Her parents, Grady and Carol, were on either side of her bed. The Howells, who had been notified by Carol of Aleesa's hospitalization, were at the foot of the bed facing her. Miles hovered near the head of the bed, holding his wife's hand.

Grady Haskins spoke up. "Baby, I don't understand"—his usual placid face was wreathed in worried frowns—"you've always been so healthy."

Boyd interrupted, "Do you think being premature

might have had something to do with this 'heart problem'?"

Lana looked shaken by the whole set of circumstances. "Premature, what about premature?"

"Sometimes babies born early may have health problems," Grady explained to her. He turned to his wife. "Leese was always a healthy child, wasn't she?"

Carol hesitated for a moment before she responded, as if remembering something.

"Except . . . remember when she had that strep throat?"

"Yes," her husband said, "and the doctor did say at that time that it was a good thing antibiotics were available to treat her, because otherwise, she could have been left with a damaged heart."

"But Leese did *everything* every other little girl did—Girl Scouts, ballet lessons, tennis, ice skating, sailing," Carol protested. "And, except for that strep thing, she was never sick!"

Aleesa wiped away her tears. The situation was almost more than she could cope with. She knew she needed time to absorb it all.

"Go home, all of you, go home!"

"I'm staying," Miles answered. "I've requested and they'll be bringing in a cot or something for me."

"I'm determined to get through this . . . this temporary setback so I can spend the rest of my life with my husband," Aleesa announced, dry-eyed. "I refuse to be cheated, so you guys go home, say your prayers, have a drink, or whatever."

"Now that's my girl," Grady said. "Good night, baby." He kissed her. His wife did the same, patting her daughter's cheek as she left.

Boyd and Lana, both fearful of losing the child they had just found, lingered a few moments longer.

"Don't worry. Please don't worry," Aleesa begged

them. "I have every confidence in my doctors. I promise I will get well. Please believe that. Be strong for me."

Lana said, "When you are well again, we will have a big celebration."

Boyd shook hands with Miles. "If you need *any-thing*, anything at all . . ." his voice trailed off. He and Lana kissed Aleesa good-bye and left. Aleesa had seen the tears in their eyes. These were people she barely knew, but their blood ran through her veins, their courage and fortitude would be part of hers.

"You're a trooper," Miles said after everyone left. "I'm proud of you."

Later that night, Miles wanted desperately to hold his wife in his arms, feel her soft, yielding body molded close to his, but the hospital bed was not designed for two. He had to content himself with holding her hand.

"Leese, I'm scared, and I know you are, too, but I believe with all my heart that the love we have for each other will pull us through. We've got a lifetime ahead of us. You've *got* to make it. I don't want to live without you."

From her bed she looked up at him. She saw his handsome face, his eyebrows furrowed with worry lines, his dark eyes pleading with her. She saw the firm mouth that had loved her with such tenderness, and she wanted so much to comfort him, to allay his fears.

"I'm not going anywhere, Miles. I have work to do."

"What are you talking about, work?"

She gave him a half smile and looked at him from beneath hooded eyelids.

"I still have to teach you how to sail. You're going

to be my first mate in the regatta race next summer, aren't you?"

"Aye, captain, that I am!" He threw her a mock salute.

She picked at the identification bracelet on her left arm.

"Miles," she said quietly, "tonight I really know what love means."

"Yes, babe?"

"To me it means that you are my life, my sun, moon, stars, my whole world. Until the day I met you, I didn't even know what was missing. Don't think I intend to give you up now that I've found you."

He kissed her then. He meant the kiss to be an affirmation of their love. He wanted her to feel the deep, abiding passion that he had for her at that moment. He prayed that all would go well. He could not lose her.

The next forty-eight hours passed in a blur for Aleesa. She was slightly aware of people doing things to her, admonishing her to move, of Miles being nearby, touching her, whispering endearments to her.

Miles was finally allowed to see his wife in the recovery room. He was accompanied by a nurse who tried to allay his fears.

"Now, only a few minutes, sir. We have our work to do. As I've said, your wife's vital signs are stable, but we still have to monitor her very closely." She placed her hand gently on his shoulder as if to reassure him. He half listened to what she was telling him. His feet felt as if he wore lead boots and he sensed his heartbeat in his throat as he neared his wife's bedside.

She seemed so tiny, so fragile. Tubes and pulsating ventilators were helping her breathe. Intravenous solutions snaking from plastic bags fed life-saving solutions into her body, that lay still beneath a taut white sheet. The ominous ticking of the machine that monitored her newly repaired heart cast blue shadows into the already dimly lit room. Its jagged line of peaks and valleys sent life signals to those whose task it was to read and assess its messages from the patient's heart.

Seeing Aleesa for the first time since her surgery, Miles felt a fear and apprehension that nearly took his breath away. He had never been so frightened in his life.

"May . . . may I speak to her?" he whispered to the nurse.

"By all means, please do. She's not fully awake, but she'll know it's you."

Miles bent over his wife's bed. He kissed her gently on her forehead.

"I love you, my darling," he whispered. He took her hand and squeezed it gently. "You are doing fine, going to be okay, I promise."

The nurse touched his shoulder and he knew he had to leave. He took another quick glance at his wife, whose lips seemed almost blue in the dim light.

"She looks so terrible," he groaned as he followed the nurse out of the intensive care unit.

"Don't worry, Mr. Kittridge. Tomorrow she will look better, you'll see. I expect even later today we'll see improvement. Healing can be a slow process, but your wife is relatively young—and you must stay optimistic."

Miles nodded, but the bleak picture of his stricken wife haunted him.

"Thank you, miss, for everything you're doing for

my wife. She's my heart and soul . . . my life," he stammered. "I want her home."

"Come back later today," the nurse encouraged.

As the cardiac nurse specialist predicted, Aleesa made steady progress. Miles gave his progress report to the family in the visitors' room.

"Aleesa's being moved! She's going to the critical care unit!"

Grady Haskins jumped up from the chair he was sitting in to shake Miles's hand.

"Oh man, that's great news!" His face beamed.

Carol, Boyd, and Lana gathered around Miles, too, each delighted with his news.

"That means we can see her more often, doesn't it, Miles?" Carol asked hopefully.

"I believe it does, as long as we take turns and stagger our visits. We don't want to overburden her. She's been through a lot," Grady said.

Boyd and Lana agreed.

"Why don't we put together a schedule so that one of us can always be with her?" he suggested. "That way, Miles, you can take a break."

"I don't want to leave her for a minute," Miles said. "I can't wait to get her home. Won't be satisfied until she *is* home."

"Oh, son," Grady said kindly, "we know how you feel. We want her home, too, but we don't want you to break down. Remember, you had us scared to death with *your* head injury."

"I know," Miles conceded with a shake of his head. "You know, Mr. Haskins," he went on, "why is it that such awful things have to happen to people? Leese and I never expected . . . we thought our lives would be perfect, with smooth turns . . . not the horrors we've had to face."

"Wish I knew, son. Life does hand out some strange, unexpected events sometimes."

"I agree," Boyd concurred. "Look at what happened to Lana and me. But, Miles, you have to have faith and trust in the love you two have for each other. That will see you through, and you'll be all the stronger for it."

Miles noted the nods of agreement from the two mothers. He felt encouraged by the support of Aleesa's folks, but he was still worried to death.

"Maybe I shouldn't say this, but I want all of you to know that I can't see my life without Aleesa. She's got to come through this. *Got to!*"

Grady placed his hand on Miles's shoulder. "We're all praying, Miles. I'm confident that she's going to be fine. You've got to believe that."

"God knows I want to believe that. I sure hope nothing else happens to us. We've been through more than enough."

The visiting schedule was drawn up and someone was with Aleesa every day. Miles's parents also sat with Aleesa, and the support from the extended family bolstered his spirits. As his father said, "We're family, and family means we care for one another. I don't know about the rest of you, but every time I visit I see a great improvement."

"She's come off the ventilator and she knows us. Knows we're around. I'm happy with that," Miles told his dad.

"She's coming along. Your mother got her to have soup and Jell-O today," he told Miles.

"Perfect!"

"What does the cardiologist think?"

"All is well. He is very pleased with her progress," Miles reported.

"She's asking about discharge, you know."

"I know, Dad. She's feeling better, that's for sure. Getting restless. But I don't want to rush things, want to be sure that everything is okay before we take her home."

"Well, you know your mother and I will be ready to do whatever we can to help."

"Thanks, Dad."

Dr. Stackworth made rounds a few mornings later. It had been one week since the surgery.

"How're you feeling?"

"All right, I guess," she whispered.

"I want you out of bed today, going to have you walk about a bit. The plan, if all goes well and your post-op tests come back with good results, is to send you home by the end of the week. Dr. Guitterez is very proud of you. He intends to see you later."

Miles grinned broadly at the news.

"All right!" he whooped. "You mean that, doctor, she can be discharged?"

"If the tests come back okay, as I expect they will, I see no reason why you won't be able to take your little lady home." He smiled. "She's as good as new." He shook Miles's hand, and Miles pumped it up and down vigorously, elated by the news.

When the doctor left, Miles could hardly contain himself. His joy knew no bounds. "I knew you'd come through, girl. Didn't reckon on anything else."

"Told you I refused to be cheated out of my life with you, didn't I?"

"You sure did, my love, you sure did. Tell you the

truth, honey, I don't think there's anything you can't do."

"Keep that in mind, buster. I guarantee you there's better days coming."

"I can't wait," he said.

Twenty-nine

Carol and Grady insisted Aleesa come to Water's Edge to recuperate from her surgery.

Miles agreed. "It would certainly ease my mind," he told them. "I have several appointments lined up for my commuter airline and most of them are overnight trips."

So it was settled. She was moved back into her old room at Water's Edge.

"It's been fourteen years since I've slept in this room," she said.

"I know," her mother said. "When you left at eighteen to go off to college, your dad and I became empty-nesters. We weren't happy about our only child leaving the nest, but we knew we had to set our little bird free to fly away and find her own place in the world."

"Thought your mother would never stop crying," Grady told her.

"It was because I didn't know whether I'd properly prepared you for the big wide world out there. I kept feeling that there was more that I should have done or said."

"I believe every parent feels that way," Miles said. "I know my mother said the same thing. 'I'm not finished with you yet,' she said. When you come to think of it, eighteen is a tender age."

"Well, I, for one, am glad to have my child back under my roof again," Grady said.

"I'm not a child, Dad! I'm an old married woman!"

Miles had insisted on carrying her upstairs, despite her protests about his old fractured leg and head injury.

"Shucks, girl, I'm as good as new, you know that!" He swept her up into his arms. She felt loved and cared for, but she persisted in her protests.

"But the cardiologist says exercise is what I need right now. I can't lay around, certainly that's not good."

Her father went over to a covered object that had been placed in front of the bedroom windows. He removed a covering.

"What's that, Dad?"

"I rented this treadmill so you can exercise right in your old room."

"Wow! That's wonderful, sir. Thanks for thinking of that, just perfect!" Miles said.

"Well, Miles, I asked the doctor and this is what he suggested."

"How often should Aleesa use it and for how long a period of time?"

"He didn't say, Miles, but he did say that the visiting nurses will be coming in to monitor her."

"So they will know . . ."

"Yes, they will have orders."

Aleesa's parents left the room so that Aleesa and Miles could have some private time together before he had to leave.

"See you downstairs, son," his father-in-law said.

"Be down shortly."

"So, you can't wait to leave?" Aleesa teased.

"If I had my way, you little vixen, I'd climb right into that bed with you. And you know that!" he said.

"As a matter of fact, if I could change my meeting up in Maine, I would, but I'm anxious to talk with the airline authorities in Portland."

"I do hope it goes well. I'm sure they are bound to be impressed with your plans and your statistics."

"I'm going to give it my best shot. What I want you to do is recuperate as quickly as you can. As the advertising goes, 'We've got a lot of living to do'!"

He kissed her then, brushed her glorious hair away from her face gently, and whispered in her ear, "I love you, Mrs. Miles Kittridge, and don't you ever forget it! Don't go anywhere until I come back."

Aleesa reached up and lovingly stroked her husband's face. "Come back soon," she whispered. "Promise you'll come right back." Her voice started to quaver when she said, "I want you here." She patted the empty space beside her on the bed. "Promise you'll come back soon?"

"Honey, I promise," he told her.

When he went downstairs, he found his wife's parents in the living room. Mr. Haskins was reading a copy of *Newsweek* and, as usual, Mrs. Haskins was working on a craft project. Something that looked like a small quilt.

"That is very attractive," Miles said. "What is it?"

"It's a wall hanging for you and Aleesa, for your home."

She was cutting, sorting, and sewing together tiny bits of cloth that were like bright jewels into an intricate, kaleidoscopic design.

"When I finish putting these together into a wheel-like pattern, I will quilt it, bind it, and then you'll be able to hang it on a wall," she told him.

"The colors are very nice. Aleesa likes blues and greens, I know," he said.

Her mother responded, "I know she is partial to the blue-green colors of the ocean, and I wanted forest greens to complement those." She pointed to a soft petal-pink print cloth. "I'm hoping this pink will bring life into the design."

"You're very talented, ma'am."

"I don't know about that," she confessed. "I like to keep busy."

Mr. Haskins spoke up. "She's talented, son. Carol always likes to turn her hand at things, and I believe she is truly gifted. Don't sell yourself short, my dear."

"I know now where Aleesa gets her artistic talent."

"Two sources, I'd say," Grady said. "Her birth parents are both musicians."

"I know. Aleesa always has music playing somewhere in the house, and she probably got her sense of order and design from you two. I've never been in a calmer, more orderly, more relaxed atmosphere than when I'm with you folks. Hope Aleesa and I will be able to have that serenity in our lives."

"You will. I know you will. Just love and trust each other."

"I have to leave soon," Miles announced, "but before I go, sir, I have to thank both you and Mrs. Haskins for your support . . . with everything. Helping to locate Aleesa's birth parents, allowing them to share in our wedding, and now helping out with her recovery. I can't thank you enough."

"You don't have to thank us, son. We love Aleesa and we'd be willing to walk on hot coals if it was something she needed. And by the way"—his eyes crinkled as he smiled at Miles—"don't you think it's time you started calling us Mom and Pop? You're a member of this family now."

"Be my honor and pleasure, sir . . . er . . . Pop. Well, I must leave. Here's the number of the hotel where I'm staying in Portland, but I'll be in touch. Be gone, I think, only a few days, but it all depends. . . ."

"We understand," Carol Haskins said. "We'll take good care of your wife."

Miles kissed her cheek. "Good night, and thanks . . . Mom."

She patted his cheek. "Good night, son."

Grady Haskins walked Miles to the front door.

"See you in a few days, Miles."

"Right, sir . . . Pop." He bounded down the front steps into the night. Grady watched as he got into the car and drove away. He closed and locked the front door, then walked back to the living room where his wife was stowing her quilting project in a large fabric bag.

"Well, honey," he sighed, "we sure have had a lot of changes in our lives over this past year."

"I know we have, but it's been quite an exciting time for us. I'm happy that things have turned out the way they have. I'm so delighted that the kids love each other so much."

"Right, and love will take them through everything. Let's check on Aleesa and then get to bed."

Arm in arm they climbed the stairs.

Aleesa made very good progress and was soon declared back to normal. Miles took her back home after two weeks with her parents and she began to think about returning to the law office.

"Only if Dr. Stackworth clears you," Miles warned.

Her doctor insisted on an electrocardiogram, another session with the heart monitor that she'd had to hide from Miles before, and finally, after completion

of all the tests, he declared she could work part-time
for two months, then be evaluated again before returning to full-time employment.

"Yours is a stressful occupation," her doctor said.

"I know, doctor, but I'm happy in my job."

Thirty

Mr. Butterworth's secretary called.

"Mr. Butterworth has asked me to let you know that he is pleased that you are doing so well, Mrs. Kittridge. He has agreed to your part-time employment until you feel ready for full-time."

In her mind's eye, Aleesa could visualize her supervisor, calendar in hand, calculating the number of half days of her employment. She still had some sick days left, but she didn't want to use them all. One never knew, and it made sense to have some leave stored up just in case.

Miles really wanted her to stay at home.

"To do what?" she countered. "Have you forgotten that I'm a professional woman?"

"Honey, I haven't forgotten a thing. The memory of you in that hospital bed, with tubes and wires stuck everywhere over your little body, no, m'dear, I'll never forget that as long as I live."

His words reminded her of the bleak days and nights she had experienced during *his* illness. Her overriding fear that she might have to face life without him.

"I know, Miles," her voice softened. "I remember those days when you were in the hospital and I thought I might never hear you speak my name again," she shuddered at the memory.

"Then you know . . ."

"I know, but I know, too, that I have to live my life, can't be bound down, afraid to live. You understand that, don't you? I promise I won't take on more than I can do comfortably. I've been cleared by all the doctors . . ."

"Sure am glad about that. Say, Leese"—his face brightened—"how about going away for the weekend, some place warm and sunny?" He gave her his familiar quirky grin.

She slanted a glance at him. "Really, you mean that?"

"Sure I mean it. Bermuda okay with you?"

"Are you kidding? I love Bermuda!"

After a smooth, uneventful flight in Miles's Cessna, they arrived at their hotel in time for afternoon tea. Miles had planned for them to stay in a one-bedroom cottage. An open veranda with attractively colored chaises, glass-topped table, and potted, vibrant tropical plants all around, made a delightful setting for the couple

"It's lovely, Miles. Nice to have privacy and yet have the hotel with everything you need right at your fingertips."

"I'm happy, my darling, that you like it."

That night, settled into bed, Miles reached for her. She snuggled close to him in her usual position. His arms around her, his hands caressed her slowly with soft, loving strokes. It had been some time since they had made love, and he was hesitant.

Her red-brown hair fanned across the pillow. She looked up into his face. Her gray-green eyes glistened with anticipation. It had been so long. But tonight it would be wonderful.

He whispered in her ear. "Is it all right? I mean, can I love you, won't hurt you?"

"Silly, the doctor said I was as good as new." She turned to face him and wrapped her arms around him as if she never wanted to let go. "I'm yours, Miles, forever. Love me tonight. It's been so long, so long."

He needed to hear no more. "I've wanted you, too, so much, but I didn't want to hurt you. Are you sure?"

"Try me. No more talk."

Their hunger for each other was so profound, within seconds it seemed, they both felt the earth move as their bursts of passion propelled them to glorious heights.

They made love again later that night as if trying to recoup the moments lost to them during her illness. The next morning, as usual, they showered together. Miles bathed her tenderly, careful not to irritate the telltale scar on her chest. After the shower he dried her carefully, applied body lotion all over her arms, legs, abdomen, back. But when he turned her over to rub the soothing, cool liquid over her breasts, she reached for him. Their lovemaking was even sweeter than the night before, their caresses deliberate, yet comforting and satisfying. Again, sated, they fell asleep in each other's arms.

Miles nudged her awake.

She opened her eyes slowly to see him standing over her. He was dressed in khaki shorts and a yellow T-shirt.

"Honey, they're bringing brunch over from the hotel. Want to get dressed?"

By the time she had freshened up, dressed in a pair

of printed cotton shorts and a white sleeveless blouse, the waiter had arrived with a wonderful tray-cart of food.

There was fresh orange juice, slices of mango, pineapple, kiwi fruit and strawberries, a covered hot dish of scrambled eggs, golden yellow with crisp bacon and tiny sausages, as well as Belgian waffles with whipped cream.

On a lower shelf of the cart Miles discovered fried chicken, slices of ham, and roast beef.

"My God, Leese, there's enough food here to feed a huge family." He poured coffee for them both, then handed her a warmed plate so she could help herself.

"Eat, eat, my love," he told her. His dark brown eyes smiled at her. She was loved by a wonderful man and she knew it. She would treasure these moments—these memories of love—for a lifetime.

At first she thought it was the overpowering perfume that Jen, her secretary, was wearing. Waves of nausea churned against her stomach wall. *Maybe it's the bacon I had for breakfast. Bacon has never bothered me before,* she thought.

"Jen, do you have any antacid tablets? My stomach is upset, feels queasy for some reason. Could be something I ate at breakfast."

The tablets helped a little and she was able to quell the nauseous feeling. A few days later the same condition hit her full force. Something told her to check her calendar. She remembered her period was due right after the Bermuda weekend. Uh-oh, it hadn't come. She realized that her breasts seemed full and sensitive. She decided to get a professional opinion.

* * *

Dr. Stackworth was pleased to see her, although a fleeting frown of concern passed over his face when he heard her reason for coming to see him.

"Of course there's a possibility that you may be pregnant, my dear. Obstetrics is not my specialty, but as your primary care physician, I'm going to refer you to a colleague who deals in high-risk pregnancies. I say high-risk only because of your recent cardiac surgery. She'll take good care of you and see you through this. By the way, congratulations to you and Miles."

Miles! She had to tell him right away. But first she would keep her appointment with Dr. Elizabeth Morton, the obstetrician she had been referred to.

"My God, Aleesa! Pregnant? God, no! I . . . I can't let you go through that! Oh God, no . . . your heart." His face broke out in beads of perspiration. He was horrified.

She tried to calm him.

"Miles, I've seen Dr. Stackworth and he sent me to a specialist who said I could have a normal pregnancy *and* delivery."

He was not convinced that all was well, and said so.

"I have to meet her and talk with her myself. It's only been a few months since your heart surgery. Leese, I should have been more careful . . . more considerate of you!" He slammed his hand against his forehead. "Dumb Miles, you're dumb, Miles Kittridge, dumb!"

"But, Miles, I thought you'd be happy to have a child of our own . . ."

He interrupted her, "I am, but I must be sure you're okay."

* * *

Miles and Aleesa were in Dr. Morton's office for a review of the plan for Aleesa's delivery.

Miles had been pleased with the confidence and assurance that the doctor showed. She was a small woman with wings of white that streaked along the edges of her otherwise dark hair. Her skin was a handsome sable brown, and her eyes always had a serious look. However, when she smiled, her no-nonsense look disappeared. Her patients always felt safe and special whenever Dr. Morton smiled.

Today, Miles and Aleesa relaxed when they saw the wonderful smile appear.

"Now, there's nothing to worry about. Your baby is of adequate weight and maturity, and I believe we can safely set the date for the C-section on August eleventh at 10 A.M."

Their faces wreathed in broad grins, Miles and Aleesa looked at each other.

"What? What is it?" Dr. Morton asked. "Something special about that day?"

"My birthday," Miles answered.

"Isn't that wonderful?" Aleesa said to the doctor, who agreed wholeheartedly.

Miles leaned toward his wife, placed his hand on her stomach in a gentle caress, and kissed her.

"Thanks, sweetheart."

"My pleasure," she grinned happily.

Thirty-one

Miles Lewis Kittridge III, later to be dubbed Trey, was born on a hot, sultry August morning. He was welcomed by three sets of grandparents.

Miles's father, Miles Sr., announced, "This baby looks exactly like Miles when he was born."

Boyd Howell countered, "Maybe he *looks* like his father, but I've already checked and he's got the long Howell toes!"

Everyone laughed. Then Grady Haskins said, "Well, Trey may look like Miles, and have the long toes of the Howells, but I'm sure you have all noticed that he has my daughter's red-brown hair!"

Each of the mothers shrugged at the proprietary attitudes of the men, as if to say, *Men!*

Two days later, Dr. Morton came into Aleesa's room. Miles was there. He had not left his wife and newborn son except to make a few phone calls.

Dr. Morton inquired, "How does it feel to have a brand-new son?" She was aware of the couple's problems and was pleased herself that there had been a successful, happy conclusion.

Miles's face sobered as he answered.

"Dr. Morton, there are not words in my vocabulary

to tell you how I feel." He stammered from deep emotion, "You have given me a priceless gift, a family of my own. Thank you, thank you."

"I'm delighted, you know that, Miles."

"But if it hadn't been for your skill and professionalism, none of this . . ." He waved his hand and gave Aleesa a loving look as words failed him.

"Only doing my job. Now, let's have a look at our new mother here."

After her examination she pronounced her decision. Aleesa could be discharged that afternoon. She asked "Will there be someone at home to help . . . give a hand?"

Both Aleesa and Miles looked at each other and laughed. "Doctor," Miles told her, "there are three sets of grandparents! Aleesa has drawn up a schedule. We're covered!"

"Then I don't have to worry. You'll be in safe hands."

After the doctor left with instructions for Aleesa to visit her office in another week, Miles let out a sigh of contentment.

"Leese, I never in this world, ever, thought I would be this happy. Do you know how much I love and admire you?" He bent over her as she lay comfortably stretched out in a reclining chair, and gently nuzzled her cheek. She turned her face to receive his kiss. His lips were warm and welcomed her response to his caress. He glanced over to the bassinet. His son was sleeping soundly. He couldn't believe it, the words still sounded strange to him. *My son.*

"Leese, I don't know how to say it, but . . ."

"Say what, Miles?"

"If I could say it everyday for a thousand years, I could never tell you how much I love you."

"I love you, too, Miles."

"You know, love, if it hadn't been for your courage, your strength of character . . ."

She could see his emotions flash across his face and she knew he was struggling to control himself. Her Miles, the strong, dependable man who supported, loved, inspired, and comforted her, was overwhelmed.

"Miles, look what love has done," she said, pointing to their child.

"For *us*, you mean, love. You know, honey, we trusted in our love and it has not failed us. We're stronger now, despite all the things that have happened. My accident, your heart problem . . ."

"You know, Miles," she interrupted him, "I can't imagine what my life would have been like if you hadn't come into it." She went on, "We found my family, thanks to your persistence, and now I can feel whole again. I've been able to feel connected to my past, a feeling that gives me the confidence I needed. Now you and I can give our son a real sense of belonging. He'll *never* have to worry about who he is."

She reached up with both arms and pulled her husband close. "Thank you, for everything," she whispered.

Trey's christening was a festive affair. Staci and Brendan were the baby's godparents, which pleased Lana and Boyd.

Everyone was waiting in the foyer of the church for the baptismal service to begin. There were several other young couples with their babies, grandparents, relatives, and godparents clustered around in several family groups.

All of the Kittridge family, aunts, uncles and cousins were present, along with Aleesa's parents and the Haskins' relatives. They were all waiting anxiously for the Howells to arrive.

"Did you give them directions, Aleesa?" her mother asked as she bounced her grandson in her arms.

"I spoke with Lana this morning," she said, checking her watch. "She said they were just leaving. Certainly should be here by now. I'll ask Miles to check."

"Miles?" Her husband, handsome and excited in a brand-new suit he had bought for the occasion, turned to his wife.

"Yes, honey, what can I do for you?"

"Would you check out in the church parking lot to see if the Howells have arrived?"

"Of course, right away!"

"Do I look okay, Mother?" Aleesa asked anxiously. She was wearing a sea-foam colored silk dress. Her hair was caught up in a French twist and her shoes were black pumps. She wore pearls and pearl earrings.

"You look beautiful, child. No one would ever know you had a baby six weeks ago," her mother said. "As far as I'm concerned, we're the most handsome family here."

"You're just prejudiced," Aleesa laughed.

"That's right, I am. Oh look, here's Miles! He found the Howells."

As she watched her biological family come toward her, Aleesa's heart swelled with love. She was so fortunate. After all these years, she had found her birth parents and her very own sister and brother, who had accepted her. Her mother, Lana, dressed very smartly in a gray silk suit, was walking beside a distinguished elderly man. He was a tall man. He had nut-brown skin coloring, with dark eyes that seemed to be noticing everything. His hair was close-cropped, a snow-white helmet in contrast to his unlined face. He was quite handsome, she thought, as Lana brought him nearer.

Lana came up to Aleesa and Miles, kissed them both, then turned to the stranger. She held on to his arm as she propelled him forward.

"Leese, my child, I want you to meet someone very special. He has traveled a long way to be here for this special day. This is Ambrose Miller, my father, your grandfather. Papa, this is Aleesa, your granddaughter." Aleesa was speechless. A grandfather!

Her grandfather reached for her and kissed her on both cheeks, in the continental style. "I'm happy to meet you, my child." His voice was soft and measured, as if his native language was strange to his own ears.

Quick introductions were made all around. Miles just beamed. "How wonderful!"

Boyd Howell told him later that he and Lana had planned earlier to send for her father a year ago when Lana's mother died. But with all the legalities and paperwork to be completed, they had just been able to get him to the States a few days ago.

After the ceremony ended, the entire family drove to Water's Edge for a sit-down luncheon. A catering service hired by Grady and Carol had set up a tent. The tables had white tablecloths and freshly cut fall flowers, yellow chrysanthemums, purple asters, and huge pink dahlias for the centerpieces. Blue and white ribbons cascaded from the center of the tent.

At the head table were all the grandparents, along with Aleesa and Miles. Grady had seen to it that a seat for Ambrose Miller was placed between Aleesa and Lana.

As host for the celebration, Grady also led the toasts to the happy couple and their son, sleeping in his bassinet, oblivious to all the excitement in his honor.

After he had completed the toast to family and relatives, he spoke again.

"Friends and family, I would be remiss if I did not

honor our special guest who has come a very long way to be with us on this special day. He is the patriarch of the family. Please, all, a very special warm welcome to my daughter's grandfather, Mr. Ambrose Miller!"

"Hear, hear," was echoed as chairs were scraped back to give the guest a standing ovation.

When the clapping subsided, Ambrose Miller stood and spoke.

"It has been many years since I stood on my native soil. I had vowed, many years ago, never to return to the country where I was born, but"—he cleared his throat and looked about at the faces before him—"many changes have taken place. Not only in my life, but in this country and to my family. This is a special day for me. I am proud of my children, my grandchildren, and I am especially proud of my great-grandson. Fortunate is the man who can look at the faces of his descendants. Today, I am such a man. Thank you."

When he sat down, his daughter and granddaughter each kissed him. His face beamed, and there were very few dry eyes at the gathering.

Aleesa and Miles decided to circulate among the tables to thank their guests for participating in their son's christening.

Grady saw them approach his table, so he got up from his seat and indicated that he wanted to speak with his daughter. He had been watching for an opportunity to do so.

"A minute, Leese?"

"Sure, Dad."

She linked her arm in his as they walked across the lawn to sit on a bench beside the wall at the edge of the water.

"I want you to know how happy I am for you, child."

"I know, Dad, it's been quite a day, hasn't it?" She sighed contentedly. "I owe so much to you and Mom."

"What we did was because we loved you, and for the joy you brought into our lives. You made us a family, my dear."

"I'm glad of that, Dad."

"Leese, honey, you know now that you have a remarkable heritage."

"Dad, I thought I'd burst with pride when I listened to my grandfather speak. To think that he gave up his country because he could not tolerate scorn or . . . indignity to be shown to his wife and child."

"Love like that is very rare," her father said. "What a legacy you have for your son. Guess we better get back to the guests."

"Guess so. Thanks, Dad, for everything."

"My pleasure." He hugged her and they returned to the tent. Her father was thinking, *With a grandfather like Ambrose Miller, no wonder my daughter has courage and persistence.*

Staci brought the baby out of the house.

"He woke up, has been fed and changed, and decided he wanted to be out here with his guests," Staci announced proudly. "So his godmother agreed. Here's Trey, everybody!"

Soon he was being cooed over by everyone. Miles rounded up family members for picture taking. "Leese, we have to have a picture of the four generations," he said.

"By all means, Miles. It will be something to treasure."

So they posed. Ambrose Miller, the great-grandfather, held Miles the Third. Lana and Aleesa stood on either side of the elderly man. Miles, Sr. knelt beside the chair. Everyone aahed as the picture was snapped.

The baby was taken back into the house because it

was getting chilly. Miles and Aleesa returned him to his bassinet and stood, arms around each other, looking down on the sleeping infant.

"Happy, hon?"

"Miles, if I were any happier I'd explode. I'll never forget this day. It's all come round full circle, meeting my grandfather on our son's christening day."

"And to think," he teased her, "all because we volunteered for Career Day."

"Because you were so fresh and bold, introducing yourself to an unsuspecting young woman, and then had the colossal nerve to propose marriage on our first date."

"Well, my dear, you know the old saying, 'Faint heart never won fair lady.' "

She retorted, "I always thought you lived by the adage, 'Strike while the iron is hot.' "

He nodded at her. "Oh my, yes, that too!" He gave her that tantalizing quirky grin that so endeared him to her and always melted her heart.

She reached up, put her arms around his neck, and kissed him. Then, arm-in-arm, they walked back outdoors into the late afternoon sun to rejoin their families and friends.

Thirty-two

"Dr. Howell, I presume?" Aleesa laughed and hugged her sister.

Staci responded with a wide grin. "Right. Take two aspirin and call me in the morning."

"I'm so proud of you, Staci."

"Thanks, Leese, I'm proud of me, too."

"Well, you have every right to be. Do you have an idea of where you'll do your internship?"

"Woodside General, in Connecticut. Bridgeport, that is."

"Not too far away," Aleesa commented.

"One reason I accepted it. Also, they have a first-rate residency program in OB/GYN."

"I'm so happy, Staci, that everything is going the way you want. And Brendan is graduating next week, right?"

"That's right. We'll all be out of the nest then. Did you know he wants to join the Peace Corps?"

"What do Boyd and Lana think of that idea?"

"They're not thrilled about it, but it's what *he* wants to do, so . . ."

"It's *his* life, right?"

Aleesa had never addressed her birth parents as Mom and Dad. They were her biological parents, she loved and admired them, but Carol and Grady, who had adopted her when she was five days old, were Mom and Dad to her. Legally, in the eyes of the law, they were her parents. The Howells understood.

Staci's long graduation ceremony finally over, family and guests were celebrating at the Howell home in Calderton. The two sisters were relaxing together in a gazebo that Boyd had built beside Lana's garden. They had the privacy they sought, a time to catch up with each other, but they could still see the party activities as the guests milled around, eating, drinking, and chatting with each other. The smell of Boyd's barbequed chicken, pungent and spicy, wafted through the air. Delicious whiffs tantalized the guests, who had their plates at the ready as they headed for the food spread out on long tables.

"The folks really put on a nice spread for you, Staci," Aleesa said, watching Boyd serve the guests.

"Dad loves to entertain. Mother, too. Glad they have lots of good friends—being 'empty nesters' will be a little easier for them."

Staci's cap of short brown curls bobbed as she shook her head, thinking of her residency choice.

"I had almost decided to settle for an internship here in Boston to be close to them, but I couldn't get what I really wanted."

"Don't worry, Staci. Miles can always fly you back and forth. You'll be able to get home easily, anytime."

"How is Miles's airline doing, anyway?" Staci asked.

"Sea Gull Airways is going great, I'm happy to say."

"Mother told me that you have been made a junior partner in the law firm. Congrats!"

"Thanks. I think Mr. Butterworth thought I was an asset to the firm after all. But I have to tell you, Staci, I could never have done it without the help of the grandparents. Always one of the folks willing to lend a hand taking care of Trey."

She spotted Miles in the group. He had their four-year-old son in tow. Staci followed her glance and saw the happy smile on Aleesa's face. They watched the pair walk toward them. Trey had inherited his mother's red-brown curls. His father's legacy, besides a slender build, included the dark, luminous, almost ebony-black eyes and a shy smile. The child was adored by his three pairs of grandparents, but Aleesa and Miles managed to keep their son from being spoiled by dealing firmly with any overindulgences. He was a lovable little boy as a result of their guidance.

"Here come my two main men," Aleesa remarked happily. "I can't believe all that has happened in four years."

Staci nodded in agreement. "You know how lucky you are, Leese?"

"I certainly do. How many people search and find their real parents? And I was a *very* lucky girl when I met Miles and fell in love with him."

"And don't forget the traumatic episodes that you both endured . . . his head injury and your heart surgery. You know, Leese, I can tell you, now I'm through med school, that was a highly experimental procedure that the cardiac specialists did on you."

"Glad I didn't know it at the time," Aleesa reflected.

"But you do feel well, don't you?"

"Like you said, Staci, I'm very lucky. I feel wonderful." Her face took on a sober look. She reached for her sister's hand.

"Staci, I always wondered . . . how did you feel when you first found out about me—having an older sister? Thank God we're close now, but I always wondered. What was it like to have someone you never knew even existed suddenly turn up and, well . . . take over as the oldest child?"

Staci rubbed Aleesa's hand. "To tell you the truth,

I tried to hide my feelings, but I was 'madder than a hatter'! Mother knew that I was and took me aside."

"What did she tell you?"

"She told me about losing you, how hard it was for her and Dad. She said the loss of her first child was horrible and it was ten years before I was born. She had despaired of ever having children. She explained that finally having me made her happy once again. She said that *I* gave her that hope . . . that happiness, and that no one could supplant that."

"She said that to you?"

"She said more, as I recall. She told me that for her and Dad to have you back in their lives, when they had been told you had died at birth, was almost overwhelming . . . hard to believe. She said"—Staci's voice took on a somber tone—"she said that she wanted me to share in their happiness, and I could do that by accepting you into the family by doing what only *I* could do."

"And that was?"

"Be a sister to you."

"What a wonderful woman," Leese said.

"Right. What a wonderful mother," Staci echoed.

Impulsively they hugged each other.

"We're two very fortunate girls to have such an unusual woman for our mother," Aleesa said.

They heard a deep baritone voice.

"Is this a private party or can anyone join in? Trey and I would like to offer our congratulations to the new doctor."

"Of course, Miles, join us." Aleesa moved to make room for them on the bench.

"For you, Aunt Staci," the little boy handed Staci a gift-wrapped package.

"Thank you, Trey. What is it?"

"Present for you," he lisped.

Staci tore away the colorful wrapping and held the gift up for everyone to see. It was a brass nameplate on a wooden desk plaque that read, STACI HOWELL M.D.

She kissed Trey, then Aleesa and Miles. "Thank you all. I'll treasure this always."

She took Trey by the hand. "Let's go show everyone what you gave me, okay?"

"Okay, let's show ev'body."

Miles and Aleesa watched the pair move into the crowd of well-wishers, showing the gift plaque, Staci accepting congratulations.

Aleesa put her arm through her husband's and held his hand.

"Staci was just reminding me of how lucky I am," she said.

He pulled her closer.

"I don't believe luck has had anything to do with it, my love. We love each other and we've both always trusted that our love for each other would see us through. And . . . it has. Luck is for gamblers. And love is for life. Don't forget that, defense counselor!"

She laughed. "I wouldn't dare, your honor."

Thirty-three

They sat inside the gazebo for a moment in quiet silence, absorbing the sights and sounds of their families around them.

Miles smiled at his wife, happy to share this special moment with her.

"Family is so important, isn't it?" he observed.

Aleesa agreed with him. "Yes, dear, it is."

"We're lucky to have wonderful families. Say"—he brightened the sober mood with a wide grin—"you'd never guess. I met someone I used to work with at Logan the other day. I was doing some contract negotiations and ran into a fellow named Arlen Gray."

"Arlen Gray?" The name was not familiar to her.

"You've never met him, honey, but I may have mentioned his name once or twice."

"I really don't remember. Who is he?"

"Aleesa, he's one of the smartest, hardest working employees WIN ever had. He was the flight supervisor that I worked under when I was flying jets for the company. We had a nice talk. He told me he was still with WIN but has been moved up to vice president in charge of purchasing new equipment. Not bad for a black man who started at the bottom as an airplane mechanic."

"I should say so. I'm impressed."

"He told me he had just left Connecticut, where he had signed a big contract for some new jet engines. Of course he'd heard about my leaving the company, and I told him all about Sea Gull Airways."

"Think he was impressed, Miles?"

"Aleesa, I believe he was. He seemed very interested. Wanted to know about it. So I told him about securing financing and all the other things besides the capital I had to line up to get started, things like the mechanics, equipment, hangar space, and the like. He asked about my aircraft and seemed to think I'd been wise in my choice of the British jets I'd purchased. He agreed with me that the BAE 14B-100 was a fine commuter plane. He said with their four jet engines, he was certain they would be adequate. I told him I was happy when I got my certificate from the Department of Transportation that my equipment was air-worthy and I could start my line."

"You know how proud of you I am, Miles. You had a dream and you've been able to fulfill that dream."

"Thanks, honey. I also showed Arlen Gray pictures of you and Trey. I'm proud of my little family. He told me I was a lucky guy to have such a family. Know what I told him?"

"What did you tell him?"

"I told him that you and Trey were better than I deserved."

"Oh, Miles, that's not true at all! We're the lucky ones!"

"I guess when you come right down to it, we're really very fortunate. I can't imagine my life without you and Trey."

"I know," Aleesa reflected. Then she said, "Miles, I've often wondered what your life would have been like had you stayed with WIN."

"Really don't know, honey. I love flying, always have

and always will. Guess it's in my blood," he said thoughtfully. "But to be honest with you, I don't know how much longer I would have been content—the long overseas flights, schedules to keep, living in hotels and out of suitcases. It was after I met you and fell head over heels in love with you that I really started to think about my future. I knew from the moment I saw you, a lovely young woman with such glorious hair and enchanting eyes—I was stunned. Leese, I knew at that moment, at that Career Day program, that you were special and would be important in my life."

She teased back, "Can't say I thought that much of you that first day. Seemed awfully fresh to me. But then"—her tone sobered—"there was something about your persistence, your self-confidence, your innate honesty that won me over. Not to mention your handsome good looks and that beautiful, vibrant body that you have and that I adore."

"Lady love, I'm at your mercy!" Miles quipped. "Keep talking like that and you've got me for life!" He looked at her loving face, her startling enchanting eyes, and kissed her. She responded, her lips soft and yielding as she accepted his caress.

"Maybe, Aleesa," he remarked after he had kissed her, "maybe it was the plane crash that helped me make up my mind to start a new career, do something I'd always wanted to do—have my own airline and my own business."

A tightly knit frown formed between her eyebrows as she stared at him.

"What are you talking about? Isn't that some price to pay for decision-making?"

He laughed. "Got you, didn't I?"

"No indeed. I got you," she snapped back. "Flat on your back, you couldn't escape me!"

They hugged each other.

"Girl, we've sure been through some tough times, haven't we?" he reflected.

"We have, but I think it's made us stronger, and we appreciate each other more."

"My mother said to me just the other day, we were talking about all the things that have happened to us, and she said, 'Steel tried by fire is strong and unyielding.' I think she's right. You and I have been tested, my sweet, and I don't think we can be found to be weak. We're a strong, deeply committed couple, right?"

"Right."

She was silent for a moment, as if thinking over what her husband had just said.

"Miles, I hope Trey will have the strength to overcome adversities."

"Not to worry, my dear. Trey's goin' to be 'the man'! With the strong legacy he has inherited, I've no doubt at all that our son is goin' to be able to handle whatever life hands him."

"I certainly hope so, Miles. We both know it can be hard."

"As I said before, both you and Trey are better than I deserve, and I'm proud of my little family." He pulled her closer to him. She welcomed him with open arms.

Aleesa knew she loved Miles not only for who he was, but for what he gave her. He was strong, purposeful, and considerate. When he made love to her, it was with tenderness and care. His gentle touch when his fingers caressed her aching breasts, eager for his touch, the fire that raced through her body when his lips met hers, the thrust of his demanding tongue as he probed the seductive sweetness inside her mouth, every nerve in her body would vibrate as a harp when the strings were plucked.

As her memory of her loving moments with her husband flickered in her mind like scenes from a movie, Aleesa sensed a deep response in her body. Her breasts tingled and, God help her, there was an unmistakable reaction in her body that she had not anticipated. It was Miles, he had changed her with his love. His love for her had lit a dormant spark that made her a real woman with desires, needs and wants that only he could give her. No other person on earth could fill that need. If she couldn't have it, she couldn't live, wouldn't want to live.

Thirty-four

Lynette Jarvis had not been so excited in months. Her new friend had invited her to spend the weekend with him at his parents' summer cottage at Oak Bluffs down on Martha's Vineyard. She expected there would be lots of parties and a chance to meet new people. She welcomed a fresh change in her life.

Her friend, Dexter, had said that Friday night they were invited to a party on a yacht. Some friends of his from Washington, D.C., had just sailed their yacht up from the Potomac and were celebrating the opening of the summer season with a party on the boat which would be anchored in the harbor.

As far as Lynette was concerned, the bleak days following her divorce should be over by now, and she was ready to move on with her life. There could be nothing more exciting than cocktails and hors d'oeuvres on a sleek, gorgeous yacht where she might meet sophisticated and congenial people. She looked forward to the weekend.

Her host and hostess, the boat owners, were very warm and welcomed her and Dexter. Dexter knew some of the guests and introduced Lynette. So many of them, men and women, were doctors, lawyers, and CEOs that Lynette was almost embarrassed to identify herself as vice-president of human services at her company. Even her host was a foreign service dignitary, and his wife was dean of the school of education at a historically black college. Her own achievements seemed small in comparison to the others. She thought, *I'll probably never see these people again, so what the heck, I'll put on a good face and enjoy myself.*

It was soon apparent that her escort, Dexter, was enjoying himself a little too much. He had started drinking the moment they had arrived on board, had finally passed out, had been dragged to a lounge chair on the upper deck, and lay in a drunken stupor. When Lynette found him, she was disgusted with him . . . and with herself. Why did she have to pick such *losers?*

She searched out the host and hostess and made her apologies.

"Oh, don't worry about old Dex. We'll take care of him," the host said. "We've known him for years. Is there anything we can do for you?" his wife asked.

"You're very kind," Lynette said, "but I'll just slip off and take a taxi. Thanks so much for your hospitality."

"You're most welcome. Come aboard any time. We'd love to have you."

Lynette had not missed the looks of pity on their faces when she left the yacht. Her pride was bruised as she ran down the gangplank to the pier and a waiting taxi. She asked the taxi driver to return for her at eight the next morning to take her to the airport.

"I want to get the first plane off the island," she told him.

"On Saturday, that's nine-thirty."

"Please pick me up at eight."

She had anticipated an exciting weekend, and here she was stuck with a lush, an alcoholic who didn't even recognize that he was one. She had practically maxed out her credit card buying a chic designer dress, plus some summer slacks outfits and a bathing suit to help her find someone new with whom to share her life.

She lay in bed in the cottage that night and reviewed her situation. How could she know that her husband, Jerry Caldwell, had problems with his sexual identity? The worst part was that she couldn't tell anyone about his sexual proclivities. She would look like a fool not to have known about his inclinations before she married him. The whole situation nearly drove her crazy. Just like her not to discover that Dexter had a problem with alcohol. Why did she make such poor choices when it came to men? Why couldn't she find someone stable . . . like Miles Kittridge, for example? She finally fell asleep with Miles on her mind.

"Leese, I've got to fly down to Hyannis today," Miles told her at breakfast.

"How come?"

"I have to meet with officials of the mechanics' union. They are threatening to strike—want a raise in pay."

"I'm sorry, Miles, I thought things were going well."

"Oh, don't worry, pet, these things happen."

"Are you going to be able to meet their demands?" she worried.

"I'm going to try to negotiate."

"Think they'll be willing to do that? Some unions are really tough."

"I believe they will. I'm going to offer them stock in the company instead of a wage increase . . . also an increase in their health benefits."

"And you feel they will accept that package?"

"I'm counting on it. I've never known a blue-collar

worker who didn't appreciate having a vested interest in the company he works for. It makes for a better, more committed employee as well."

"I wish I could come with you, Miles, but I have a case I'm working on and really can't spare any time away from it. The Cape is so nice this time of year."

"I know, honey. I would like that, too, but perhaps soon we can squeeze in a weekend down on the island. Should check on the house, see how the builder is doing. Didn't he promise we'd be able to be in there by the middle of July—only a few more weeks?"

"He did say that, but it seems there are always delays," Aleesa fretted.

"Look, honey," Miles had gathered up his briefcase and overnight bag and stopped at the kitchen door to the garage to kiss his wife good-bye. "I should be home by Saturday sometime, but I'll call you tonight at any rate. Love you, babe."

She heard him raise the garage door, then she heard the car engine turn over. Miles backed out of the garage and blew the horn good-bye as she waved at him from the window.

She suddenly realized that this was the first time since Trey had been born that they had been separated.

She sighed deeply and prepared to leave the house herself to get to the law office. Trey was already in nursery school and would be cared for by the babysitter, a high school student who would be with him until Aleesa got home.

Lynette Jarvis was able to secure a standby seat on the plane and soon landed safely in Hyannis. She picked up her car at the Hyannis airport. *Damn,* she thought, *now what am I going to do?* She didn't feel like driving back to Boston to her empty apartment. She had noticed the paper said that Luther Vandross was appearing that night at the Cape Cod Melody Tent. Maybe she would take that in, have a quiet brunch at the hotel Sunday morning, and leave before one o'clock in the afternoon to beat the traffic over the Sagamore Bridge.

She was able to get a room at a hotel near the airport and she checked in, optimistic that her weekend might still yield some surprises.

"I'm so glad that you agreed to have dinner with me tonight," Miles told Lee Marcus, the union officer in charge of negotiating the package Miles had proposed.

"No problem. The sooner we can wrap things up, the better, I always say," the man smiled affably.

"I'm delighted that your men saw the merit in the package, and I want to thank you for your support. Couldn't have done it without your help."

"We want this airline to succeed. It's our bread and butter, provides a decent living to those of us who want to live and raise our families on the Cape."

A waiter appeared to take their orders.

"What will you have, Lee? Dinner is on me."

"I've heard that the prime rib here is excellent."

"It is, sir," the waiter said.

"You know, it's been a long day and negotiating is hard work. Prime rib, medium rare, sounds good to me," Miles said.

"Me, too. Only make mine an end piece, well done, if you can," his guest told the waiter.

Thirty-five

By the end of the dinner meeting, each man was satisfied with the progress he had made. They shook hands and said good night with high hopes that the union membership would agree with the contract negotiations.

Miles saw the union official to his car and returned to the lobby of the hotel. From the nearby lounge and bar area he heard a jazz band. He thought he might stop in and listen for a few minutes, then he remembered he had not called Aleesa as he had promised.

He went to a pay phone in the lobby, and with the seductive sounds from the band, he dialed home.

"Hello?" Aleesa's voice answered.

Miles closed the door of the booth to shut out the music.

"Hi, babe," he said cheerfully.

"Hi yourself, Miles. How did everything go?" she wanted to know.

"Very, very well, I'm glad to say. As a matter of fact, I've just finished dinner with one of the union officials. It's been an all-day session, but I think he and I ironed out most of the details tonight."

"That sounds good."

"Yes, and once the contract is approved by the union membership, we'll be all set."

"You must be very tired, Miles."

"Well, I am. It's been, like I said, a long day, but I'm pleased with the outcome. I'm really too tired to fly home tonight."

"You shouldn't try to, Miles. Get a good night's rest."

"I think that's the best idea, Leese. I should be home by noon tomorrow at the latest. How's Trey?"

"Oh, he's fine, misses you and . . . so do I."

"Well, that's good to hear. Love you, Leese. See you tomorrow."

He bounded out of the telephone booth feeling extremely fortunate. He had everything he wanted in life: a beautiful, loving wife, a healthy, adorable son, and a business of his own that promised to do well. Dame Fortune was smiling on him.

He walked from the lobby to go into the lounge and bumped into a young lady coming toward him around the corner.

"Oh, please excuse me, so sorry," he mumbled. "Lynette! Lynette Jarvis!" He had not recognized his childhood friend at first in the subdued lighting of the room. He put out his hand to steady her.

"Miles?" She peered at his face in the dimly lit room. "Miles Kittridge? Is that you?"

"Sure is. Girl, you look good!"

"Well, you look good yourself, Miles."

They hugged each other.

Miles said, "Come on back to the lounge. Let's have a drink and catch up with each other."

"Okay. This band is pretty good. I've been sitting here by myself, listening to them. I never expected to run into anyone I knew."

"You never know who you'll run into here on the Cape," he said. "What are you doing down here, business or pleasure?"

He noticed how beautiful she looked. She had always had an enticing figure, and the Donna Karan number that she had splurged on accentuated her very attractive body. She wore her hair in a sleek, severe cut which called attention to her pert, pixielike face. Gone was the tomboy rambunctious girl next door with whom he had grown up. Lynette Jarvis was a lovely young woman, he noticed.

"Buy me a drink, Miles, and I'll tell you all about it," she said.

He signaled the barmaid and ordered their drinks, a gin and tonic for him and a rum and coke for her.

They were quiet for a moment, then both spoke at once. "Lynette—"

"Miles—"

Then Miles said, "Go ahead, Lynette. What were you about to say?"

Their drinks arrived and the awkward moment passed.

Lynette absentmindedly twirled her swizzle stick around in her glass. "I must tell you that your wedding was certainly one of the most beautiful I've ever attended."

"It was a great day for us, that's for sure."

"Yes, and it was especially so when you both stood by the wall and released those two white doves into that bright blue September sky, well I'll never forget that sight. It was breathtakingly beautiful!"

"It was Aleesa's idea. She said she wanted to create a memory and I believe she did."

"I know I'll never forget it."

Lynette looked at him for a moment.

"Miles, how have you been after your dreadful accident and all?"

"I'm fine, kiddo. Never felt better."

"And Aleesa? Mother told me she had heart surgery before your son was born. She doing all right?"

"Oh, thank God, yes. She's fine, and so's our son, Trey."

"That's wonderful," she said.

"I'd heard you relocated after your divorce. I was sorry to hear about that. But now that you are back in the area, you'll have to visit us. I know Aleesa would be glad to see you."

"Since Jerry and I divorced, Miles, it seems nothing is going right for me."

"I'm sorry, Lynette." He clicked his glass against hers. "Here's to old friends and better times ahead."

"I'll surely drink to that," she said. "You asked me how come I'm here at the Cape. I came down with a friend, hoping for an exciting weekend over at Martha's Vineyard. We were invited to a dockside party on one of his friend's yachts. But my 'friend' turned out to be a dyed-in-the-wool alcoholic. I sure can pick out the worst men on the planet," she sighed.

"Don't talk like that, Lynette," Miles tried to console her. "You have a lot to offer, and when the right man comes along . . ."

"I'll be old and gray, looking at him through my bifocals."

"Don't talk such nonsense. You're a beautiful, attractive, very smart young woman. You've run into some bad luck, that's all. And that's not your fault. I've always considered you one of my best friends."

Friend, yeah right, she said to herself. *Never knew I was in love with you all these years.*

"Miles, would you order me another drink?" she asked.

"Sure." He signaled the barmaid.

"Another round, please, miss," he told her.

"The band is real good, isn't it?"

Miles observed, "Can't tell you when's the last time I've been to a nightclub. But tonight I really feel relaxed. Good company, good music." He tipped his glass in her direction. "Want to dance? This music is too good to waste."

"You know I love to dance, Miles," she said, rising from her seat and allowing him to lead her to the dance floor. "This is like old times," she murmured as she settled into his arms.

Miles was surprised at how naturally they fit together. As teenagers, growing up next door to each other, they had often practiced together, taught each other new dance steps. He noticed how much he still enjoyed dancing with her. For one thing, she felt comfortable in his dance embrace, and the other, she followed his dance movements very well. But then, he remembered, she always had. Both were reluctant to separate when the music ended. They seemed to hesitate in moving back to their table. Finally, they slowly returned, the magic spell broken. Miles spoke first when they sat down.

"That was great, Lynette. You're still a remarkable dancer, and you're still a good-looking woman."

"You mean, after all these years?"

"You said it, I didn't," he bantered. "For one thing, you still have the moves you had as a teenager," he added.

He glanced at his watch.

"Getting late, Lynette."

"Right, it is."

"Let me settle up the bar tab and I'll see you to your room. Okay?"

"Be fine, Miles. I'm in 728, on the seventh floor."

"How 'bout that! *I'm* in 740, down the hall."

He paid the bill and they walked together toward the bank of elevators. Anyone looking at them would assume they were a couple. Miles's right hand cupped Lynette's elbow in a protective manner as he led her into the elevator.

Thirty-six

"Can you come in for a minute, Miles? It's been so long since we've had a chance to talk. Remember when we were kids, you used to help me sell all my Girl Scout cookies?" She smiled at him.

"Even if I had to get my folks to buy all the extras you couldn't sell?" he said.

"Yes, and remember us sneaking over to Logan Airport so you could watch the planes taking off and landing?" She gave him the identification card to slip into the slot to open the door. "You always were in love with airplanes, Miles."

They entered her room and Lynette slipped off her high heels, throwing her handbag on the bed.

"Sit down, Miles, you don't have to go far now. You're just down the hall, almost home, as a matter-of-fact. I'll never forget, Miles," she reminisced, "the day you told your folks you had signed up for flying lessons."

He laughed at the memory. "I thought my mother would have a fit! 'You can't even drive a car and you're talking about flying—up in the sky!' she said."

"Your father agreed, though."

"I think Dad knew me well enough to see just how determined I was, so he had to give his permission. He realized it was what I wanted."

"You're very lucky, Miles, to have been able to get what you wanted. It seems to me that I've never had . . . what I wanted. Maybe I've always wanted the wrong things." She moved over to the liquor storage cabinet and took out a nip of rum. "Want anything?" she asked him. "Please say yes. I don't want to drink alone."

Miles saw a flash of despair flicker in Lynette's eyes. He answered, feeling sorry for her, "Well, since I've been drinking gin, I'll have one for the road. I'm flying home tomorrow at noon and I'll need a clear head."

"You were always the one with a clear head, Miles. You always knew what you wanted. Not like me, addle-brained half the time. Didn't know what I wanted," she repeated.

She handed him his drink and sat down beside him at the foot of the bed. She sipped at her drink. She gave him a steady look. He wondered what was coming.

"Miles, you know you are my oldest friend. I mean, I've known you all my life. We could always tell each other . . . things. Probably because we were only children."

"Guess so, Lynnie."

"I've never"—she drew a deep breath—"I've never told *anyone*, not even my parents, about me and Jerry . . . why our marriage failed. We . . . we were very happy at first, our sex life was adequate. Jerry was not overly excited . . ."

"Lynnie, you don't have to tell me this," Miles interrupted her litany.

"But I want to. I need to tell someone. I've kept it bottled up all these years, and if I don't speak of it, I'm going to explode one day!"

She sipped more of her drink. Miles could see she needed the alcohol to bolster her courage.

"Like I said, Jerry was always tender, kind, and considerate of me, but there was something missing, I could tell. There was no fire, no flames of passion that I had expected from the man I thought I loved. Then"—she hesitated, as if reluctant to go on—"we'd been married for only six months when he started coming home late. He had a meeting in town that was running late, or his work schedule had been interrupted and he had to work late to finish up some last-minute details for his boss. And, finally, he began to stay out all night. His office is in Burlington."

"He works with computers, doesn't he?" Miles asked.

"Yes, with a company that's working on genetic codes or something like that."

"I imagine that's stressful," Miles opined.

"Guess so. Anyway, whenever he stayed out all night, he'd usually call me from one of the hotels out on Route 128 to let me know where he was."

Miles waited for her to continue, knowing that the confession was difficult for her. Sympathetically, he put his arm around her.

"I . . . I thought he was having an affair, Miles. I was certain of it. In fact, after he'd stayed away several nights, I confronted him."

"You did?"

"Yes, I did, and he admitted that he was—having an affair, that is. So I had to know more. I asked him with whom, and he said it was no one that I know. I kept insisting that he tell me. Miles, he finally told me that he was truly in love for the first time in his life—with a man!"

She sobbed openly then. "Miles, another man! How come I didn't *know*? What was wrong with me that I married a . . . a gay man? Tell me," she pleaded, "what's wrong with me?"

"There's nothing wrong with you, Lynnie. Nothing

at all," he tried to reassure her. She threw her arms around him and sobbed. Her slender body shook from the depths of her sorrowful pain.

Miles felt sorry for her. He had known her since they were kids playing together in a sandbox. He was distressed by her pain.

"Hold me, Miles. Please hold me," she sobbed into his chest. For a moment Miles was stunned. He did as she asked. He held her. "Don't cry, Lynette, don't cry," he said softly. "Please, don't cry."

"What's wrong with me that I couldn't tell, couldn't see Jerry's inclination? I never dreamed . . . oh, Miles . . ."

"Not your fault, Lynnie." He kissed her forehead, trying to comfort her, ease her pain. She held on to him like a frightened drowning victim. He felt so sorry for her. He kissed her cheek as her tears streamed out of her eyes. He'd never seen her like this. She started to gasp for breath, and her grief seemed to border on hysteria. Her anguish was tormenting her.

Miles tried to calm her.

"Let me get you a glass of water," he said, and started to reach for the carafe on the table.

"No, don't leave me. Oh, please, Miles, don't leave me. Stay with me tonight. Please don't . . . don't"— she hiccupped—"don't leave me, Miles. I need you. You're my friend, the only friend I have. Oh, please stay!"

The sight of the near-hysterical woman, her makeup smudged, tears furrowing the makeup on her face, and alcohol evidently clouding her thinking, moved Miles. This was not the self-assured Lynette Jarvis he had grown up with. What should he do? How could he leave her in the state she was in? How could he stay? He certainly didn't belong there. Nor did he want to be found there. What should he do?

Luckily, the room had an automatic coffee maker with packets of instant coffee. He filled the coffee maker with water and put the instant coffee in a mug. He forced Lynette to stand up. He removed her dress and her stockings.

"Oh, Miles, you're so good to me. Oh, thanks, Miles." Her speech was slurred by now, and she could hardly stand. He went into the bathroom, wrung a face cloth out in cold water, and grabbed a negligee from the bathroom. He made Lynette put on the robe. All the while she was trying to take her bra off.

"No, Lynette. No, I said!" he shouted at her. He washed her face vigorously and turned back the coverlet. He made her sit on the side of the bed and drink the coffee.

"It's hot, hot," she protested.

"You need it," he told her. "Drink!"

"Aren't you goin' sleep with me, Miles?" she slurred. "I need . . . need a real man tonight. Please, not a homo or a drunk. Please, Miles, you're a real man."

"No, Lynette," he answered, "I will not sleep with you, but I'll stay until you fall asleep. All right?"

"Aw right," she mumbled. "Love you, Miles . . . good man, Miles. Aleesa is . . . lucky woman. Should have married me . . . not Aleesa, Miles, shoulda . . ." She dozed off.

Miles put out the lights, left the nightlight on in the bathroom, and quietly closed the door behind him.

When he got to his room, he called the front desk for an early wake-up call.

What a narrow escape, he thought. *I never knew.*

Thirty-seven

Miles checked out of the hotel at six-thirty the next morning. He had coffee and a bagel while his Cessna 400 was being readied for takeoff. Thank God he had his flight plan registered and could leave as soon as his plane was prepared.

He thought about Lynette Jarvis, her problems, and how she had wanted to seduce him. As a teenager, Lynette had more boyfriends than she knew what to do with. Too bad she chose Jerry Caldwell. He hoped now she was all right after last night, but she was a grown woman. He had his own problems to think about.

What would he tell Aleesa? How could he tell her of his narrow escape? Would she believe that nothing had happened? She always had a slight suspicion where Lynette was concerned.

He thought about his marriage. How lucky he was. Both he and Aleesa were tuned into each other's hopes and dreams. Aleesa wanted to be a partner in the prestigious law firm where she worked, and he encouraged her in her dream. He was happy to be in the business he loved. They were both aware of the worries and stresses each of them faced. Even better was the fact that each of them admired the other's talents and skills. Miles marveled at the way his wife approached her legal work, and she admired his management skills that had made his commuter airline the success it was.

Aleesa delighted in giving unusual little surprises, too, like the birthday cake she created for him in the shape of a commuter plane with SEA GULL AIRWAYS inscribed on the fuselage. He hadn't wanted to cut the cake.

He wanted nothing more in this world than to make Aleesa happy. It scared him when he realized how close he could have come to losing his whole world.

He walked around the plane to make his visual inspection, climbed aboard, checked the switches on his instrument panel, and radioed his readiness to the control tower.

He arrived at Logan and was on his way home, all within the hour. As he drove he thought of the near miss, the devastating episode with Lynette.

He hugged Aleesa as if he dare not let her go.

"Honey, I'm *so* glad to be home. So glad. Had an awful experience."

Surprised, his wife looked at him.

"I thought you said that everything went well. That's what you told me last night, Miles."

"Oh, my union business went very well. I'm very pleased with that. It was something else that happened to me."

She looked more closely at him then and saw the troubled look on his face. "I can see that you're upset. What on earth happened?"

"Lynette Jarvis," he said. "That's what happened." He sat down abruptly and put his head in his hands.

Aleesa joined him on the couch.

"What about Lynette?"

"Ran into her at the hotel I stayed at last night."

"Well, that was nice, wasn't it? An old friend. How is she?"

"Turned out to be anything but nice. It was right after I had phoned you. I was feeling so upbeat, the union thing almost settled, I was coming home to you and Trey. There was a little combo playing in the lounge and I had decided to listen for awhile, have a drink before going up to my room."

"And?" Aleesa prompted.

"That's when I ran into her."

"She was alone?"

"Yeah. Said she'd been invited over to the island for the weekend. But it seems her date turned out to be a first-class drunk, so she ditched him and flew into Hyannis."

"If I know Lynette, she really was upset."

"She was upset. But, Leese, it got worse, much worse."

"What do you mean, worse?"

Miles got up. "Do we have any hot coffee?"

"Sure. I made a pot this morning. I'll get a cup for you. Thought you might want some."

"That's all right. I can get it. Would you like a cup?"

"Yes, that would be nice."

They both went into the kitchen. Miles poured a steaming hot mug for each of them.

Aleesa perched on a stool and placed her mug on the counter to cool. She waited for her husband to finish his story. She had an inkling of what may have happened, but she knew he would tell her.

Miles was pacing back and forth around the kitchen.

"Like I was saying, it got worse. I think I had two gin and tonics—you know I don't believe in drinking when I'm going to fly the next day—and Lynette had two rum and Cokes. Of course I don't know whether or not she had been drinking before we met, but she did seem to be sober. Anyway, we danced a couple of times . . . the music was real good."

"So," Aleesa said, "I can tell already that something went wrong. What happened?"

Miles stopped pacing. He looked at his wife. "Aleesa, sometimes I think I can be so thick, so dumb . . . I *never* in God's green world thought *anything* could go wrong. I should have known when I escorted Lynette to her room. Turns out she was on the same floor that I was . . . was only polite to see her to her door, never thinking . . ."

"But Lynette was thinking, wasn't she?"

"How do you know?"

"Buster, that girl has always wanted you. Didn't you know that? I did."

"But . . . I never dreamed. I always thought of her as a sister, *never* any other way! You don't sleep with your sister!"

"She was all over you, wasn't she?"

Miles nodded. "Like white on rice." He hated the picture.

"So what did you do?"

"I suddenly realized that she was very drunk. So, I made some coffee, made her drink it, and put her to bed. She literally begged me to sleep with her, Leese! Begged me! She was crying all over the place, saying she had made poor choices. Told me that Jerry, her ex-husband, turned out to be gay. She kept saying that I was the only real man she ever knew and that she had always loved me. Honey, I tell you it was awful! I checked out of the hotel at six-thirty the next morning. Couldn't leave there fast enough. I sure hope our paths don't cross anytime soon."

"She probably won't remember if you do see her."

"But what if she does? She's bound to be embarrassed."

"Tell her you saw her to her room and said good night."

"But what if she remembers how she acted, tried to come on to me?"

"All you have to do is stick to your story," she said in a sly tone of voice, her head tilted to the side as she peered at him. "Your story is true, isn't it, buster, my boy?" she teased him, a wide grin on her face.

"You know it is, Aleesa. You do trust me, don't you?"

"With my life."

"That's all that matters to me," he said as he put his arms around her, tilting her face toward his to kiss her. It was a deep and loving embrace that reaffirmed their commitment to each other.

"You always trust the one you love," she whispered in his ear.

"I think, my love, the song goes 'You always *hurt* the one you love.' "

"Now none of that," Aleesa murmured. She had her husband back where he belonged, safe, in her arms.

Stability had been restored in her family, and it was the trust they had in each other that had put it there.

"Trey is over at Mom and Dad's house. Dad is taking him sailing today." Then she looked at him, impishly. "How would you like to keep an appointment with me . . . in our bedroom?"

"My love, you do have the most exciting ideas. Lead on!" Miles said, unbuttoning his shirt and tie as he walked down the hall with his wife.

"I'm so glad to be home," Miles confessed, relieved that his wife understood what had happened. How fortunate he was to have the love of a woman like Aleesa.

"Where you belong," Aleesa responded.

Adding actions to her words, she helped him shed his jacket and shirt. Then she ran her fingers over his chest to stroke the silky mat of dark hair. Miles moaned with desire as he in turn peeled Aleesa's robe from her shoulders. Her tawny skin gleamed like pure silk in the morning sunlight streaming into their bedroom.

Never, Miles realized, had this woman, his wife, looked more beautiful, more alluring to him. Her red-brown hair fanned out like wild wheat on the white pillow beneath her head, and her enchanting eyes bewitched him. He knew she watched him step out of his trousers and fling away his underwear. Then he approached, aroused and impassioned, as she lay waiting.

His fingers moved slowly over her breasts. Aleesa felt flaming tips of fire wherever he touched. She responded by arching her body upward and placing her arms around his neck. She wanted him closer, but Miles was content to continue his exploration of her body. His fingers traced the length of her legs, her soft inner thighs, her feet, and returned to cup each mound of her lovely breasts. His touch increased her yearning, and she responded to his caresses with soft whimpers. She wanted more from Miles . . . needed more, and when she began to gasp with desire and longing, the way she hoarsely repeated his name made him realize that he alone had the awesome power to grant her wish and appease her need.

"Leese, Leese, my own love, it's been so long. Too long. Let me love you." His voice failed.

"Yes, yes Miles!" she hissed between clenched teeth. She could not say more because her husband silenced her with his mouth. His tongue circled hers as he tasted and savored her honeyed sweetness.

"God," he murmured into her ear as he moved his mouth to caress her ear's circles with his tongue. "Never knew I could love a woman the way I love you, Leese. You're mine forever and I want you to know that. Say you're mine forever. Say it, my darling, my sweetness," he pleaded.

She whispered, "I'm yours forever, Miles." Her breath came in gasps, "Always and . . . forever."

His response to her almost took her breath away. With a sure thrust he crushed her to him as she accepted his ardor with a responding cry that came from the depths of her very soul.

She curled her body into his then, skin to skin, thrumming heart to heart, her legs and feet aligned along his muscular suppleness that delighted her. Their bodies had been fused as one by the white-hot heat ignited and fed by the soaring need they had for each other.

Thirty-eight

It had been a long, eventful day for Miles. The commuter flight to Portland, Maine, had gone well and he was pleased. He could hardly wait to get home to Aleesa and tell her all about it. There was one more special occurrence that he had to tell her about.

After dinner he played with Trey until Aleesa said it was their son's bedtime. After settling their son for the night, Miles followed his nightly ritual of checking the house—doors, windows, appliances, the security system, before he moved down the corridor to their bedroom. As he neared the bedroom wing of the house, he could smell the soft, alluring fragrance of Aleesa's after-shower body lotion. He smiled to himself as he felt his body quicken in anticipation. The clean, enticing odor stimulated him, and he quickly shed his clothing as he strode into their sanctuary.

Aleesa smiled warmly at him over a magazine she was reading. Her emerald-green eyes invited him, and when he saw the way her hair cascaded around her shoulders, he groaned, "Be with you as soon as I get rid of this travel grime."

He threw his clothing down on a chair and hurried into the bathroom. A few minutes later he bounded out wearing white pajama pants. His skin was damp and cool to Aleesa when she opened her arms to him. He framed her face with both hands and kissed her.

"Ah-h-h, home at last," he breathed into her ear. "Been waiting for this all day."

"Long day, Miles?" Aleesa asked as she wove her fingers through the soft, silky mat of curls on his chest.

He moaned into her hair. "Sure was, but it is a good run, Boston to Portland. Had almost a full planeload to Portland and a good number returning to Boston this afternoon. Not bad for a new commuter line, I'd say."

"So, you're satisfied."

"Yup, I am. But let me tell you who I ran into today."

"Who?" Aleesa asked as she continued to run her fingers across his chest.

"Lynette Jarvis."

Aleesa bolted upright. "You saw *who?*"

"Lynette. I was on my way to do some flight business and as I went inside the terminal, I saw someone I knew. Pete Warren. Remember him? He's the guy that was with me when we crashed in Iceland."

He pulled Aleesa back down on the bed, folded her soft, supple body close, and continued to talk, his chin resting on top of her head. Aleesa closed her eyes and listened as he spun out the stunning news.

"I do remember Pete. How was he?"

"Just fine. I said, 'Pete! What are you doing in Maine?' Last I heard he was still flying for WIN. We were glad to see each other, hugging, slapping each other on the back, and he told me that he had quit the airline freight company, that now he was working in insurance, that he and his wife were in Portland to attend an insurance seminar."

"Lynette?"

"Right. He said, 'My wife just stopped in the gift

shop—oh, here she is now.' Honey, I almost choked when I saw Lynette coming toward us."

"What happened?"

"We both spoke at once. 'Lynette,' I said, and she said, 'Hi, Miles!' Pete looked at both of us. 'You two *know* each other?' 'Pete, we grew up together, we were next-door neighbors,' I explained to him. 'We were raised almost like brother and sister. Our mothers were best friends.' Then Lynette gave me a hug. 'How have you been, Miles? It's been such a *long* time since we've seen each other.' "

"She said *that*?"

"Yes, she did. And I said, 'I've been fine, Lynette. And look at you, looking great and married to one of my old friends, my copilot friend. Congratulations to both of you.' "

"So, evidently the Cape episode is in the past. How did she really seem? Happy?"

"Yes, she did seem happy, and I noticed Pete seemed to be very much in love with her and she with him. You can tell when couples are on the same wavelength, I think."

"I guess you really did have an eventful day."

"Um-m-m, right," Miles said softly. "Now, it's time for an eventful night. I want to make love to my beautiful wife." He nuzzled her ear as she settled into his embrace. He kissed her, a long, satisfying sealing of their lips until they were each breathless.

"Oh God, you taste so good!" Miles continued to lavish her sweet body with searing kisses that made Aleesa's skin quiver. She knew she was helpless, melting, dissolving into a state of nothingness because of this man who was life itself to her.

"Miles," she breathed as his lips sought the delicate, rose-tinted peaks of her breasts, first one then the other, until Aleesa thought she would not be able to live with the blazing fire that burned within her. She was unaware of what she was doing, but sensed her fingers pushing and pulling at the pajama trousers that impeded her search for the treasure she wanted.

Miles swiveled his hips to release them from the bonds of his pajamas. He hissed in utter anguish as he felt her delicate fingers caress his throbbing desire. He kicked the restraining trousers to the foot of the bed and pulled her nightgown over her head.

Skin to skin, heart to heart, they aligned their bodies.

"My beautiful one, I've loved you since the moment I first saw you," Miles whispered.

"Miles, love me now, please, love me now. Don't ever stop or I'll die," she pleaded.

He ran his fingers over her body as if creating harmonious music from a delicate instrument.

Her response was to cling to him, to clutch him as if she feared to let go. She whimpered in ecstasy as his fingers sought the secret moist haven that quickened soft as a butterfly's wing when he touched it.

Soon their white-hot passion knew no bounds, and his hoarse cry of release mingled with hers and they were both hurled to heights neither had ever envisioned.

Sated, they lay in each other's arms as their heartbeats slowed to a normal cadence and their body temperatures cooled. Miles pulled the sheet and blanket over them as they recovered from their tumultuous ascent.

Aleesa curled close to Miles, her head resting on his chest. He pushed her moist, tangled hair away from her damp face. He kissed her closed eyelids.

"Sleep, my lady. Our love is true and will be ours forever."

"Um-m-m, Miles, you always say the nicest things," Aleesa whispered sleepily.

" 'Sposed to—you know that."

They slept, secure in each other's arms. They both knew that the trust and love they shared would be theirs always—no matter what circumstances they might ever have to face. They had each other.

Epilogue

The Thanksgiving season was approaching. Aleesa decided to visit her grandfather, Ambrose Miller, at her birth parents' home in Calderton. She wanted to spend some time with him.

The old man, now nearing his ninetieth birthday, remained spry and agile. His mind was vigorous and alert. He was curious about everything and was planning to visit his remaining family member in Georgia, a sister several years younger than he, after the holiday.

"Pleased that you wanted to come see me and visit with me, granddaughter," he told Aleesa.

"You are a family treasure, Grandfather, and, of course, I want to be with you as much as I can."

He nodded his head in agreement and his dark eyes showed a twinkle that assured Aleesa that indeed, he wanted to be with her.

"Yes," he observed, looking at her, "you have your grandmother Annaliese's hair and eyes, there's no doubt of that, but I reckon from what your folks have said you got your stubborn, independent nature from me. I got it from *my* folks."

He chuckled at his own comment, a deep, throaty sound.

"You know, I always believed in myself. I figured

there were plenty of folks as *good* as me, but none better than me!"

"I've always had pride in myself, too, Grandfather, even though for thirty-two years I didn't know who my real family was, where I had come from, or who I belonged to. Now"—she smiled at him and patted his leathery hands—"what a joy to know that it's *your* blood that runs through my veins. I'm so proud of that."

She studied his tobacco-brown skin, smooth and unlined, despite his ninety years. She was intrigued by his dark brown eyes. They seemed to sparkle from his years of wisdom and experience.

"I must tell you, my dear, that I am very proud of you for the strong values and courage that you seem to have. But you came by them honestly."

"I did?"

"You did." Aleesa placed a pillow behind his back. He settled more comfortably in his chair.

"More comfortable?"

"Perfect," he said. "Thank you very much. Let me tell you. You are very like her in your ways, your nature. Your great-grandmother, my mother, Lucile Miller. She was the strongest woman I ever knew, physically and mentally, and she was not a very big woman, either. 'Bout your size. They say she worked side-by-side with my father to build a log cabin. Chopped down trees, helped Pa put up the log walls, chinked the logs with tar and mud . . . did everything she could. She wore a pair of Pa's overalls. She didn't care who saw her in pants, they say. Tied her hair up under an old hat and went to work helping Pa build the house. You know she was a rarity in those days. Her father was a Confederate general and her mother was a housemaid, but he—her Pa—saw to it that she was educated. Her father sent her to school. She learned Greek and Latin, which didn't help her much, but she never let on to strangers the amount of education she had, just went on living her life. One day, though, somebody out riding went by, saw her out there working, asked my Pa who the worker was, and could they hire 'him' when Pa finished building. Pa laughed. 'Ain't no worker. That's my wife!' My mother never stopped, kept working. It was important to her to get her house built. She didn't have time to worry about what anyone else thought. I believe you're like that, too, Aleesa. I know I am. Always wanted to live my life *my* way as long as I wasn't hurting anyone else or treading on anyone's toes."

"I'm like that."

"I know you are. I can tell. I figured I had to find a way to live with dignity, like a real man, or else I'd just as soon not be around."

"Was that why you decided to go to Russia?"

He nodded. "I had to, my dear. I was offered a chance to find a life that would allow me to live as a man, equal in standing to any other man."

"So, did you find that in Russia?"

"At first, child, I did. The cotton seed that I'd helped develop produced the type of cotton that could flourish and grow in that climate. But then there were changes in the Communist leadership, and I began to notice that I was not being credited for the seed I had developed. The credit went to a Russian agronomist instead. Incidentally, the man had been one of my students at the university."

"But you didn't come back to America?"

"No, I didn't. For one thing, I'd vowed not to return. Things were not that much better here, and by then I had been in the Ukraine so long and then . . . there was your grandmother, Annaliese. I couldn't interrupt her life. The incident in Georgia when we had to flee for our lives had really frightened her. In truth, she had to be persuaded that Boston was a safe city for your mother to come to for school."

"I can understand her fear," Aleesa agreed.

"She could never get over what happened to us. But," he sighed, "they tell me things are different now, with new civil rights laws and such-like. This change is hard for me to believe."

He asked her, "It is true you can ride the buses and trains, eat in restaurants, attend the cinema like anyone else? This is so?"

"Yes, Grandfather, it is so. When you get to Georgia you probably won't recognize it."

"It is hard for me to believe all these changes. And I must say I never dreamed that my children and grandchildren would do so well. Of course, I had hopes and dreams, but never did I think that I would have a granddaughter, you, my dear, who would be a lawyer, and another, Staci, who would be a physician. And a grandson who will serve in the Peace Corps. He will be like me, eh, his grandfather, taking his skills abroad to share with others . . . to show his value and worth." He shook his head at the wonder of it all.

Aleesa smiled and reached for the old man's hand. "See what a legacy you have given us, Grandfather?"

"Yes, my dear, and let us not leave out that wonderful husband of yours! Imagine, owning an airline! I can't believe such a feat is possible. How did he ever do it?"

"Grandfather, I believe next to me and Trey, my beloved husband loves airplanes with a passion. His dream was always to own his own business . . . his own airline. That's all he's ever wanted to do. I love him very much with my whole heart, so I've encouraged him even though I knew there would be tremendous sacrifices . . ."

"How did he get the airplanes? You say he has three?"

"Yes. He leases them. They are commuter planes, four jet engines called British Aerospace number one-hundred-forty-six. I've seen them and they are sleek, beautiful aircraft. Each plane has eight first-class seats and eighty-six coach seats."

"And you tell me his business is doing well?"

"Very well, Grandfather, I'm happy to say. Especially the Cape and Islands run. The economy, you see, is good. People have money to spend and they want to start their vacations as quickly as possible."

Her grandfather shook his head.

"It's very hard for an old man like me, coming from another generation, to take all of this in . . . such unbelievable changes," he murmured.

Aleesa answered softly, "You started it all, Grandfather. You had the strength to leave what you hated and accept the challenge of change, whatever that change happened to be. The courage, the stamina, the fortitude you had to do that is alive in each of us, your descendants."

She leaned toward him and kissed his soft cheek. "I'm proud to be your granddaughter. I accept my legacy,' " she said quietly.

Silently, he hugged her.

As she returned her grandfather's embrace, Aleesa's mind reeled back to Miles, her perceptive, understanding husband. Miles, who comforted her, championed her, and loved her, had been right from the beginning. He had always said that he would accept whatever facts were revealed about her birth and adoption.

"What really matters, my love, is the true, lasting love that we share. That's what matters most."

In her mind she recalled his firm pronouncement,

"My love, it's you and me, babe, and how we feel about each other that counts."

How right Miles was, she thought, *and how very, very lucky I am.* It proved that one's trust in love made it all possible.

Coming in July from Arabesque Books . . .

__ISLAND MAGIC by Bette Ford
1-58314-113-8   **$5.99US/$7.99CAN**

When Cassandra Mosely needs a break from her work—and from her relationship with Gordan Kramer—she vacations in Martinique and finds herself in a new romance. But Gordan is determined to win her back and with a little island magic, the two just may rediscover their love . . .

__IMAGES OF ECSTASY by Louré Bussey
1-58314-115-4   **$5.99US/$7.99CAN**

Shay Hilton is shocked when her ex-fiancé is murdered in her apartment, but when she comes face to face with her prosecutor, Braxton Steele, she is overcome with desire. When a storm traps the unlikely couple together, it's the beginning of a passion that will change both of their lives forever . . .

__FAMILY TIES by Jacquelin Thomas
1-58314-114-6   **$5.99US/$7.99CAN**

When Dr. McKenzie Ashford discovers that her new boss, Marc Chandler, may be responsible for her mother's death, she is determined to obtain justice. She never imagines that her quest might uncover long-hidden family secrets . . . or that her heart might be overcome with love for Marc.

__SNOWBOUND WITH LOVE by Alice Wootson
1-58314-148-0   **$5.99US/$7.99CAN**

After a car accident, Charlotte Thompson develops a case of amnesia and seeks comfort in the arms of her handsome rescuer, Tyler Fleming. But as they fall in love, Tyler realizes her true identity as the person he holds responsible for the tragedy that nearly destroyed his life. Will he be able to give his heart to this woman that he has hated for so long?

Call toll free **1-888-345-BOOK** to order by phone or use this coupon to order by mail. *ALL BOOKS AVAILABLE JULY 1, 2000.*

Name_____

Address_____

City_____ State _____ Zip _____

Please send me the books I have checked above.

I am enclosing	$_____
Plus postage and handling*	$_____
Sales tax (in NY, TN, and DC)	$_____
Total amount enclosed	$_____

*Add $2.50 for the first book and $.50 for each additional book.
Send check or money order (no cash or CODs) to: **Arabesque Books, Dept. C.O., 850 Third Avenue, 16th Floor, New York, NY 10022**
Prices and numbers subject to change without notice.
All orders subject to availability.
Visit our website at **www.arabesquebooks.com**